ANYONE BUT THE BILLIONAIRE

SARA L. HUDSON

Boldwood

First published in 2022. This edition first published in Great Britain in 2023 by Boldwood Books Ltd.

Cover Design by Head Design Ltd.

Cover Photography: Shutterstock

Every effort has been made to obtain the necessary permissions with reference to copyright material, both illustrative and quoted. We apologise for any omissions in this respect and will be pleased to make the appropriate acknowledgements in any future edition.

A CIP catalogue record for this book is available from the British Library.

Paperback ISBN 978-1-83751-733-6

Large Print ISBN 978-1-83751-729-9

Hardback ISBN 978-1-83751-728-2

Ebook ISBN 978-1-83751-726-8

Kindle ISBN 978-1-83751-727-5

Audio CD ISBN 978-1-83751-734-3

MP3 CD ISBN 978-1-83751-731-2

Digital audio download ISBN 978-1-83751-725-1

Boldwood Books Ltd
23 Bowerdean Street
London SW6 3TN
www.boldwoodbooks.com

To the women who love to laugh while having both their hearts and their panties melted. You are my people.

1

CHASE

My pussy is anti-social.

Don't be crass. I mean my pussy cat.

He's a sphynx, so basically a hairless pussy. Yeah, I know. There are a lot of jokes there. They're all funny. But that isn't the point.

Right now, the point is I'm sitting on a bench in Central Park watching all these beard-growing, man-bun douchebags score with the ladies all thanks to their playful puppies jogging up to everything with boobs. Boobs encased in wonderfully tight and revealing Spandex. And I'm stuck with a hairless cat that refuses to budge from under my hoodie.

Yes, I put my cat under my hoodie. What would you do with a hairless cat on a cool spring morning? Let him freeze his hairless balls off? You're heartless.

Anyway.

You might be wondering what a thirty-five-year-old heterosexual man is doing with a hairless cat. I wonder that every morning when I wake up to his wrinkly butt in my face at the crack of dawn.

Pun intended.

Truthfully, he's my ex-girlfriend's cat. Well, I got him for her 'cause she was crazy allergic to everything. Ownership had been iffy until she gave me an ultimatum—marriage or it's over.

I chose over.

She tried to backpedal *real* quick, but it didn't work. Especially as I'd found out she was banging my business partner. When confronted, she broke down, saying I'd forced her to cheat on me. That I had commitment issues.

Commitment issues? *Hello?* I bought you a cat.

Also, I hadn't been the one with a side piece. And my business partner? When you stoop that low, you better sure as shit know that I'm taking said cat. Hairless or not.

So now here I am, trying my hand at rebounding with Mike Hunt, the sphynx.

See what I did there? Yeah, I know. Not very mature. But considering my ex had named him Fluffy, which I thought demeaning rather than ironic, I think Mike Hunt is an excellent upgrade.

I hunch over and talk to the bulge under my hoodie. This causes a few passersby to give me the side-eye.

Whatever, keep jogging, man-buns.

"Listen, Mikey. You're not doing either of us any favors right now." The wrinkly ball of skin burrows deeper. "Okay, you asked for it." I fish my phone out of my back pocket and start an online search for cat sweaters. This is what my life has come to. Buying sweaters for hairless pussies.

God, that's depressing.

But just as I'm about to PayPal an entire wardrobe for Mr. Hunt here, my phone vibrates, and my father's name flashes on the screen.

Not "Dad" or "Father," but his legit, legal name: Stanley W.

Moore. That should give you some clue as to how close we are. Or aren't, as it were.

Since my outing today seems to be a lost cause for all types of pussy, I slide my thumb right and answer. "Stan."

"Chase."

"To what do I owe the pleasure of your cheerfulness on this fine spring morning?"

"Jesus."

I love riling the old man. It's the only thing he's ever let me know I'm truly good at. Gifted even.

"Shareholders' meeting at noon today," he barks into my ear. It's the same tone he's used with me since I was a kid. When I accidentally (on purpose) blew up my science fair project by mixing too much vinegar and baking soda. When the police brought me home for toilet papering the principal's house. When I got caught in tenth grade with my hand up Megan Dumphrey's blouse in the janitor's closet. It's even the same tone he used when I graduated high school with a 4.0 GPA, was voted valedictorian, made varsity soccer all four years of high school, and went on to graduate at the top of my class at University of Pennsylvania on academic scholarships.

Growing up, I quickly learned that no matter the situation, I'd be thought of as the flunky, the spare, the good-time kid. So why not act like it? Way more fun than trying to please the perpetually disgruntled Stanley Winston Moore.

"So a family lunch?" I muse into the phone. "Considering all the shareholders are family members. Right, Pops?"

I can almost hear his teeth grinding. "You are required to be there."

He says it like if it were up to him, I wouldn't be there. Which is probably true. Color me surprised when at eighteen I inherited shares in the family company, Moore's, a luxury retailer world-renowned and based in New York. Think Harrods, but American. I love the damn store, even though it was drilled into my head from a young age that it wasn't my destiny. I was the second son. The spare. The just-in-case. They let my younger sister Liz and me know, repeatedly, that our older brother would be given the reins. Liz, because not only was she third in line, but worse, a girl. Me, because... well, I'm me. My father had no choice but to divvy up the shares. My maternal grandfather made sure of that. But control? Hell to the no.

I blow out a quick breath and force a smile into my voice. "I'll be there, Daddy-O."

"Thomas has some information he wants to go over. Try to at least act professional."

Professional like having created a multimillion-dollar app? Like successfully investing in start-ups since I was twenty, without a dime of family money?

But I refuse to take the bait. Instead, I reply cheerfully, "Will do, Stanley."

Dead air. No goodbye.

Nice.

I wish I could say that this type of passive aggressive conversation is unusual between the old man and me. That Stan is normally a friendly, loving father, proud of my accomplishments and always inviting me over for family lunches and golf outings with his cronies.

But if wishes were real, I wouldn't be sitting on a park bench ordering argyle sweaters for Mike Hunt.

* * *

Bell

Momma always said there's an Elvis lyric for every situation. And right now, sitting in my lawyer's office, in front of the man representing a thief and my former employee, I can surely feel my temperature rising. Well, *temper* is more like it. And he for sure isn't a hunk of burning love.

Not with more hair on his upper lip than a 1970s porn star.

"Listen here, little lady…"

Annnnnd, I zone out. It's either that or strangle the bastard.

Look, I live in Texas. The odds are stacked against me that at some point I'll be referred to as "little lady." If I was lucky, it would have been by a cute, wizened old man playing chess in a rocking chair who means it with dignity and respect. However, luck is not on my side today.

Reminding myself that lawsuits are serious, even if his has no real foundation, I try to refocus on what the pompous, beer-bellied lawyer across the table is saying. But all I see is his 1970s porn 'stache and fake gold Rolex. John, my former employee, is underestimating me if he thinks he'll win his ridiculous countersuit with this ambulance chaser.

"So if you drop the suit, my client will—"

"No."

Porn 'stache blinks. "Excuse me, missy?"

"My name isn't missy, and it sure as hell isn't little lady. It's Campbell King. Ms. King to you. I'm not dropping the lawsuit. And frankly, your client's countersuit is laughable at best. Your client, my ex-employee, is guilty of corporate subterfuge. There are records, emails, and security footage." I glance over at my lawyer, Leslie Peterson, who is trying to hide her smirk by looking down and shuffling the stack of evidence in front of her.

"This is simply a misunderstanding. My client assures me that you just didn't know the system in which he was—"

"Trying to take credit for my work and poach clients? Yes, Porn 'stache, I one hundred percent understand the system he was using."

A laugh bursts from Leslie, and she tries to hide it with a cough. Shoot, I said Porn 'stache out loud. Not very professional. When provoked, I have a tendency to say what's on my mind without much thought. It's a habit I developed after staying quiet one too many times in the past.

But seeing as Porn 'stache isn't a client, has called me little lady *and* missy, and works for my asshole ex-employee, I don't have one fuck to give.

Leslie clears her throat and addresses the 'stache. "On top of which, your client, Mr. John Dudley, who, I may add, didn't even bother to show up at this meeting *he* requested, signed an ironclad agreement not to compete during his two-year contract with King Marketing." Leslie's crisp East Coast accent cuts through the room. A clear contradiction to 'stache's and my Southern drawls. "So Ms. King's lawsuit will stand. Mr. Dudley will cease his unlawful marketing start-up with King Marketing's client information, which was taken illegally, and he will pay the penalty for his subterfuge against my client's company."

Porn 'stache narrows his eyes. "This is what happens when you let women in business. They make a play for a guy and then get all emotional when he doesn't feel the same way." His cheeks get bigger, his eyes smaller, so I can only assume he's smiling under that overgrown caterpillar on his lip. "Oh yes," he says, looking at me, "Mr. Dudley told me all about your little crush on him, *Ms. King.*" He looks at Leslie, who is no longer smiling. "We could always add sexual harassment to this suit if this is how your client wants to play it."

I choke down a surge of outrage at Porn 'stache's blatant lie but remain visibly calm. John had been hired as an intern. When my former assistant left on maternity leave, then fell in love with being a stay-at-home mom to her sweet little girl, John applied for her job. As he'd just barely had the necessary qualifications and I'd been in need of an assistant ASAP, I gave him the job. Much to my current dismay. Though he'd always given off a skeevy vibe, it hadn't been until IT made me aware of his illegal activities that I'd fired him.

I take a deep breath through my nose, not wanting to appear *emotional*, as accused. Although I do have a pretty big emotional need to stab Porn 'stache in his turkey neck with his gold fountain pen.

I stand up and turn to my attorney, whose narrow-eyed expression makes even me want to pee my pants a little. I figure it's time to let her earn her salary. "Leslie, you want to finish this up?"

"With pleasure." She doesn't look at me, keeping her gaze on Porn 'stache, who now squirms in his seat, much to my satisfaction. He has no idea the whoop-ass he just rained down on himself and his client. I was being nice. Leslie doesn't do nice. Best thing I ever did was hire her. Stupidest thing I ever did was hire John Dudley.

No, I take that back. Stupidest thing I ever did was eight years ago.

Elvis Presley once said, "Those people in New York are not gonna change me none." Even now, with all my current success, I wish I'd had more of the King's wisdom with me in my youth.

Fifteen years ago, I'd trekked clear across the country to the Big Apple, to one of the best business schools in the country. In my six years there, I made my parents proud, earning scholarships, winning competitive internships, and graduating at the top of my class. I'd foolishly thought all of that had prepared me for the real world.

It took only a few months at my first real job in a major marketing firm to prove me wrong.

I'd felt a lot of things at the time—shame, humiliation, disbelief, hurt. But the one that got me through it, that got me to my current level of success, was anger. I like to think I hadn't come home to Houston with my tail between my legs, but rather with a fire under my ass.

Throwing Porn 'stache a withering look, I gather my briefcase and stride out of the room. Once I clear the conference area, I spot my weasel of an ex-employee flirting with one of 'stache's secretaries. Guy would rather chase tail than show up to his own lawsuit mediation.

I slow my steps as I pass her desk, drawing a questioning glance from the secretary and an arrogant sneer from him. I lean in toward her and say in a whisper that's loud enough for the whole room to hear, "Make sure you're stocked up on penicillin. Otherwise it takes *forever* for it to go away."

Both of their mouths drop open in unison as I continue on to the elevator, humming a happy Elvis tune.

2

CHASE

Okay, surprise of the century. The golden boy, the family savior, my brother Thomas (not Tom or Tommy, but *Thomas*), is a total douche.

My sister, Liz, leans back in her chair and sighs. "God, what a douche."

See, I told you.

"Liz, manners." Even in the face of financial ruin, my mom can admonish with flair.

"Sorry, Mom, but, I mean, I thought he was the one groomed to run the business, and now he just wants to sell?" Liz looks genuinely bewildered, like a kid on the cusp of discovering Santa isn't real. Which pisses me off, as I spent the larger part of my high school years perpetuating that fantasy of Santa for her. She'd been the only kid in middle school who'd gotten into a fistfight defending Santa's honor.

I'd been so proud.

Stan makes a strangled sort of noise, and I wonder if my next step is 911. Mom pours herself another mimosa from the sideboard before sitting back down in the high-back dining chair. And by mimosa, I mean straight champagne. She usually doesn't drink. Except when around my father. Seeing as we all wish our glasses contained vodka instead of champagne, we turn a blind eye to Mama's happy juice.

A moment ago, Thomas sat down at the dining room table and disclosed that Moore's is in financial trouble. He *then* dropped the bomb that he would not be taking over the company as previously planned. Furthermore, there's an offer on the table from some retail conglomerate, and he wants to sell. Then he got up and left to the sounds of Stan sputtering, Liz cursing, and Mom tipping another back.

I should be enjoying this moment. But I'm not.

Growing up, Thomas always had the right grades, said the right things, joined the right clubs. He didn't waste time on things like childhood and fun. After I'd had a particularly bad set-down/lecture from Stan in my middle school years, I'd stormed into Thomas's room and asked, "Can't you do anything *wrong* for a change?"

Thomas had simply quirked a superior eyebrow and replied, "Can't you do anything right?"

Touché, Thomas. Touché.

So now that Thomas has finally gone against the family's wishes, and in a big way, I should feel some sort of validation. But since Thomas's fall from glory seems to be taking the family's legacy with it, I can't summon up any feelings of triumph. I grew up in Moore's, which is way more than a store—it's over a million square feet of prime Manhattan real estate.

Spending time at Moore's was the highlight of my childhood, sad though that is. I played hide-and-seek with Liz in the clothing racks. Mrs. Gilman, the women's floor manager, always snuck me sweets when my parents weren't paying attention (which was often), and West, the men's tailor, had taught me how to dress to kill. Both for the ladies and in business.

I may have been told, *repeatedly*, that running the store wasn't in my future, but it still had always *felt* like mine.

Stan's mouth is working, but no sound emerges. Probably still recovering from what must have been the blow of a lifetime. When words finally form, I'm not sure if he's responding to Liz or just talking to himself when he starts babbling. "Sell... maybe. Downsize staff... could work..."

His words become a buzzing sound in my ears as I think of Mrs. Gilman, West, and the rest of the loyal staff who make Moore's.

"No." Everyone jumps at my interruption. I even startled myself.

There's a beat of silence while everyone looks at me.

"Excuse me?" Stan does not look pleased.

Am I really going to do this? I glance at Liz, who smiles encouragingly. *Sigh*. I guess I am.

"Look," I say. "If you want to increase sales, you don't take away the people making them." Stan opens his mouth, but I just keep going. "Thomas may have had a point when he said family-run, stand-alone luxury retailers are a thing of the past, but that doesn't mean we can't bring it into the future. It doesn't mean we have to sell."

Stan sneers. "Please. And you know all of this from your porn site?"

Okay, so that app I developed? It could be considered porn. It's basically the equivalent of Hot or Not, that asshole app that rates a girl's appearance on a scale from one to ten—but for dick pics.

That's right, ladies and gentlemen, now women the world over can turn the tables on those assholes and upload all those unwanted dick pics to my app and rate them on a scale from one to ten.

It's pretty fucking ingenious, if I do say so myself. But yeah, you could also say it's porn.

Liz pipes up, "You mean his multimillion-dollar social media application?"

My sister is awesome.

Stan rolls his eyes while my mom widens hers at my sister in warning. The app I created is worth millions. And while it's true it was my creation, after the whole girlfriend/partner dirty deed, I walked away with a fraction of what I was owed. Honestly, money isn't that important to me. True, I recognize that I can say that because I was lucky enough that my early investments helped me buy an apartment outright in Manhattan and I have enough in savings that I really don't have to work right now. Which I thought would be cool, but it so isn't. The idle life is not for me.

But I'm not wealth-obsessed like my father.

A young woman in a catering uniform comes in to clear our plates, breaking my train of thought. Yes, our family lunch has been professionally catered by my parents' personal chef. A personal chef who has three underlings who serve meals in Stan's five-hundred-square-foot dining room dripping in crystal and gilt.

And they wonder why the business isn't financially stable. Insert internal eye roll here.

"Lizzy," my mother murmurs before taking another sip.

Chastised once again, Liz looks down and tucks her hair behind her ears. My mom and my sister have a pretty good relationship. Mom is old school and from a generation where women defer to their husbands. And though Liz has more backbone than that, she craves our mother's approval. Maybe it's a mother–daughter thing. Even so, Liz still reaches over and squeezes my hand for encouragement.

I take a deep breath and prepare for battle. "Say what you want about my app, but you can't say it wasn't lucrative. I knew what I was doing."

"*Was?*" Stan asks, gearing up for a put-down. "Couldn't stick with it, could you, boy? Got run out from your own business? That sounds about right."

I want to smack Stan in the face, but that would probably lessen my credibility. Liz opens her mouth to speak up, but I shake my head at her. I don't need her putting her foot in it with our parents. And Stan doesn't need to know that I'd sold because my ex-business partner couldn't keep his snake in his trousers and my ex is a certifiable serpent charmer.

"That's a little bit of the pot calling the kettle black now, isn't it?"

He blusters, and I *do* get a bit of satisfaction from that.

"Listen. I just finished selling off my app, and I've been thinking about my next venture. Moore's could be it."

"Could be? *Could* be?" Stan thunders. "We should all just stake our futures and the billion-dollar offer on the table because this *could be* your next venture?"

Sigh. "Okay, wrong choice of words. Moore's *is* where I want to be and also where I'm needed. Which is more than golden boy Thomas can say."

Stan is really working those nostril muscles with all the flaring he's doing.

"Let's vote." I gesture to the door Thomas has recently stormed out of. "You already have a vote to sell. My vote is to allow me to take over, increase our bottom line, and bring Moore's into the twenty-first century."

Liz glances at our mother. Mom shakes her head slightly, making my stomach clench. I knew it was a long shot, Mom going against the old man, but I didn't think she'd disapprove of Liz standing by me.

"Two votes for Chase," my sister says, not meeting our mother's eyes.

Yep, love my sister.

Stan's fingers tighten around his glass. "If you think I'd let you anywhere near—"

"If you don't let me take over, the only other option is to sell."

"I'd rather do that than hand over the company my family has built from the ground up to some no-account playboy like you. You'll get distracted by the first floozy who bats her lashes at you, and Moore's will have the same fate as everything else you've ever started and never finished."

I could win millions in Vegas with my poker face.

Masking the sting of his words with a smile, I lean back in the ornate dining chair. "Please, old man. You've already started the wrecking ball with your laughable management skills."

"You—"

"Enough."

Everyone blinks at my mother's voice. It hadn't been raised, but it had been firm. Even Stan creases his forehead in surprise. I don't think Mom has ever used that tone with him, or any of us, before.

A long sigh escapes her perfectly painted pink lips, and I swear her eyes cut to the bar cart by the door. "Let's not be vulgar." She straightens the multiple tennis bracelets on her slim wrist before continuing. As if petting diamonds gives her strength. Heck maybe it does because I've never seen her get involved in business before. "Truthfully, I am not as surprised as the rest of you that Thomas wants to sell. He never really did like the store."

When Stan opens his mouth to speak, Liz shushes him, surprising him again. Seems like the women are running this show.

"And it also doesn't surprise me that Chase wants to take over. He *has* always loved the store." She gives me a small smile. It almost looks apologetic. "I never said anything because"—she looks forlornly at her empty glass— "well, because." She straightens in her chair, which is hard to do as she already has perfect posture.

Silence.

When no one speaks up, and my mother doesn't continue, Stan starts in again.

"Do neither of you understand the damage he could do?" He actually points at me, like they don't know who "he" is. You've got to hand it to the guy, even with all his children against him, outnumbered both bodily and with shares, he's still trying to find a way to *not* let me take over.

I bite the inside of my cheek. Am I really that bad?

Stan drops his hand to the table with a thud, the crystal glasses shaking. "If we give over control now and he fucks it up, like he undoubtedly will, the offer on the table will be lowered. Or even withdrawn. Moore's would be forced to declare bankruptcy."

For a second, panic freezes my chest. What if I *did* fail? What would happen to Mom? To Liz?

"Dad, Chase won't let that happen. He's smart. He graduated the top of his class. From *U Penn*." A sigh dripping with exasperation escapes her. "I don't know why you think he's going to mess up."

My little sister smiles at me, and the panic evaporates. She's right. I can do this. I know it. And more importantly, I know Moore's.

Mom gives up on getting a refill from the elusive staff and pushes back her chair to get it herself. She might have gone quiet again, but I don't miss the slight nod of encouragement she gives me behind Stan's back. My mother is sending mixed signals today.

Stan rolls his eyes. The juvenile move would be comical if it weren't directed at me and his complete lack of faith in my abilities.

Ugh. Fuck Stan for getting in my head. He may not like his family's legacy in the hands of the spare, but I don't have an ounce of sympathy for the guy. He brought this on himself with bad business management and nonexistent fatherly support. So I lean back again, this time with my arms behind my head, and smirk. "Yeah, old man. Don't worry, I got this."

"Really?" He narrows his eyes. "Just how sure are you about that?"

Mental sigh. Why is nothing ever easy with this guy?

But I take the bait. "What do you mean by that?"

His eyes are intent on mine when he leans forward. "You've got until the end of the year to improve the bottom line. If you don't, we sell. We'll have to. But if it comes to that, or I should say *when* it comes to that, you forfeit all your shares."

I don't blink. I don't move. I just stare back.

I'm not stupid. I know I don't have to take this deal. I already have the majority shareholder votes, what with Liz and Mom having sided with me. Nothing he can do at this point can stop me from taking over. But he's just so damn sure I'm going to fail. Just because I'm not Thomas. And if I don't put money where my mouth is, he'll think I agree.

Damn it.

"You got yourself a deal, Daddy-O."

* * *

Bell

Porn 'stache folded. As I knew he would. You can try to pull the *women are overemotional in business* card all you want, but you can't argue cold, hard evidence, which is what I have. Security footage of John in the building after he was fired and his digital footprint all over my clients' information files sealed his fate.

I blink against the sun as I overlook the city skyline, visible from the prominently located high-rise in Houston. In the eight years since I started this company, I've gone from working out of my bedroom to being the youngest female president and CEO of a marketing agency in the country. Now my personal offices are housed in Houston's prestigious Galleria, though I have staff across the United States. That's the beauty of business these days—you can do it from anywhere in the country. Especially when your business focuses on online marketing.

Even so, I'd always thought the city skyline outside my office window would be a bit bigger.

And it was—for a moment.

"Ms. King, call on line two."

Closing my eyes on the bright Texas sun, I let the black dots dance behind my lids as my eyes adjust. I swivel in my chair, reaching for the intercom button on my phone. "Who is it?"

Forbes just ran an article citing King Marketing as one of the top ten innovative companies to watch. Which means lately I've been getting a lot of cold calls from businesses wanting my company's help.

"A Mister... uh, oops!" She giggles. "I forgot his name."

I roll my eyes at the recent temp the agency sent. Who giggles at their own ineptitude? I don't bother replying. I disconnect with her and pick up the receiver, pressing two. "Campbell King here."

"Hello, Ms. King. Thank you for taking my call. Glad I could catch you before lunch."

Sex. That's what the voice sounds like. Tingles shoot across my skin. All roads lead to Rome? Well, all tingles lead to my hoo-ha.

"Ms. King?"

"Hmm, what?" I shiver. "Oh, yes. I'm here." I shake off the trance his voice put me in and uncross my legs, planting both feet firmly on the floor under my desk. I finally register what Sexy-voice said and glance at the clock on my desk. "Yes, well, I usually don't leave for lunch until noon."

"The time difference." He pauses. "I forgot. It's already noon here in New York."

My stomach drops. New York?

"I recently read the article about your business in *Forbes*," Sexy-voice continues. "Your company's really been making a name for itself, thinking outside the box and reinventing businesses by enlarging their digital presence. That's exactly what we need. I wanted to call as soon as I was ready to set up a meeting. I'd like to discuss the possibility of your company coming on as consultants in developing a new marketing plan for Moore's that utilizes social media. Something Moore's has been sorely lacking."

Moore's? He couldn't mean *the* Moore's, could he?

"I'm sorry, Mr....?"

"Moore. Chase Moore."

Holy shit.

"I'm sorry, didn't your secretary tell you?"

I take a deep breath. "No, *I'm* sorry. I recently lost my amazing assistant to maternity leave, and the temps haven't been... well, up to par, so to speak."

He chuckles, and it does something to my insides. "I understand. Moore's has recently undergone a few personnel changes of its own."

"Hence your phone call to King Marketing."

Another laugh. "You're quick."

"You have to be, in this business." Feeling more in control, I pick up my fountain pen and scratch out 'Moore's' on my legal pad. "So, Mr. Moore, just what exactly are you looking for?"

* * *

First class has ruined me for life. I spent the flight curled under a cashmere blanket, my feet toasty in complimentary slippers while the stewardess served me glass after glass of champagne.

I mean, I've traveled for work plenty, but usually business class. However, after I established that Chase Moore was not a phone sex operator with the wrong number and truly was the acting head of the largest family-owned department store in Manhattan, I got with the program.

We talked for quite a bit. I mentioned the work King Marketing did in New York over the years, though all of it was conducted remotely on my end. I named my New York-based strategists he'd want to meet with, and he agreed, as long as I was there too.

I never actually said I was hesitant to fly out to New York, but he must have sensed something in my tone, so he pressed.

"I know what you did for Cavendish's. Six years ago, they were a mom-and-pop business with only a few locations across Texas. That's it," he said. "Then you came in, reinvented their website and developed a whole social media marketing plan, and in two years they opened six more stores across three states. And they're still going strong. That was you, not your staff. I want *you*."

And really, when a billionaire with the voice of a sex god offers you the deal of a lifetime and a chance at redemption in the city that once chewed you up and spit you out—you go.

So that's why, after taking the conveniently pre-arranged limo from the airport to my sumptuous hotel room overlooking Central Park, I spent an evening eating room service and sleeping off the plane's champagne.

Now, having showered the travel grime off, I'm dressed and sitting in a cab ready to do some recon before the meeting with Chase Moore tomorrow. I know my end of the business is online, in the ether of the Internet, but just as I shopped for cowboy boots and belt buckles at Cavendish's before taking on their account, I aim to do some hands-on research under the guise of shopping at Moore's.

Moore's. Just thinking the name has me salivating. The publicity, recognition, and prestige of taking on such a company.

And being able to charge hours for shopping is a great perk too.

"Get your head out of your ass, woman!" The cab driver leans on the horn, then gestures rudely toward another driver.

My smile stretches wide. Ahh... New York. There would be no little lady-ing or bless-my-hearting here. New Yorkers keep it real.

"Is that Elvis?"

I stop mid-hum. "Ah, yes, it is. Sorry. I tend to hum Elvis without realizing it. Habit I picked up from my mom, I guess."

"No need to apologize. Better than most of the stuff I hear in this cab." He makes a jerk-off sign to a fellow driver. "Besides, Elvis was the man. They didn't call him the King for nothing."

"Yes. My mother and I thought so." As usual, a little pang of loss hits me, but anytime Elvis is mentioned, it's always tempered with great memories. Mom and me dancing to "Blue Suede Shoes" in my bedroom. She and Dad swaying in the kitchen while "Love me Tender" played on the record player.

"Move it, jackass!"

After a few more minutes and a lot of colorful exclamations from the cab driver, I hop out in front of one of New York's more impressive buildings. Moore's.

I have to crane my neck back to take it all in. It isn't a skyscraper, but to me, it's more imposing. Moore's takes up an entire block. Nearly one million square feet, set in the ridiculously expensive real estate of Manhattan. Just the property value alone humbles all but the one percent.

Though huge, it's really the Beaux Arts architecture that sets Moore's apart from most buildings in New York. Built in the Gilded Age of America, when iron barons ran rampant, Moore's opulence is what defines it. Balustrades, columns, and pilasters all combine to foreshadow the equally lavish interior. I might know the time stamp of design due to research, but the rest comes from memory.

Once I pass through the gold-framed rotating door, I'll find finely polished marble floors and a tuxedo-clad employee whose sole purpose is to welcome guests and guide them to their destination. Like a shopping butler.

Though it's been nearly a decade, my memory proves correct as I push through the heavy door and tell the handsome elderly gentleman I'd like a cup of coffee before I begin my shopping. He gives me directions to the café on the main floor. Directions I've followed a hundred times before. It's the same café I used to study in during my college years, where I'd sit and people-watch the rich patrons I was so sure would be my own clients one day.

Other students had piled into the campus coffee house or the closest Starbucks. Me? I'd made two subway changes and walked three blocks just to sit in Moore's.

My sandals slap as I walk down the white and black marble hallway and hang a right into the Italian Renaissance-themed café. I take in the surroundings, noting that the hand-painted ceiling, white marble columns, and gold metal chairs with white leather seats arranged thoughtfully around marble-topped tables haven't changed in the eight years since I've been here. But all the luxury around me pales when I see the most decadent element in the room.

Chase Moore's fine ass.

3

CHASE

Today is going to shit.

To start, my brother tried to contact me. He left a message about wanting to discuss family stuff, but that's bullshit. He didn't even blink when he voted to sell the company. Now he probably heard through the rich and lazy's gossip mill, aka my father, that I'd taken over. And being the control-freak jackass that he is, he probably wants to dictate my business decisions. Well, too bad. He can dictate my dick.

Get it? No? Yeah, me either. I must be too tired for funny this morning.

That's why I'm standing in line at Moore's first floor café, waiting on an extra dose of caffeine to jump-start me out of the knee-deep crap Stan made of our family business. The family business I may not get to be a part of if I don't pull this off. I'm kicking myself for making the deal with the devil, again, aka my father. I knew better. After watching Thomas walk away, you'd think he'd at least be happy with his second son picking up the slack. But nooooo. He'd rather sell than trust me with our legacy.

Which brings me to the other reason today is shit. I spent the whole week going over Moore's financials as well as our marketing plan. Or lack of one, really. It's sort of embarrassing to realize how long Moore's has been coasting on its old-money reputation. And it's just as obvious that Stan hasn't been hands-on in years. His remark that I'd never worked hard for anything is so ironic it isn't funny. All he's ever done was leave it to "the good old boys" to run his family's legacy while he played a round of golf.

My meeting this morning with said good old boys, aka the corporate managers, was the cherry on top of the shit sundae that is my day so far. The idiots all wanted to lay people off. That old-school way of doing business really chafes my ball sack. So… I may have fired more managers than I'd planned on.

But then again, I'd just been taking their advice, hadn't I?

I chuckle at the thought. And then chuckle some more when I think of all the phone calls Stan will get from his work buddies, all bemoaning that his son fired them.

Maybe today isn't such a shit day after all.

I grab my coffee from the young barista at the counter and put a twenty in the tip jar. Technically, they aren't supposed to have a tip jar on the counter. But as I know them all to be college students working for their bread (literally), I'm not about to enforce yet another archaic rule.

However, I must move too fast for the next person in line because we bump into each other when I turn to leave.

Do you know what happens when you're holding an extra-hot cappuccino and your momentum is impeded by a strong force in the opposite direction?

Burnt mother-fucking man nipples is what.

"Fuck!" I yell at the same time as the person who ran into me. The chorus of profanity is enough to turn everyone's head in the café, making us the entertainment of the morning, I'm sure.

For a moment, my brain is too busy trying not to go into shock from the scalding hot coffee dripping down my shirtfront. But once my synapses start firing correctly, the important things come into focus.

Like the slim hands currently dabbing at my chest with paper napkins. Or the way those hands lead to slender wrists and toned arms. And how the top of this woman's head is covered in the most beautiful shade of hair I've ever seen. Like all the sunset colors and stuff.

What? I'm a dude. That's as descriptive as I get.

Then she looks up, and my brain shuts down again.

Because holy hell, not even boiling coffee can stop my dick from twitching when I look into those eyes.

Brown eyes. Which no one ever writes odes about, except for good old Van Morrison. But they should. Because these chocolate brown eyes, lit up by golden flecks, deserve a fucking sonnet. No, a symphony, written in their honor. I'm lost in them, hearing the pretend orchestra in my head playing a score to this moment in time that I'm pretty sure will change my life.

That is, until said eyes squint with concern, and I realize the woman has been talking to me this whole time.

"I'm sorry, what?" I ask. Her stunning eyes widen, and she takes a step back, letting me know I may have just shouted. But when you've got a symphony in your head, you've got to speak up.

"Sorry." I mentally lower the volume on my internal sound-track I've got going. "What were you saying?"

Her full lips twist to the side in amusement. "Well, I said quite a few things, but I'll just remind you of these two." She holds up one of her hands, leaving the other pressed to my chest with a napkin. A napkin that's already soaked and useless, but I'm not about to bring that up. "One, I'm terribly sorry. And two, are you okay?"

At this point, she's probably questioning my mental acuity as well as my burnt chest with her last question. She has a Southern accent, her words moving a bit slower, more sensuously out of that wide mouth than the edgy, quick-worded New Yorkers I'm used to. Something about that accent stirs in the back of my mind, but I shove it aside and focus on the woman in front of me.

I cover her hand on my chest with my own and say, "Baby, I think you just made my day."

I'm pretty stoked at my charming comeback. The barista watching us sighs in delight. Out of the corner of my eye, an old lady clasps her hands to her heart at the romantic scene she's witnessing. Hell, the angelic cherubs painted on the café's ceiling start singing (or maybe that's my soundtrack again).

But the lady who could've sent me to the emergency room with third-degree nip burns? She just tugs her hand out from mine and rolls her eyes.

"Yeah, you're okay."

She steps back, and that's when I see I'm not the only one covered in cappuccino.

Just like the nipples currently visible through the shirt the woman is wearing, my day is starting to look up. She catches my glance and looks to her shirtfront. With a sigh, she crosses her arms over her chest, cutting off my personal wet T-shirt contest.

"This isn't exactly the introduction I was hoping for," she murmurs.

"I beg to differ. I think this was a spectacular way to get my attention." I wink at her, but unlike every other warm-blooded woman in New York I've tried it on in the past, it just seems to annoy her. I clear my throat, smile still in place, and try again. "I'm Chase."

"Yes, I know who you are, Mr. Moore. That's why I wanted to introduce myself."

The smile slides from my face. "Oh." It doesn't happen all that much. When I was younger, right out of college, women who knew my last name would approach me hoping for the connections and lifestyle my name had come to represent. But it's disappointing to realize that this fine woman is digging for mine or Moore's gold.

"Yes. I got here early to do some recon on the store and saw you. Didn't want to be rude." She gestures between us, exposing one perfect nipple from under her soaked white blouse. "But apparently that ship has sailed." She straightens her shoulders and drops her arms. The look on her face says she'll be sorely disappointed if I can't keep my eyes on hers and off her chest. Though I desperately want to be the perv Stan thinks I am, I never like to disappoint a lady. I meet her golden-eyed stare.

She sticks out her hand for me to shake. "I'm Campbell King."

* * *

Bell

"As in King Marketing?"

"That'd be the one." I have to give it to him; he isn't looking at my chest. I mean, I caught him glancing earlier, but really, who wouldn't? I'm probably high-beaming the man. And just to say, if he'd been wearing white pants and I could see *his* junk through them, I'd have looked too.

Dear lord, I'm thinking of his junk. Off to a great start with my new client.

I clear my throat. "Yes. I like to get a feel for the businesses I work with, especially those that have a tangible base of operations. As you probably know from the *Forbes* article, I've built a niche in the social media marketing world with businesses that deal in consumer goods. I like to think a lot of my success comes from doing my homework. Both on the ground and online."

I'm trying desperately to act professional here. You know, like I didn't just soak us both in hot coffee. I'm also trying not to notice that his face doesn't just match his sexy voice, it surpasses it.

His crazy good looks aren't a total surprise. The guy showed up in the papers frequently when I lived in New York. As soon as he said his name over the phone, I had a mental image to go along with his sex-operator voice. And after a mildly stalkerish Google image search, I also had a lot of recent photos of Chase Moore to go by as well. Photos I may have thought of while in bed. Alone. (Sigh.) But just as I like to think supermodels and celebrities don't look as good in real life as they do in magazines, I've been hoping the same would be true of Mr. Chase Moore.

No such luck.

Not that I wish he'd been beaten by an ugly stick or anything, but trying to remain professional in the face of, well, his face, is quite trying.

"I appreciate your dedication. It's no wonder *Forbes* wrote that article."

Gone is the good-time-boy charm. His voice seems stilted, and his eyes are staring at some place over my shoulder. My nipples are making him nervous.

I giggle. Well, shit. That isn't very professional either.

But my laugh makes his eyes return to me, and I like that. I like that a lot.

"And I appreciate *your* dedication to not ogling my boobs, Mr. Moore." I'm treated to a full-blown smile at that. Holy hell. I cross my arms over my chest again, sure the traitors have cut through the thin cotton by now. "But I should probably head back to the hotel before security arrests me for public indecency. I'll see you tomorrow."

"Oh no you don't." Chase steps quickly between me and the door, tossing his empty cup in the trash. "I won't let a little spilled coffee stand between you and your research. I think with the seven floors we have here at Moore's, we can find you something to wear."

"That really isn't necessary. But thank you." I try to move around him, but he shifts again.

"I insist. Especially if it's going to help you build Moore's a fantastic social media marketing plan."

And that is how, three minutes later, I find myself in the women's department, standing next to Chase while he explains to the very attractive, very put-together older saleswoman why I resemble a high-priced flasher. At least, I hope I look high-priced.

Because it isn't lost on me that I'm in the women's *luxury* department. The carpeted area, where they keep all the merchandise priced over a grand per item. Honestly, a T-shirt from the athletic department would've sufficed. But as the coffee has cooled and the air-conditioning is pumping, I'm not about to start an argument about cost while I literally freeze my nipples off.

The conversation finishes and Chase turns to me. "Susan will take care of you." He looks down at the giant brown stain across the front of his dress shirt. "I'll be back in a minute." He winks and walks off.

I want to slap him when he winks. Not because I feel it's chauvinist or insincere, but because it makes me want to jump him and ride him like I'm at the Texas Rodeo.

"Miss?"

Oh yeah. Susan. She's looking at me in a friendly way. Probably way friendlier than I would've interacted with a stranger soaked in coffee and flashing some nip. But then again, it *is* her job. And when the boss says jump...

I clear my throat for what feels like the twentieth time today and say, "I really just need a T-shirt."

This time, her smile is a mix of sympathy and condescension. "I'll see what I can do."

* * *

Apparently, what she can do is set me up in the largest dressing room with a plethora of blouses, dresses, pants, and even lingerie. I know they don't sell bras and panties on this floor, so I wonder what exactly Chase had instructed Susan to do.

That'll teach me to stare at his ass while the adults are talking.

I spent the better part of ten minutes sitting in a robe after Susan took my clothes, including undergarments, and said she'd be right back. I really didn't see why she needed my panties, but as the robe was warm and fluffy, I hadn't cared.

And now, with a multitude of choices before me, all beautiful and made in sumptuous fabrics, I decide to spend my recent tax refund on a new wardrobe. Who needs to deposit into their retirement account when La Perla lingerie and Stella McCartney blouses are staring you in the face?

I've just put the first outfit on, complete with neon-pink lace panties, when Susan returns with a knock on my door.

"Ms. King? When you have the first outfit on, I need you to come out to the platform please."

"The platform?"

"Yes, the room with the three-way mirror? We passed it on the way in. I need to see what you have on."

Great, she probably thinks I'll steal something and wants to catalogue everything I'm wearing. I hadn't even gotten to try on the Gucci pussy-bow blouse yet. I pout into the mirror but reply, "Sure thing, Susan. Be right out."

In the mirror, I take inventory of what will probably cost me half of said tax refund. A black Tom Ford pencil skirt and an Alexander McQueen blush-colored silk blouse. I'm no slouch in the wardrobe department, but I've never owned anything this nice. Or should I say, this expensive.

It's the stuff I dreamed of buying while wearing an Old Navy hoodie and Walmart jeans while I studied for my finals a few years ago and a couple floors down from here.

I take one last longing look at the clothes I've yet to touch and exit the dressing room, humming to myself.

Resolved to spending a fortune, I shuffle in my bare feet down the corridor and into the platform room.

"I'm wearing the bright pink La Perla panties, so you can definitely put those on my bill, Susan," I say while looking down. I run my hands down the length of my body, enjoying the feel of the expensive fabrics. "And this pencil skirt is in serious contention, though I can't wear it today. It would look odd with my flat sandals."

"Then we'll have to get your shoe size so we can bring you a selection of shoes to go with that outfit," says a deep, familiar voice.

I close my eyes and count to five, hoping that when I open them Chase won't be there. That I hadn't just announced what color underwear I'm wearing to my new client. Slowly, I open my eyes... and sigh.

Not only because I had, indeed, announced the color of my panties, but because it isn't fair that my new client looks this good.

He's sitting on one of the pink velvet couches behind me, relaxed against the plush cushions, legs crossed like only men can get away with in public. He's changed suits entirely, going with a navy so dark, it's one shade this side of black. The top button of his new white shirt is undone, and I can see the hollow at the base of his throat. I spend a weird amount of time looking at his throat. I mean, who gets turned on by a hollow?

Me, apparently. *I* get turned on by a hollow. (Internal eye roll.)

"What are you doing here?" I cringe at my sharp tone.

He just grins. Great. Now I'm contending with a sexy hollow *and* a charming smile.

"I thought we could have a *Pretty Woman* moment." He gestures to the room, which I have to admit, does remind me of the shopping scene in that iconic movie. But wait a minute...

"Did you just call me a hooker?"

4

CHASE

"I, uh..."

Campbell erupts into a fit of laughter so hard she doubles over.

"Oh my god... you should see... your face," she says between deep breaths as she tries to control her laughter.

A second before, my mind seized in panic. Now, watching her previously guarded face transform in delight, I find myself grinning back at her. This isn't who I was expecting. I mean, I *was*, but I wasn't. *Forbes* had highlighted King Marketing, the company. Sure, most of it had been about its president, CEO and founder, Campbell King, but the focus was on her business acumen, her savvy marketing strategies, her prestigious educational background and awards. The magazine hadn't focused on Campbell King, the woman. On her laugh, her eyes, or her sexy Southern lilt. (If they had, they'd have sold a thousand more copies.) There'd been a picture, but it was a group shot. I hadn't thought to look through all the names under the picture to figure out which person was Campbell. It hadn't mattered what she looked like; it mattered how she did her job.

And besides the article, all my other searches had come up

with company background information and her personal résumé. No pictures. So although I am quite familiar with her impressive marketing talents and credentials, I'd been unprepared for her... everything else.

"So glad I could amuse you," I tell her.

Her laughter ebbs, and she wipes a hand under her eyes. "Amuse? Yes, definitely that."

A minute passes as we just stare at each other, smiling.

"I'm pleased you like the ensemble, Ms. King. So glad to have gotten the sizing right."

I start, having forgotten Susan is still in the room, standing some distance behind the couch I'm on. From the look on Campbell's face, so had she.

"Oh, uh, yes. Everything fits fine." Campbell turns toward the floor-to-ceiling mirrors, arranged so the customer can see every angle of herself. As can the people on the couch. A fact I am very much loving at the moment.

Back to ignoring me, Campbell engages Susan in a conversation about the latest fashion, while I sit back and enjoy the view. Whoever invented pencil skirts should be given a commendation. Every librarian fantasy I ever had is busy streaming through my mind as I watch her twist and turn in the mirror.

"It really is lovely on you. But please, do try on the other garments I hung in your dressing room. I know the Diane Von Furstenberg dress would look amazing. The blue one with the asymmetric hem? It just came in, and the coloring would be fabulous on you."

"I don't know..." Campbell's glance meets mine in the mirror.

"By all means, please try on all that Susan brought you." I lean back further into the plush couch. "That *is* why you're here, isn't it? To do a bit of recon, as you said."

She looks longingly toward the dressing room, where the rest of the clothes hang. "Well, yes. But I wasn't going to spend the entire day in the women's luxury department. I should really get a feel for the rest of Moore's as well."

"We have plenty of time for that," I reply. The way she's already inching toward the door, I know I don't have to push much.

"Well, maybe just one more outfit..." she says, scurrying back to her dressing room.

Susan and I share a smile. It seems our new marketing guru is a bit of a clotheshorse.

I can work with that.

* * *

I *cannot* work with this.

For an hour I've been suspended between pleasure and discomfort, watching Campbell model clothes. Clothes that look so good on her curves that my dick can only sit up and take notice. Thank god for the throw pillow I placed on my lap to hide my situation.

Closing my eyes wouldn't have helped either. She hums Elvis tunes in the silence. I don't even think she knows she's doing it. I've been too intrigued to call her on it, afraid she'd stop. And don't even get me started on the pleasure of just listening to her talk. With her sweet Southern accent inciting fantasies of her talking dirty to me with that sexy twang.

And we've talked. A lot.

At the beginning, we stuck mostly to business—sales projections, media campaigns. Her interest delved further than just marketing, though, asking questions about the store's buyers, in-house restaurant management, and more. She picked up the new information with a nod and a smile, quick to make connections and extrapolate the information into further-reaching marketing analysis.

In short, Campbell King is smart as fuck.

And damn if that isn't twice as hot as her ass in that pencil skirt.

I'm not sure I've ever enjoyed my time in the store more. Even when Susan interrupted with embarrassing stories about me as a kid getting into trouble amidst the clothing racks. Including one when my little sister pants me in front of a cute, college-age sales associate when I was seventeen.

Campbell's laugh went straight to my dick.

Between the conversation, Campbell's body modeling the latest fashions, and the sound of her laugh doing things to my insides, by the time she carefully selects a few items for purchase, I'm desperate for distraction.

"Lunch?" I ask as Susan wraps Campbell's new clothes in tissue and gently places them in our signature black and gold bags.

"You needn't bother. I hadn't meant to take up your whole day."

"No bother at all."

Her teeth bite into her lower lip. I try not to think inappropriate thoughts. Key word: *try*.

I clear my throat, looking over Susan's shoulder to a sales associate who is rehanging the outfits Campbell decided not to purchase on a separate rack, as I instructed. "We can discuss your initial thoughts on Moore's and its much-needed marketing update."

Campbell pauses, just long enough that I'm certain she'll say no. Like she's running through a list of excuses in her head to pawn me off. So I'm pleasantly surprised when she squares her shoulders and says yes.

"Is that Thai place on 39th still there?"

"Thai's Pad?"

A small laugh escapes her. "Yeah, that's the one."

"Still there. And still making some of the best curries in Manhattan."

"Okay," she says with a decisive nod. "Business lunch. We can order in." She thanks Susan for all her help before taking her bags. "Do you have an office or conference room we could commandeer?"

"Of course." I smother my triumphant grin, which is probably wildly inappropriate for a business lunch, and turn to Susan. "Thanks for your help, Susan."

The too-knowing older gal with her perfectly coifed silver hair turns a sly look my way. "My pleasure, Mr. Moore." She smiles at Campbell. "You two enjoy your *business* lunch."

"We will. And call me Chase, Susan." Ignoring her amused snort, I hold out my hands to take Campbell's bags from her.

One finely arched, auburn brow quirks up as she hands them over. "I can carry those myself, you know."

"Yes, I know." But I don't give them back.

She rolls her eyes but does it with a smile. With a final nod to Susan, who looks far too pleased with herself, I lead Campbell away from the counter, happy with today's turn of events.

That good feeling stays with me for all of five minutes.

That's how long it takes for the wolves to descend. Or should I say cougars? But that isn't accurate either. Moore's hires a diverse selection of men and women. And while only a few of the men want to shake hands with the new boss, *all* of the women do. Or shake something, as we work our way out of the store.

"Mr. Moore!" a saleswoman calls to us from across the department. "We just received an absolutely fabulous selection of silk boxers this morning." She runs her hands down the sides of her tight dress. "Would you like me to select a few for you?"

Unfortunately, the route to the elevator takes Campbell and me right past her. "No thank you, Ashley," I say, squinting to read the name tag on her chest she's thrusting at me.

"Oh." She blinks rapidly. "Perhaps you're more of a boxer brief man, then?" There's a hopeful note in her voice. I can tell she wants me to play along. To laugh. Flirt.

Usually, I'd be that guy. I'd play the part that I often do just to rile my father. I'd tease a bit, smile at everyone, even wink at the older gals who've known me since my diaper years. But today I don't want to be that guy.

Today, in the presence of Ms. Campbell King, a woman with the reputation of a marketing genius, I want to be the guy who impresses with his business acumen, who takes the time to listen to a publicity plan without having to fend off lingering arm touches and innuendo.

I smile tightly at a disappointed Ashley before moving past her. Unfortunately, Ashley isn't the last to stop us on our way.

"Your staff is very... dedicated," Campbell says, her voice dripping in Southern syrup, after I played dumb when stopped by an overly eager furniture saleswoman asking about how hard I liked my wood.

"They're, uh, still getting used to seeing me on the floor," I manage, relief flooding through me when I catch sight of the gold-framed elevator doors that lead to the office floors.

The corner of her mouth twitches. "Mmm-hmm."

I insert the special key card to operate the elevator and stand back to let Campbell through. Her brown eyes are sparkling, the light taupe-colored freckles highlighted by the small chandelier in the elevator foyer. And when I catch sight of her backside, clad in her new form-fitting pencil skirt, my dick decides that her mouth shouldn't be the only thing twitching.

Especially when Campbell starts humming "All Shook Up."

5

BELL

"Coming?"

My new Jimmy Choos trip over the low pile carpet outside his office, but I quickly right myself. The bastard smiles, like he knows what that one little word did to me. Actually, that isn't quite fair. It's a nice smile. A professional smile. One that turns concerned at my small stumble. I'm the one with the one-track mind, apparently.

"Ah, yes. Coming." *I wish.*

Leave it until this moment for my body to finally decide to make sexual attraction a priority. I've been in business over eight years, and never once have I been distracted like this. I'd be able to overcome his general good looks if he wasn't also so *nice*. I've done business with plenty of good-looking men. I've even done business with good-looking men who'd made it obvious they wanted more than just my business strategy.

Leslie likes to joke that I'm lacking in sexual mojo. And maybe I'd believe her if I wasn't so thoroughly enamored of playing with my battery-operated personal massager while binge replaying Jason Momoa's scenes in *Game of Thrones*. Or Stephen Amell from *Arrow*.

Both of whom are bad boys. Not nice guys. Like Chase, when he over-tipped the barista earlier, or made sure to find me new clothes, and then played along when Susan told embarrassing stories of him as a kid. Then there was the rest of his staff.

He was stopped multiple times on our way to the staff elevator. And true, a lot of that had been women flirting with him, a bit outrageously even. But he'd stopped every time with a kind word and a genuine interest in their lives.

I've always heard nice was the kiss of death. That nice boys finish last.

I'm pretty sure this nice boy might finish last, but only because he'd let you finish first.

Chase closes the door behind me, and I find myself alone in a small space with my charming new client and my wickedly improper imagination. Probably not the best combination.

Although one couldn't really call his office small. It's bigger than my first apartment in Houston, the very place I started my company. Floor-to-ceiling windows behind the desk, showcasing the best of New York up close and personal. Walnut bookcases, oddly empty, line one wall. Opposite them is a richly appointed sitting area with furniture straight out of *The Great Gatsby*. You could probably fit a lap pool in here.

But still. The door is closed. And that's all I need to feel claustrophobic with a man like Chase Moore. I should say goodbye and call it a day.

"Why are your bookcases empty?" Damn it. There I go blurting things out again.

Chase glances at the wall of shelves, an uncharacteristic frown on his face. "This wasn't really my office until a few weeks ago. It used to be Stan's."

"Stan?"

"Stan Moore."

"Isn't that your father?"

"Yes." His tone is so flat, so un-Chase-like, that I mentally search for some witty comeback to make him smile again.

Before I can think up a humorous retort, he turns a frame around on his desk to face me. A handsome older couple, two pre-teen boys, and a young girl. They're sitting in this very office. The man looks bored, the mother has a plastic smile, and one of the boys seems mad at the world while the other, and the girl at his side, look like they're trying not to laugh. He taps the bored-looking man. "That's Stan."

I nod and point to the smiling girl with the puffy dress and big bow on her head. "The pantser?"

Chase laughs softly, a loving smile on his lips. "Yeah. That's the pantser. Otherwise known as my sister Liz."

I'm inordinately proud that I got him to smile again. "And I guess that's your brother?" I ask, pointing to the proud-looking, handsome kid with Stan's hand resting on his shoulder.

The smile is gone; Chase's shoulders stiffen. "Thomas. My older brother."

"Older? Then why isn't he—" Chases flinches, and I immediately regret my question. I hadn't meant anything by it. Family-owned companies like this are still pretty archaic. The eldest inherits and all that.

But before I can smooth things over, a buzzer sounds, followed by his secretary on the intercom. "Mr. Chase, your fa—"

The older man from the photo, a man of medium height and with a slight paunch, throws open the door. "What the *hell* have you been up to, boy?"

I can't help but wince as his booming voice reverberates around the large office.

"Ah... speak of the devil," Chase mutters.

His father *does* look slightly demonic with his red-flushed face, but luckily, I'm able to stifle my laugh and remain unnoticed. He storms past me without a glance, stopping just short of Chase.

"I have been getting phone calls all day from people informing me that you have fired the majority of my management team!" Stan slams an open palm on the desk, and the family picture crashes forward. Glass breaks.

Chase's eyes track the overturned picture before his carefully blank expression morphs into one of gleeful insolence. I actually have to blink to make sure I'm seeing him correctly. *This* is a bad-boy look.

"Whatever do you mean, Pops?" Chase sits down in his large leather chair and props his feet on the desk.

"You know exactly what I mean, you little—"

"Ah-hem."

Both men turn to look at me. Oh shit, *why* did I open my mouth? Ugh, I know why. 'Cause I didn't want to hear Chase get chewed out. Like he isn't a grown-ass man capable of dealing with his angry father. I fight hard not to roll my eyes at myself.

"And just *who* are you?" Stan asks, obviously not impressed as his hard gaze rakes over me from head to toe.

I look down at my chic, Moore's assembled outfit. Joke's on him if he finds fault with my attire.

"Campbell King, Mr. Moore." I stride across the Persian rug on my new Jimmy Choos, arm outstretched. "I'm the owner of King Marketing, here to develop your new social media campaign and consult with overall marketing strategy."

Ignoring my offered hand, Stan turns back to his son. "Social media campaign? Are you serious with this crap?" He gestures in my direction, and I can't tell if 'this crap' refers to the campaign or if I'm somehow included.

I'm pretty sure Chase is thinking the same thing as his expression blanks out again, and he stands.

"Watch yourself, old man."

Silence.

I can't see Stan's face, but Chase's remains hard.

Mouth firmly closed, I fight my need to fidget, hating the silence.

Stan loses the weird, macho staring contest he has going on with his son by turning to me. "Angelica, is it?"

Really? Misremembering my name? *Such* a cliché dick move. "Actually, it's Campbell. Campbell King." I don't offer him my hand again, but I totally deserve another pair of Jimmy Choos for keeping the disdain out of my voice.

"And just what do you think you can bring to the table that five of my most loyal managers can't? Hmmm?" He snorts. "Five managers that *this* one"—he thumbs over his shoulder to his son — "fired today."

Chase opens his mouth, but I stop him with a look. No man needs to save me. Especially when my business intellect is questioned.

I raise one eyebrow, matching Stan's condescension. "Why, customers, of course." His eyes narrow, and I maintain eye contact. "It seems you've been lacking them lately."

Chase coughs back a laugh.

"Think this is funny, do you?" Stan turns his disgust back toward his son. "Fire the men who can actually keep this place running and hire a nice rack to waste money on social media?" Stan snorts again. Calling him the devil may have been giving the man too much credit. Between his nasal noises, belly, and red face, he looks more like one of those personified pigs from Beatrix Potter. "Seems like something *you'd* do."

Chase's fists clench, and though his anger is almost palpable, his expression remains calm. I realize he doesn't trust himself to speak.

Taking a breath, I walk over and right the overturned family portrait on Chase's desk before fluttering my lashes at Stan, now only inches away. "Better than a bunch of swinging dicks with carpal tunnel and inflated paychecks."

Both men's jaws drop. Then Chase starts chuckling again, which turns into a full-out guffaw. Stan just turns a deeper shade of red.

"So nice meeting you, Stan." I'm proud to have kept my parting words civil. "Chase, we'll have lunch another time. I'll see you tomorrow for our scheduled meeting."

He frowns a moment before glancing at his father and sighing. "Tomorrow, Ms. King. Can't wait." He winks.

Stan starts to bluster and stutter, probably trying to think of something nasty to say. Before he can, I walk my nice rack out of the room.

* * *

Chase

"Even when you're in charge of the whole damn company, the only thing you focus on is bedding a hot piece of ass disguised as a businesswoman, huh? Where'd you find the foul-mouthed woman? On that porn site you're so proud of?" Stan eyes the door Campbell just closed a moment longer before piercing me with his next set-down. "I don't know why you can't be more like Thomas. He'd never hire a woman like that."

"That's rich considering the only reason I'm here and have made these changes is because of Thomas and his desire to have nothing to do with the company."

Cue Stan's nostril flaring.

"And let me guess: You think a beautiful woman can't work for Moore's unless she's on the sales floor. Convincing customers they can either *be* her or *have* her if they just buy what she's selling." His facial expression tells me I'm right in my assessment. "Is it truly beyond your comprehension that women can be as good as, hell, *better than*, men when it comes to business?"

"Please," he scoffs. "Any woman worth her salt knows her place. And it's sure as shit not in the executive offices of *my* company."

Her place. I roll my eyes. My optic muscles are always under threat of strain when dealing with Stan. "Do you really think that? Because you only got a foothold in Moore's boardroom door because you married Mom." I pause, thinking over our last family lunch. "Maybe that's why Mother hits the bottle when you're around. Sad that this is where you've taken her legacy."

His eyes narrow to slits. "Shut it."

I throw him a smirk I know will annoy him before sitting down and kicking my heels up on the desk again. *His* desk. "Besides being unbearably rude and sexist, was there something you wanted?" I really shouldn't have given George the morning off to go to the eye doctor. My administrative assistant could've squinted a bit longer. Clear eyesight is overrated, anyway. Especially when it means he isn't here to act as a barrier to my father just waltzing in like this.

He glares at my feet a moment before throwing me a smirk of his own. Anything even resembling a smile on the man is quite unnerving.

"You want to throw your weight around like a toddler with a tantrum, fine." He extends his hands out to his sides. "Go ahead. Fire those men."

"Thanks for permission to do something I've already done, Stan."

The would-be smile leaves his face, but his eyes continue to gleam.

I'm instantly alert. "What have you done, old man?"

"Me? I've done nothing. But you, with all your rash decisions, you could be responsible for your poor, dear sister becoming... well, destitute."

I put my feet down and lean forward over the desk. No use pretending he doesn't have my attention. It's a well-known fact I've always favored my sister. I glance at the family portrait, now cracked, on the desk. We may be further apart in years than Thomas and myself, but as soon as she was born, I hovered over her, protecting her at an early age against the coldness of our father and the easily bowed backbone of our mother. "Explain."

"I just got to thinking this morning, after all those phone calls from my colleagues."

I hold back a snort. Colleagues would imply my father had actually worked alongside them. My father has never sullied his hands with work.

He continues, "You may have the majority of shares held hostage at the moment, but I have something even better."

The smile returns to his face, and it's downright frightening. I'm not sure if it's the awkwardness of his facial muscles attempting something they've rarely done, or if the man is truly evil, but I swear to god, goosebumps dance along my arms at the sight of it.

"Don't keep me in suspense, Daddy-o, what is it you think you have that's better than our shares?"

"Money."

"Really, Stan? Money? Is that even a threat? Everyone in this family has money, even Liz."

"No, not Liz. Not her own, anyway. Every dime she spends she gets from me."

I still for a second before feigning nonchalance. But it's too late. The old man caught my reaction. His grotesque smile widens.

"So?" But I know. I know what he's about to say. I'm not an idiot. I made sure as soon as I took over to look into the laws regarding the shares. And what can and can't be done with them if Moore's is sold at a loss. I saw the loophole he could exploit if he wanted to. And for some reason, even after a whole lifetime of him disappointing me, I'm still hoping he won't stoop that low.

"Liz is only twenty-three. She can vote, as she did in your favor to take over the company, but she doesn't control her money or her shares in the event of a sale before she's twenty-five." He pauses for effect. "I do."

And that's it. That's the last shred of hope that my father isn't a complete dillweed, up in smoke.

"So... if you fuck this up, *boy*, not only am I taking *your* shares, as per our deal, I'm cutting your sister off as well."

A sigh of disappointment escapes me. "You really are one horrendous excuse for a father, you know that?"

Something flashes in his eyes, and that shred of hope wants to forge itself back to life again. But then my father scoffs, and the hope is gone for good. "Legacy and business are what matter. Your problem—well, yours and Liz's—is that you're too caught up in *feelings*."

I wonder, not for the first time, what the hell happened to this man to make him the way he is. But I shove the disquieting thoughts aside. "Well, as lovely as your threat is, it isn't much of one. Remember, I can take care of Liz."

"Can you?" He rocks back on his heels. A little too carefree for my liking. "If you let your dick get in the way, like you did with your pornographic app, you won't be making any money at

Moore's." He chuckles at my expression. "You didn't think I knew you let your previous *business* go tits up because of a woman?" He waves his hand in the air. "It may have been porn, but at least it was profitable. And then you let your delicate *feelings* get in the way, walking away with not even a quarter of its worth." He sneers. "Who cares who the bitch slept with?"

Honestly, this is a side of my father I've never seen. I hadn't thought it possible to dislike the man more than I already did. "You are one cold bastard, Stan. But that isn't anything new." I walk around the desk, closer to the man I share blood with. "But I *will* take care of Liz. Always. Even if you're not man enough for the job."

His eyes narrow. "You could. That would make Liz beholden to you. Asking for handouts from you, rather than being in charge of her own money. She'll just love that." His smirk has me clenching my teeth.

I shake my head, not sure why I'm so sad to have the fact that my father doesn't know or care about his daughter confirmed so thoroughly. "Liz has never cared about money."

Stan scoffs. "Please. She's a self-proclaimed *artist*." He rolls his eyes. "You think she doesn't care about money? Wait until she doesn't have any. Until she has to support herself." His eyes narrow. "What do you think will happen when she finds out the cold, hard truth that being a hippie won't pay the bills? She may be a free spirit, but she's proud. She'd never let you support her."

I try to take a calming breath, but it's no use. As much as I want to refute what he's saying, I can't. If on the outside chance I don't make Moore's more profitable, and Stan goes through with yanking her shares, Liz won't have a dime. And even though it would be my fault, Liz would never agree to let me help her financially.

Stan gloats before continuing. "She'll have to give up her

dreams and get a real job. And since all she knows how to do is swish paint on a canvas, it'll be a shit job at minimum wage." His lip curls. "And she'll have you to thank for her lot in life."

A weight settles in my stomach. I've never worried about money, and a lot of that has to do with the free education I got and my last name. I never fooled myself into thinking Stan paid my way through college out of the kindness of his heart. It was expected in our level of society. He needed to keep up with appearances. Besides the degree, I'm smart. I don't need family money. Haven't even used it except for college tuition. But Liz. She's still in school. And if things go wrong and she doesn't let me help her with the bills, she probably won't be able to finish.

And even as I think this, I realize there are ways around it. Liz is smart, and her art is well thought of by her professors. She could get a scholarship, take out a student loan. But the money wouldn't be the worst part.

The worst would be the moment she realizes just how easily her father could cut her so cleanly from his life.

Liz is sensitive. It's one of the things I cherish most about her, how she remains so kind and warm in the midst of the barren wasteland that is the Moore clan. Knowing how unapologetically cruel her father could be would change her in ways she'd never recover from. And just like I kept her believing in the magic of Santa Claus for as long as humanly possible, I've protected her from the reality of our father's controlling dickheadedness.

My expression must show my thoughts because the smile on Stan's face becomes more genuine.

It's truly terrifying.

"Yes, your sister may side with you, and she may love you the most, but she's a godforsaken, free-living hippie who still loves her family." He glances to the door where only a few moments ago Campbell had left. "You were never my first choice to run this company, but it seems not just two, but all three of the Moore children have become disappointments." His fists clench, probably thinking of his beloved Thomas's abandonment. He opens the door and, like the villain he is, throws back one more parting shot. "So keep your dick in your pants and do the job you were so smug about being able to do."

6

BELL

"Hey sweet thing, looking good!" a man shouts from scaffolding as I pass underneath. This statement is punctuated with a wolf whistle and some barking.

Damn, I've missed New York.

I know. I know. The construction workers' comments are crude and objectifying, but it's also so... New York.

Plus, I *am* looking good. Slim-cut cigarette pants with zippers at the ankles hug my hips, and my feet click with every step in my new shoes. New shoes that had been laid out on my bed when I'd gotten back to the hotel yesterday.

Seems the clothes I hadn't purchased yesterday had been boxed up and sent over.

Normally, I'd refuse. I'd maintain professional boundaries. Not muddy the waters, as it were, by accepting such a lavish gift. Except the note hadn't said *From Chase*. Or *Mr. Moore*. It had said, *From the grateful staff at Moore's, please accept with our thanks for all that you will do.*

How the hell do I send *that* back?

I can't. So I didn't. Instead, I have yet another new pair of

Jimmy Choos on my feet, these a modest two-inch-heel slingbacks in red.

And though these shoes are truly fabulous, my absolute favorite part of my new outfit is the top.

It's one I hadn't even seen yesterday, let alone tried on. Because if I had, I would've purchased it in a heartbeat, no matter the cost.

The cream silk blouse has a Peter Pan collar and dainty pearl buttons. But what gets me is the print. It's almost like a modern toile print, but instead of an English countryside, it's cowboys riding horses.

Though not the most professional of blouses, I couldn't help but wear it today. Maybe being back in the city I love so much is making me feel both whimsical and homesick. So a top that celebrates Texas and shoes that symbolize my new client seem like a good omen for my first official day on the job.

The bakery door chimes as I enter. Fresh-baked bread and pastries perfume the air. I inhale deeply. The sweet tune of "I Just Can't Help Believing" plays in the background, solidifying my good feelings. It's like Mom is with me whenever I hear Elvis. And as a Texas girl born and raised, she'd also love this blouse.

"Can I help you?" A middle-aged man behind the counter in an apron and hairnet leans his forearms on top of the bakery case.

"Yes, please." I step closer, pointing to the top basket in the case. "A dozen plain bagels and three medium containers of cream cheese. One of plain, one of strawberry walnut, and one of your lox spread."

"Love a girl who knows what she wants." He gives me a friendly wink and starts packing my order.

The wink reminds me of Chase. Specifically, the last one he threw my way yesterday after his father had barged into his office. As much as I didn't like meeting his father, I think the interruption was for the best. Things were getting too... intimate?

I pull my card out of the inside pocket of my soft-sided brief-case slung over my shoulder and pay, asking for the receipt. Being able to write off New York bagels for work is a definite perk of the job.

Again, I think of Chase.

Chase is *not* a perk.

"What was that, dear?" the lady at the cash register asks. Her brown hair is cut in a bob, with small streaks of gray woven through it. Her pleasant smile creases the corners of her eyes.

Great, I spoke my thoughts out loud again. "Oh, uh... nothing. Just, um, reminding myself of something."

"You business gals, always going a mile a minute, never a rest." She shakes her head, her bob swinging.

"And what do you think you are, Midge?" the man asks, handing me my bag of goods. "You're a business lady, and thank god for it. Without you, I'd run this place into the ground." He kisses her cheek.

"Oh, stop it, John." Midge playfully pushes him away.

"Family business?" I ask.

"It's been in my family for three generations." John puffs his chest out proudly before deflating it fast. "Though it never turned a real profit until this one started working here." He puts his arm around Midge. "Had to marry her to make sure she stuck around."

Midge rolls her eyes. "Honestly. There were easier ways to turn a profit than marry me."

"Yeah, but none with so many benefits." He waggles his eyebrows at her, making her laugh. It's obvious this is a timeworn argument, loving and playful.

"Here now, don't let us keep you." Midge hands me the receipt. "Come back soon!"

I nod. "I'm in New York for business, but I'll be sure to come back." I gesture to the bakery case. "Those black and white cookies are calling my name."

John tries to give me one on the house, but I manage to resist. "Gotta keep me wanting more, right, Midge?"

She agrees with a smile and a nod, going back to playfully fending off her husband's advances as the bell rings with my departure.

The cab ride to Moore's is made more pleasant by the smell of warm carbs.

* * *

"Ma'am."

I smirk at the security guard, a straitlaced, buttoned-up, suit-wearing guy (no mall cop uniforms for Moore's). He is about as far from Texan as you can get in his shiny oxfords, but the ma'am gets me every time. Instead of arguing, though, I just nod back, determined to get these bagels to our scheduled conference room without any nipple-exposing incidents.

"Could you tell me where the security office is? My team and I have an appointment this morning with Mr. Moore. I need to sign in and get an elevator key. I'm Campbell King."

He places a finger at his ear, like a CIA agent on assignment. I purse my lips in amusement. Moore's has secret agent security but no social media plan? That's just crazy.

Two women glide into Moore's wearing more diamonds than Beyoncé and Rihanna at the Grammys. One has an Hermès Kelly bag on her arm, the other a Fendi Selleria. How do I know about these bags and their five-figure price tags? Personal dreams and professional research.

So maybe high-end security isn't *that* crazy.

"This way, ma'am."

"King. It's Ms. King."

"Yes, Ms. King." He gestures forward. "This way."

Tamping down my annoyance at having to be escorted, I follow the security guard's well-fitted dress pants down the hall and past the restrooms to an Employee Only marked door. Security-man slides a key card next to the door and stands back to let me through.

Feeling slightly childish for thinking he'd been escorting me because I am a woman, not because there's actual security proto-col, I shuffle forward in my slingbacks.

"This is Ms. King. She needs her key card."

The man behind the desk jumps up. "Ms. King?"

Wondering at his enthusiastic reply, I simply nod. "Yes, that's me."

"Here, let me take that for you." He reaches for my bag of bagels and places it on the counter. "I'll get your key card for you. I just need your license for verification."

"Sure." I retrieve my ID from my briefcase and slide it toward him. "All this to get to the office?"

"The office elevator doesn't just access the offices. It also accesses inventory. And as some of our inventory can be worth quite a bit, we need to verify everyone who gets access."

"Oh. That makes sense." It does, but it doesn't help the twinge of anxiety rearing its head again. Social media campaigns can focus on many different things. I've marketed oil companies, state colleges, and yes, clothing stores. But I hadn't needed security clearance at Cavendish's or been surrounded by diamond-wearing clientele.

"Mr. Moore asked to be informed as soon as you arrived." He reaches for his phone. "I'll page him now."

"Oh no, don't." I pause when his eyebrows shoot up, surprised at my outburst. I take a deep breath. "It's just, I'm early. No need to bother the boss, I'm sure."

The man smiles right back, oblivious to my unease. "No bother. Mr. Moore gets here early every day since he took over." He slides my ID back, along with my new key card, and continues his call.

I try for a smile, though I'm sure it looks more like a grimace. "That's... great." I slip both cards in my briefcase before grabbing my bag of bagels.

Usually, I would love to hear that my new client is reliable and hands-on. But this is different. Because usually I don't want my clients hands-on on me.

"Good morning, Ms. King."

Tingles spread under my skin. Stupid phone-sex voice.

I try and calm myself by taking a deep breath of the fresh-baked goods in my arms. For the first time in my life, the scent of carbs does nothing to soothe my frazzled nerves.

Figures.

Pushing my body weight onto the balls of my feet, I pivot around to face him. Clean-cut. Tailored. Expensive. Yummy.

Let's pretend I directed that last at my bagels.

"Morning, Mr. Moore."

"You look lovely today."

"Thank you." I rake my eyes over his sapphire blue suit, white shirt, and skinny black tie. The man even has a pocket square. I squint trying to make out the pattern.

He follows my eyes to his chest and tugs out his pocket square. Cats. All different breeds of cats playing with blue balls of yarn printed over white silk.

"That's... adorable."

He shrugs. "I'm adorable."

You sure are.

Chase's eyebrows shoot up. Security-man chuckles.

Damn it. I have to stop doing that.

Taking pity on me by not addressing my slip-up, Chase turns to Security-man. "How are you, Sam?"

"Just fine, sir."

"How's Chrissy?"

Security-man Sam lets out a long-suffering sigh. "Fine. Just started a new daycare and probably planning a coup to take it over."

They both laugh. "That sounds like your daughter, all right," Chase says, clapping Sam on the shoulder. He turns to the security guy behind me. "Scott, can you see that Ms. King's belongings are sent to the conference room?"

"Sure thing, Mr. Moore." The guy who made my key card, Scott, rounds the desk and takes the bag of bagels from me.

"You don't have to do that." I adjust my briefcase shoulder strap.

"It's no problem, Ms. King." He walks toward the back of the room, where I see a maintenance elevator.

"You wore it." Chase's eyes light up at the sight of my blouse. With the bagel bag out of the way, he has a better view. "I'm glad. I saw it yesterday, and it reminded me of you. I had Susan put it in the care package last minute."

"Wait. *You* put that together?" I look down at my new, beloved blouse. "The note led me to believe the package was from the staff of Moore's."

"Yes. Though I may own shares, I do have an office here." A full-blown smile now. "As you know." A shrug. "Technically, I *am* staff."

"Technically, huh?" But I'm smiling too. Only Chase could get me to smile when I should feel tricked. Maybe it's his voice. His smile. Or the fact that it's hard to get mad at a man wearing a cat-printed pocket square. But knowing he personally picked out my favorite shirt ever sends shivers down my spine. The good kind.

"'Return to Sender'? Good song, but don't even think about it."

Crap. My cheeks heat, but I smile it out, like I was conscious of my odd habit.

Why do all my weird quirks have to rear up around this man?

Chase checks his watch. "We have some time, why don't we order coffee at the café for your team before heading upstairs?" He steps back, gesturing me to the doors leading back to the retail floor.

Shaking off my embarrassment, I give him a sly look. "Returning to the scene of the crime, huh?"

He coughs. "Uh, yes. I guess we are." Once through the doors, he walks beside me. "Although I wouldn't call it a crime. Much too serendipitous for that."

"I'll be sure to use serendipity as my defense if I get arrested for flashing any more nipple today."

* * *

Chase

I'm getting side-eye from a barista.

It's the same girl from yesterday. I think she's hoping for another incident. And as much as I wouldn't be opposed to seeing Campbell's nipples again, I'm extra careful with the carrier of coffees as we exit the café.

"Tell me about yourself, Ms. King. We didn't get to talk much what with the wet T-shirt contest we had and then being interrupting by an irate, portly man."

One side of her mouth quirks up.

"Why did you decide to start your own business?"

Her mouth flattens. "Same as anyone, I suppose. Be your own boss and all that."

"True. I'm just surprised no one snapped you up out of grad school."

Is it the light from the overhead chandeliers or did her eyes just darken?

She glances down, like she's watching her step, but I'm pretty sure she's just trying to hide her expression. "What do you mean?"

"You aren't the only one who does their research. I know more than just what the *Forbes* article highlighted." I nod at a cosmetic counter, where two saleswomen are waving enthusiastically. "Graduated top of your class from NYU, with a bachelor's in business and a master's in marketing. Scouted right out of college to—"

"Yes. I am aware of my education and résumé, thank you." She stops at a shoe display featuring the shoes currently on her feet. "This display is great. Very artistic. This should be shot and posted on the store's social media account."

"Moore's doesn't have social media accounts."

"I know." The look Campbell gives me makes me feel chastised and aroused all at once.

If anyone else took that tone with me, or insinuated incompetence, I'd make a joke and move on (cough *Stan* cough). But when Campbell takes me to task, I want to prove her wrong. Do better. "Well, that *is* why I hired you. I expect social media accounts to be a part of the marketing plan you'll be pitching."

"Yes. A big part of it." She waves toward the display again. "But back to this—who's in charge of displays?"

"I'm not sure." I scan the floor and catch sight of Raymond, the floor manager. He sees me as well and makes his way over. While we wait, I realize Campbell has done it again. She's avoided talking about herself. Interesting.

"Yes, Mr. Moore?" Raymond asks, his posture bordering on military precision.

I try not to cringe but fail. "Chase, Raymond. Call me Chase."

One perfectly quirked eyebrow tells me he is not in favor of my request. He never is, but, as always, he nods in acknowledgement of it.

"This is Campbell King, of King Marketing," I continue.

"How do you do, ma'am?" Raymond inclines his head in her direction.

Campbell surprises us both by laughing. *Damn*, she has a great laugh. Big and gusty, unfettered by self-consciousness. "I came all the way from Texas only to be called ma'am in New York. Several times." She chuckles again. "I'm Bell, Raymond. Nice to meet you." She adjusts the bag on her shoulder and sticks her hand out to him.

Raymond, usually stoic and borderline taciturn, smiles warmly at Campbell and grasps her outstretched hand between both of his. "A pleasure." He brushes a kiss across her knuckles.

A weird feeling slinks through my gut. It takes me a moment to realize I'm jealous. I'm jealous that Campbell King invited Raymond to call her Bell, but not me. I'm jealous that she seems relaxed and unguarded around my sixty-something-year-old floor manager, but not around me. And I'm extremely jealous that he's touching her, kissing her, even if it's totally innocent.

The corner of Raymond's eyes wrinkle in a large smile when he looks up from her hand.

It better be totally innocent.

Ugh. Chase Moore does not get jealous. He didn't even get mad when his ex cheated on him. In fact, he'd even go so far as to say he'd been relieved. But here he is, not only thinking of himself in the third person, but also very fucking jealous.

Instead of opening my mouth and biting off either Raymond's or Campbell's head in my sudden, covetous man-fit, I let *Bell* take the lead while she questions Raymond on the displays.

"I've been through a few departments, and while none of the displays are necessarily bad"—her tone suggests otherwise— "none have this artistic quality. It really draws me in. Do you know who created the display?"

"You have a great eye ma'a—Bell." He shakes his head, like he can't believe he just called a lady by a nickname. And now I have an urge to punch the man who once helped me figure out the perfect sixteenth birthday present for my little sister. "Moore's doesn't actually have anyone in charge of creating displays. We usually receive reports from management on what styles or designers to promote and are told to do so simply, without fanfare."

I blink at the longest-running employee at Moore's. "You're kidding." Incredulity has shoved my jealousy aside for the moment.

Raymond shifts uncomfortably. "No, sir. The inventory manager thought anything else would seem... garish, I believe was the word he used."

Before I can respond to this latest nonsense, which I am sure originated from my father, Campbell interjects, "So how did *this* happen?" Once again, she gestures to the shoe display featuring Jimmy Choos hanging from the ceiling with fishing line, making them look as if they're floating. A bunch of different styles and colors dangle at different heights from the top of the alcove posi-tioned at the front of the shoe department. It makes for a more impactful presentation than the standard shoe shelves that usually grace the area, especially when the shoes rotate on the threads, under the glow of lights.

Bell starts humming "Blue Suede Shoes." She's fucking adorable.

"One of our youngest sales associates has been, well, rather tenacious, in wanting to try her hand at display." Raymond shrugs, making me smile at the glimpse of tenderness in the otherwise stoic gentleman's demeanor. "I'd been putting her off for some time, but when young Mr. Moore took over, I thought, at the very least, no one would get in trouble for trying something a little different under his management."

"I'm so glad you did. This is amazing." Campbell's Southern drawl thickens as she studies the display, stepping back a bit, tilting her head. "What's her name? Is she working now?"

"Her name is Alice, and yes, she's currently shelving stock, I believe."

Campbell's eyes light up. "Would it be okay to ask her about the display?" She turns to me as if just remembering I'm here. "That is, if you don't mind, Mr. Moore?"

I grind my teeth. "Chase. Please. And yes, that's fine."

A few minutes later, a woman who looks like she's fresh out of high school scurries out onto the floor.

"He had nothing to do with it!" Alice begins, waving at Raymond. "Mr. O'Neil here didn't know anything about my rearranging the display. It was all me." She's panting a bit, her eyes huge.

"Well, that is a shame, as I was going to applaud Mr. O'Neil for letting such a talented designer create such a brilliant display," I tell Alice, whose mouth is now hanging open.

Campbell steps up, placing a calming hand on the girl's shoulder. "Please tell me more about your display, Alice. What made you think of it? And do you have any training in design?"

"Um…" Alice looks to Raymond.

"It's okay, Alice. Mr. Moore—" Raymond pauses when I clear my throat. "I mean, Bell and *Chase*"—he looks visibly pained at using our given names in front of his staff— "were just saying how much they loved your design."

Alice's body visibly relaxes, one hand reaching out to hold on to the edge of the display table. "Oh, that's good. I really need this job." She takes a deep breath before stepping back and looking at her display. "I'm really glad you like it. I'd been thinking of it for a while. I thought if I could make the shoes look comfortable, more inviting, then maybe more people would try them on. And let's face it, once you try these shoes on, you aren't going to take them off." She looks pointedly at the Jimmy Choos on Campbell's feet. "And that's when I got the idea to make the shoes float. Look lighter than air."

Though that sounds a bit far-fetched to me, the look on Campbell's face tells me she is one step away from swooning over Alice.

"That's brilliant." She turns to Raymond. "Is it possible to look over the sales numbers for Jimmy Choos since the display has been up?"

"Of course. But without specifics, I know for a fact that we have had to order more stock than normal. The inventory manager informed me yesterday. That is what Alice was stocking before she came out to join us."

Alice blushes, her fair skin pinking from the top of her hairline and disappearing into her high-necked blouse. It makes her look even younger.

"How old are you?" Campbell's blunt question takes us by surprise. "Sorry," she says, her own blush highlighting her cheekbones. "Didn't mean to be so forward."

Alice laughs. "It's okay, I've been getting asked that a lot since I got my hair cut. I think it's the bangs." She raises her eyes, trying to look at the thick fringe lying on her forehead. "I'm twenty-six."

"You don't look a day over eighteen," Campbell says. "Where did you study?"

"I'm sorry?"

"What college did you attend?" Campbell asks.

"Uh, I didn't." Alice looks down at her feet. "College wasn't in the cards for me."

Campbell smiles at her kindly. "That's okay. In fact, that makes your idea and application even more impressive." She turns to me for a second, then back to Alice and Raymond. "Would you excuse us for just a minute?" Campbell takes the coffee carrier from me, placing it on a display table, then drags me by my arm to the other side of the shoe department. I say drag because I slow my steps. I tell myself that it's so Campbell doesn't turn an ankle in her heels, but I know it's to stretch out this moment, enjoy her arm linked in mine.

Sometimes I think flannel-wearing lumberjacks are going to come and revoke my man-card.

"I want her," Campbell says once we are out of hearing.

My eyebrows shoot straight up my forehead, while a knot forms in my stomach. I hadn't known what she wanted to talk about, but it wasn't *that*. I guess her age question makes sense now. "Um, well, you technically aren't a Moore's employee, so I guess there's no problem if you want to ask her out." I know we work together, and therefore getting involved is never a good idea, but the thought of Campbell playing for the other team and being truly out of reach romantically seriously depresses me.

Campbell stares at me for a solid minute, unblinking. Then she surprises me yet again by saying, "You're an idiot."

"Excuse me?"

"I can't believe you just said that." She leans back on one heel and crosses her arms over her chest. The universal pissed-off pose. I'm used to seeing it from my parents, but when Campbell does it... let's just say *all* of me comes to attention.

"That makes two of us."

She snorts. It's delightful.

"I *meant* I want her for my team. My *marketing* team I'm building for you. She would be a better asset to Moore's in display than in sales."

"Oh." If I blushed, I'd be fire-engine red right now.

"Yes. 'Oh.'" She rolls her eyes, and the goofy look on her normally serious face makes me smile. I smile wider when I realize not all hope is lost for this spark of attraction between Bell and me.

Her eyes narrow. "What's that smile for?"

"Oh, nothing." I wink, my smile remaining unchanged. As is the semi in my pants.

"It looks like you're up to something." She sounds wary, unpleased with my cheerfulness.

If I were honest, I'd tell her I'm incredibly happy that of the two of us, I'm the only one well-versed in the art of female cunnilingus. Or that I'm currently trying to strategize a way to both get to know her better and for her to climb me like a jungle gym naked. However, I'm pretty sure saying any of that on the very first day of us working together makes me a total douche. Hell, just thinking about it probably qualifies.

So I keep it all to myself.

"I don't know what you mean," I say instead. Ignoring her look of distrust, I take her arm and link it with mine once more, directing her back to Alice and Raymond. "Let's go get you your girl, shall we?"

7

BELL

My wooing skills need work.

Chase's wooing skills? They need no help.

After Chase realized his mistake about my interest in Alice (I can't *not* laugh when I think of it), he'd simply ushered Alice and me up to his office and laid on the charm. When I tried persuading Alice to move into marketing, she'd been reluctant. Then Chase mentioned a salary increase, more benefits, better insurance, and *poof!* A huge smile overtook Alice's face as she received a copy of my schedule, the agenda for the upcoming meeting, and a few words of encouragement from Moore's head honcho.

Chase may wink and laugh with ease. And yes, the ladies may love him. But he was nothing but professional while talking with Alice, knowing exactly what she needed to hear to boost her self-confidence, recognize her abilities, and take the chance on a new position.

Watching him be both professional and courteous is a serious turn-on. Which is bad. There's already this informal camaraderie between us that shouldn't be there. It's the reason I haven't given him permission to call me Bell. I don't need to blur any more lines.

It's as if we've known each other a lot longer than two days and a phone call. Maybe it's because he saw my nipples. Or knows what color panties I like. Whatever it is, I can't let myself be less than professional. Even if he is charming and has the physique of an Olympic swimmer, with dark hair that's a day or two past needing a trim, and large, graceful hands...

No. Not going down that road. Going down... Shoot, now I'm thinking about going down on Chase Moore. My dirty, dirty mind is obviously against me. I really should've listened to Leslie and opened up an online dating profile. This sex drought I'm experiencing must be affecting my professionalism.

"Thanks so much for this opportunity, Ms. King, Mr. Moore," Alice says, hugging the folder full of paperwork to her chest and, thankfully, pulling me out of my dirty daydreams.

"No, thank you, Alice. You just did me a solid, putting your artistic talents to better use for the company," Chase says smoothly while guiding her to the door. "And remember, it's Chase, not Mr. Moore."

Alice nods, still wide-eyed, thanks us again, and leaves to finish her shift in the shoe department before reporting in with the rest of my team tomorrow in the conference room.

"The coffee's probably cold by now." Chase gestures to the drink carrier I'd placed on his office coffee table and picks up the phone. "I'll get my assistant to have more sent up."

I want to protest, but honestly, I know my team. They need to be properly caffeinated. "Thanks."

"No problem."

While he's on the phone, I walk over to the mostly empty shelves. I say mostly, since whereas there was nothing but shiny mahogany glaring at me when I was here yesterday, today there are three photos scattered on one large shelf. In one photo, a younger Raymond, maybe thirty or so, though still as stiff-looking as ever, is bent at the waist, eye to eye with an elementary-school-aged Chase. The older man's stern but loving expression is at humorous odds with Chase's impish grin.

At first glance, the second photo is of a random clothing rack. But on closer inspection, two pairs of shoes peek out from beneath the clothes—one pair of red girls' sandals and one of scuffed-up boys' sneakers.

The third photo makes me chuckle. It's a teenage Chase, standing next to a slightly younger Susan. Susan is smiling at the camera, but Chase's eyes are cutting to the side where an attractive salesgirl, maybe in her twenties, is working.

"As you can see, Raymond and Susan have known me most of my life."

I jump, not having heard Chase move up behind me.

"Our conversation yesterday reminded me of these photos." His finger drags along the side of one of the brass frames.

"It did?"

"Yep." He picks up the one of him and Susan. "What you can't see in this photo is my sister, crouched just off camera, ready to pounce."

"Your sister? All I see is a hormonal teenage boy ready to pounce on an unsuspecting salesgirl." I look closer at the picture, taking in Chase's slightly leaner frame and longer, shaggy hair. His expression is just an older version of the mischievous grin he gave Raymond in the first photo.

"Yes, I was planning my next attempt at seduction with Serena." He taps on the girl in the picture. "But I shouldn't have bothered. Liz took care of it for me in the end." His grin is rather sheepish. "Remember that story I told you yesterday? Well, this was the moment just before she pantsed me."

"Oh my god. No." I laugh out loud, imagining the confident,

handsome boy in the picture getting taken down a peg by an equally mischievous sister.

"Oh, yes. But not to worry." He places the frame back on the shelf. "I had the last laugh."

"And how's that?"

Hands in his pockets, he rocks back on his heels. "I had been pestering Serena for a good month to go out with me. Even though I was seventeen and she was twenty-two. Each time, I was shot down."

"Oh, poor you."

"Yes, my poor, tender heart was bruised beyond belief."

Scoffing, I pat him on the shoulder. "I bet."

"Then Liz pants me. Managing not only to take down my trousers, but my boxers as well."

"No!" My laughter erupts once again. But instead of looking embarrassed, Chase just smirks. "So how did you get the last laugh? Did you pants her back or something?"

He shakes his head. "Nope. Didn't even have to come up with a plan for revenge. Serena did that for me."

"What do you mean?"

"One look at me with my pants down, and I had a date."

"Seriously?" Now I'm shaking my head. "You were seventeen!"

He strolls over to his office door, still open from when Alice left. "But I was seventeen with a nine-inch dick."

With that parting shot, he walks out, turning down the hall. "Coming?" he calls.

"If I had nine inches, you bet your ass I'd be," I mutter.

He pokes his head around the door frame. "What was that?"

"Nothing! Nothing!" Eyes determinedly fixed away from said nine inches, I hustle out the door and past him toward the elevator.

8

CHASE

Buzz.

"Mr. Moore, sorry to interrupt you, sir, but your brother is on the line."

Sighing, wishing it was yesterday with Campbell in my office, I push the intercom button. "Tell him I'm not in, George."

"Yes, Mr. Moore."

"Thanks. And remember, call me Chase."

Nothing. George won't outright tell me no, but he isn't afraid to go radio silent when he disagrees with me. I'd thought George, being a younger guy who grew up in the days of leisure wear as everyday wear, would embrace informality. I should've known better when it came to light that he was Raymond's nephew.

I swear the kid had been more offended than his uncle when I'd asked him to call me Chase.

The intercom buzzes again.

"Yes, George?"

"Now your mother is on the line, sir."

"Tell her the same, I'm out of the office." I tap the fountain pen in my hand on the desk. "In fact, whenever they call, tell them that.

I'll only answer for my sister. All other family members get the new party line. Got it?"

"Yes, Mr. Moore."

"Chase."

Silence.

Why the hell is my brother calling? My mother I might understand. Every once in a while, she gets it in her head to invite me to lunch. But more than likely it's because I'm not answering my father's calls and he's managed to bully her into calling me on his behalf.

But Mom calling right after my brother? My brother who's never once called me? That's just weird.

I grab the family picture on my desk, running my finger over the crack in the glass. It runs diagonally, perfectly dissecting my image from the rest of the family.

Metaphor, anyone?

Instead of the usual resentment about my family dynamic, I find myself chuckling, remembering Bell in here with my father, holding her own as he blustered on. Was that really only two days ago?

She's something else. Something different. I knew it the moment my nipples became third-degree burn statistics.

She's also interested, even if she might not want to be. Don't think I didn't hear her comment about my dick yesterday morning. I'd just played the gentleman card and pretended I hadn't.

I also pretended not to notice how we traded glances in front of her team as they ate the bagels she'd brought and drank the coffee I'd had sent up fresh. It was like high school, each of us cutting our eyes away when the other looked.

Duty had called me away to handle some accounting issues yesterday, but George, and his newly adjust eyeglass prescription, had stepped in and given Campbell and her team a formal tour of all the departments at Moore's.

Blinking, I redirect my focus to the spreadsheets on my computer, wishing I'd been there to give the tour myself, seeing Bell's face as she took in my family's legacy. The only place that had ever felt like home to me.

I glance at the silent intercom. George said the tour went well. When I pushed for more details, he just raised his eyebrow over his flashy wireless frames. Curious bastard.

Today he's back manning his desk and screening my calls, and Bell and her team are holed up in the conference room down the hall, just a few steps away. They've been there since early this morning. I hung back when I heard them walking by my office, not wanting to seem overeager, or worse, micromanaging. I made sure George sent up more hot coffee.

Did Bell bring her employees bagels again today? She seems like the kind of boss who'd take care of her team. But I wonder what kind of boss she is when it comes to getting work done. Is she cutthroat and demanding? Quietly assuring? Is it weird that any and all of those scenarios is arousing to me?

In the little I've seen her and her team interact yesterday morning, I can tell there's mutual respect. She didn't go around hugging everyone, but her smile was genuine and their handshakes friendly. Her team, Chris and Ben, work in New York while she's based in Houston. Yet she still asked about their lives, their families. Showed she cares. They didn't do the same, but I'm not sure if they didn't feel comfortable doing so because she's their boss, or if they hadn't known what to ask. Even so, there weren't any stiff formalities or tie straightening and posturing like when Stan usually enters Moore's. On those rare occasions he deigns to enter the building.

Shaking off thoughts of my family, I place my broken family

picture face down and glance at the clock. Almost noon. The stack of papers I have to go through and the amount of emails and calls I need to answer means I can't sneak away and check on the King Marketing team, much as I want to. But after getting Bell thinking about me in a nonprofessional manner, I don't want her to think I've forgotten her either.

A quick Google search gives me the phone number I need.

"Thai's Pad. May I help you?"

"Yes. I'd like to order for delivery please."

* * *

* * *

"We could literally do anything, and it would be an improvement," Ben says, pausing only to shovel noodles into his mouth. "I mean, they don't even have a Facebook page, let alone a Facebook ad." My fresh out of undergraduate marketing strategist looks bewildered, and it would be comical if it didn't highlight just how much work we have ahead of us. "Damn, this is good Thai food." He swallows. "Where is this from again?"

"Thai's Pad," I answer automatically. Best not to think too much on how Chase remembered me mentioning it. Focus on the task. "Chris. Thoughts?"

Chris pauses in mid-reach for a takeout container. "It's weird. I'd like to know how they've stayed in business this long." He grabs the box. "I don't get it."

"Old money." I try not to pounce on all the Thai goodness spread out on the table. I give up and grab the shrimp spring rolls and a container of peanut sauce. I don't even offer to share. I fully plan on double dipping.

Ben and Chris are both based in New York. They'll travel where

I need them, but it's fortunate that they both love New York and made it their home.

Clients are usually surprised at the small teams I run, but to me, too many cooks in the kitchen gets confusing. Whichever coast I'm on, and whatever team I use, it usually only consists of two to four people. Though I have to say, together, Ben, Chris and I make up most of the marketing strategies around. They're the best of my best. So it's handy they're local, as it looks like King Marketing needs a verifiable battle plan to bring Moore's into the twenty-first century, and it would cost a mint to house them in New York for a long period of time.

Alice, who met me at the conference room door this morning carrying a book bag full of notebooks and pens like it was the first day of school, hasn't touched the food, refusing to put down her pen or stop taking notes. Though I see her eyeing the yellow curry. I push it closer to her with my chopstick. She smiles guiltily before giving in and pushing her notebook aside.

It's been a long morning. Yesterday we toured the store. It takes a long time to walk through almost a million square feet. We didn't bother with the office space or restaurants, just the retail departments. George, Chase's assistant, showed us around. He was... efficient. I was surprised how mature he is for his age. We left late afternoon to drum up ideas and first impressions so we could hit it hard this morning.

But our morning was mostly slogging through the archaic advertising Moore's has been using and their current situation analysis. They've been in business for a lot of years, much longer than any of my other clients. There's a lot of information to analyze.

"Moore's reputation of catering to socialites and celebrities has kept them going. It's like a status symbol. And even if they don't have social media accounts, celebrities do, and luckily they post where they purchased certain items." I nod to Chris. "But you're right. It isn't enough. Even the wealthy are shopping differently. Looking more to what's trending on social media and one-clicking their purchases online." I take a large bite of spring roll. Dear lord, I've missed this peanut sauce. Best I've ever had.

After I swallow, I look up to see everyone staring at me.

"Enjoying that, are you?" Ben smirks.

I flush, realizing I may have moaned as I ate. "Yes, well." I clear my throat, moving on. "Let's look on the upside. We have a completely clean slate. We don't have to overhaul what's already there and debate about what to keep, what to lose, and so on. We can build fresh."

Yesterday we dealt with tangible goods. Now we're dealing with the corporate side, running numbers and making sure all our information is up to date. Comparing them with those of the competition.

"We'll be meeting with Moore's contracted marketing team, Warren and Baron, soon, right?"

I nod at Chris.

"Though who knows what they've been doing to earn their money," he mutters.

Ben snorts, looking at his laptop. "Nothing, if I had to guess from the apparent lack of information at hand."

"You know they're going to have more than just three people, right?" Chris asks me, making me pause in my next bite. "They won't be happy we're here, and they'll try to intimidate us. By sheer numbers if necessary."

"Yes, but until I know how well Warren and Baron is willing to work with us, I don't want to assume they'll be difficult. Besides, I have assurances that *we'll* have full control, not Warren and Baron." Though if W&B is unwelcoming or unwilling to play ball under new management, it won't be the first time I've had to 'bitch up' and take a more authoritative stance.

I tap my pen on my laptop, thinking as I chew. This time silently. Swallowing, I change directions. "Moore's is unique in that due to the overwhelming assortment of products they sell, we have a huge option for cold prospect marketing."

We've reviewed the company's target audience, strengths and weaknesses, and now we're on to strategies. All of which we've studied before, but it's good to do so again after seeing the product and company firsthand.

"The best numbers are in the high-end departments," Chris says, putting the now empty container down. "But there's a big decline everywhere else."

"Most of the high-end customers are in the forty to sixty age range." Alice looks up from her furious note-taking. When everyone's eyes meet hers, she looks back down, blushing.

Ben nods, looking lost in thought. "That's a good point. Moore's is basically alienating two generations. They may not have the money to shop in luxury goods, but there are a lot more departments than just the ones with the carpeted flooring." He taps on his keyboard. "The gaming area and café are pretty cool, but I don't even think those are listed on their basic website. Or if they are, they're not prominent."

"Then let's target those areas. Instagram, Facebook, Twitter. We need to set up a social media plan anyway, seeing as Warren and Baron never made one for Moore's."

Ben and Chris look at each other, eyebrows raised.

"I know. When I talked to Cha—I mean Mr. Moore, he was pretty determined that social media would be our primary focus."

I catch Alice's smile at my near slip. Thankfully, young, recent male graduates are oblivious to those sorts of things. Ben simply states, "Awesome. Social media marketing is my jam."

"It's everyone's jam, Ben," Chris says, rolling his eyes. "It's literally what King Marketing does."

"Whatever. I'm excited, okay?" He rubs his palms together. "Moore's is pretty huge. And as Campbell said, we have a clean slate. That's pretty much a marketing man's dream."

"Yeah, if Warren and Baron let us do our job," Chris adds, always the optimist.

"Don't worry about that." I close my laptop and scan the room, bringing all eyes to me. "I'll handle Warren and Baron."

* * *

Walking out the front doors of Moore's and into the smoggy New York air, my mind is filled with visions of room service while cocooned in my sumptuous hotel room bed with an action film on in the background.

Those daydreams stutter when I see Chase leaning against a town car that's parked at the curb.

My first thought? *Damn*, he looks good.

My second? He brings new meaning to "Hound Dog."

I haven't seen him all day. And I'd be lying if I said I hadn't noticed his absence. I'm a little mad at myself about how often I scanned the room or looked over my shoulder for his dark head of hair and charming grin. He'd sent us my favorite Thai food, but he never showed. I spent too much time worrying if he was avoiding me. If between me talking back to his father and mumbling about his nine-inch dick, he'd been offended.

By the time my team and I were ready to call it a day, my anxiety was clawing at me. So instead of dwelling on whether or not Chase Moore was upset with me, I made plans to relax in bed, in my sweats, listening to theatrical soundtracks of Bruce and Arnold quipping one-liners amid explosions of mass proportions.

Wine and action movies. This girl's dream night in.

"Have a productive day?"

My answer comes a bit slow, because most of my brain power is occupied with eyeing his tall body, clad in gray trousers and a light blue plaid, button-down shirt with the sleeves rolled up.

Forearm porn. It's a thing. I swear.

"Um, yes. Yes, I did." I gesture to the car. "What's this?"

"One of your perks. Much better than a cab."

I nod, studiously ignoring his forearms. "Thank you. I guess I'll see you tomorrow." I step toward the rear door of the car.

"Actually, more like two hours."

I pause, my hand on the handle, which is seriously close to his ass as he's still leaning against the car. "Excuse me?"

"I managed to stop Chris and Ben on their way out, too. Alice can't make it, some pre-established plan." He finally pushes off from the car and turns to open my door, grazing my hand in the process. "You'll be picked up in two hours for dinner at Winston's." His free hand gestures to the top of Moore's. "The restaurant on the top floor. Chris and Ben too."

I stare up at the imposing building, ignoring the heat from where he touched my hand. Finally, I get my shit together and step back. "That's nice and all, but no need."

"I insist. Dinner is the perfect place to catch me up on what you and your team came up with today. Plus, George told me you didn't have time to visit the restaurants during his tour yesterday."

That makes sense. It really does. But I can't help but push back. "I can just email you the notes we've made and see Winston's another time."

The corner of his mouth lifts in that easy way he has, and this time when his hand reaches out to touch mine, it's deliberate. "Why do I get the feeling you don't want to spend time with me, Campbell?"

The way he says my name sounds like a prayer. I haven't been too good about praying to baby Jesus lately, but right now, with Chase's hand on me and my name on his lips, my brain is screaming *Hallelujah*.

"No, it isn't that. I…"

"Then what is it?"

I haven't taken my eyes off him, and I swear he hasn't moved, but he suddenly seems so much closer now, his question too probing. The fact that I so desperately want to say yes makes me wary.

"Ben and Chris are coming?"

He nods.

Disappointment flutters, and I squash it down. I don't need any more alone time with Chase Moore. I've had too much as it is. Plus, he's correct. I haven't yet seen the various restaurants Moore's runs, and Winston's is supposed to be the most well-known.

Resolute, I clear my throat and pull back from his touch. "Dinner will be fine, Mr. Moore. I'll be ready in two hours." I pivot around him, avoiding eye contact as I slide into the cool leather seat. I lean forward to give the driver my hotel's address, not trusting myself to look Chase's way. But that doesn't stop me from feeling Chase's amused smile through the tinted windows.

I'm in trouble.

9

BELL

When I think Winston, I think Churchill. Which doesn't inspire the appetite. However, Winston's at Moore's is a whole different story.

Large golden chandeliers, dripping in crystal, hang from the ceiling. No linen tablecloths, just polished, well-worn wooden tables, dressed with bone-white china and crystal goblets. The old parquet floor patina glows under the dim lighting, with candles in honest-to-god brass candelabras illuminating the table. Between the decor and the breathtaking view of the city from the panoramic windows, it's a magical place.

Oddly, it's not crowded. Now, or when we sat down to dinner two hours ago.

When I mention the lack of patrons to Chase as the waiter clears our plates away, he simply says, "That's why you're here."

Indeed.

"Thank you all for dining with me tonight on such short notice. I really appreciate you rearranging your previous plans to bring me up to speed."

Chris and Ben nod enthusiastically and brush off Chase's

concerns. "No, man, this was great," Ben says, smiling wider than I've ever seen him. "Much better than what I had planned."

Not to be outdone, Chris offers, "Anytime, man. I'll have to take my girlfriend here sometime."

"I apologize, I should've extended the invitation to your plus-ones. I'll make sure to tell the manager that you have open reservations anytime you want. On me, of course."

"Wow, really? That's so cool." Ben's mid-twenties enthusiasm is showing.

Chris punches him in the arm. "You'll need an actual plus-one first, Xbox King."

Ben scoffs. "Don't be hating on my mad gaming skills, dude. No one likes a whiner." He straightens his shirt, running his hands down his skinny tie. "Besides, I can get a date anytime I want. Chicks love the nerd look these days."

Chase chuckles, a delightfully low rumbling sort of sound, and says, "Good to know, Ben." He winks at me before addressing my employees again. "If you wouldn't mind, I have a few more things to go over with Ms. King before the meeting tomorrow. But I've had the car pulled around to take you both home."

"Wow, man. Cool." Ben tosses his napkin on the table. "No late-night subway."

Before I can find an excuse to leave with them, Ben and Chris tell me to have a good night and shake Chase's hand, then amble out of the restaurant.

Chase Moore and I are alone.

My palms grip my knees under the table while I dream about assigning my two young employees the next female hygiene company to market in retaliation for abandoning me. Oblivious to my turmoil, Chase simply watches Ben and Chris leave before turning his attention to me.

"Your employees admire and respect you."

"Oh." Not what I'd been expecting him to say. "Thank you."

"You sound surprised."

I shrug. "I wasn't sure what you wanted to talk about, so I hadn't been expecting a compliment."

"You should always expect compliments."

I roll my eyes, but I'm smiling.

"I mean it." He pauses, as if unsure, before continuing. "You look beautiful tonight." Smoothly he moves from his seat across the table to the chair next to me that Chris vacated.

At first, I'm relieved. He's been across from me all night, and his eyes, when taken straight on, are hypnotic. They make you forget things that you should very much remember. But when he angles the chair next to me, so I'm once again the only thing in his line of sight, only much closer, I feel the pulse at my neck jump.

"Thank you." I drag my gaze from his eyes and look down at the blue dress Susan talked me into. It really is lovely. "Moore's does only sell the best."

"It isn't the dress." A quick glance shows him smirking. "Though I might give Susan a raise for getting you into it." His smile turns softer, his eyes heavier. "You'd be beautiful in anything."

I don't know what to say to this, so I say nothing. But that doesn't stop my body from *feeling*. I haven't felt this kind of attraction in... well, never. In the words of the immortal King, I'm all shook up. I haven't been able to get my footing where Chase is involved. All day yesterday and all through dinner, with each charming smile and audacious wink, I've felt myself forgetting the reasons why professionalism is so important to me.

"So, um. Your father. He's... interesting."

Chase lets loose a short bark of laughter. "I don't think anyone would call my father interesting. He is as boring and stereotypical as every other silver-spooned white guy from his generation."

His eyes become distant, and I feel like an ass for bringing Stan up, but I have to know.

"Will he be inserting himself into the new overhaul at Moore's?"

Chase gives me a questioning look.

"I just want to prepare my team if we need to be on the lookout for more of Stan's, um, input."

Smirk in place, Chase shakes his head. "No, Stan-the-man doesn't *do* productive work. The only input he likes is what you heard the other day. Rude comments, judgments, and your basic chauvinist attitude."

"Oh." I shift in my seat. "I'm sorry."

"No, no. I'm sorry. I really should've apologized for his behavior before now. I just didn't want to spoil the evening by talking about my father."

"Oops."

We both chuckle. Our laughter dies out slowly as we stare at each other in the candlelight. The shadows flickering in his eyes only highlight the warmth and smolder already natural to him. It would be so easy to lift my palm to his jaw, feel the light five o'clock shadow with the pads of my fingertips. Trace my fingers down to that damn hollow at the base of his neck.

I blink, breaking my train of thought. What am I *doing*? I need to go.

As if sensing my imminent retreat, Chase launches into a new subject. "So are you and your boys ready for me to set up a meeting with Warren and Baron?"

The tension eases at his playful, friendly tone, and I settle back in my chair, not realizing my legs had already been braced to stand. "My boys? You mean my highly qualified, top-notch educated, award-winning marketing team?" I throw my own smirk in his direction. "Yes, we're ready. Or we will be. You didn't really have a lot in place, marketing-wise."

He chuckles, the sound sending a warm buzz through my body. "In the past few months, I've been able to get rid of or change most of the antiquated inefficiency that's plagued Moore's. But the previous managers contracted our marketing to Warren and Baron, and there's still a year left on the contract. I could break it and pay a penalty, but as Moore's is already trying to come back from a decline in revenue, and we don't have an in-house marketing department set up *yet*"—he gives me one of his seductive winks—"I thought working *with* them, instead of firing them, would be best."

I nod once. "That makes sound business sense."

"Why do I feel like you want to add a 'but' to that statement?" The man has a million types of smiles, and the one he gives me now is playful.

"*But*"—I draw out the word, smiling back at him— "Warren and Baron is a well-established, traditional company. They do well with established businesses not looking for or needing expansion into other avenues. They deal more with referral advertising. Honestly, I'm not sure why Moore's hired them to begin with— they don't have any real retail background. And I'm not sure how well they'll play with the new team in town." I gesture to myself. Unintentionally, my fingers graze across the skin below my collarbone. Chase's eyes follow the movement, his gaze lingering.

In that moment, the emptiness of the restaurant surrounds us, the silence once more stringing out the tension that has been building since our first hello.

"I don't know, Campbell," he says, his sex operator voice going full-tilt, "I think you underestimate your appeal." He swallows, and my mouth parts as I watch his Adam's apple bob above that maddening hollow at the base of his throat. "I know *I'd* want to play with you." He raises his gaze. For once, his full lips aren't pulled back in a smile. Instead, his face is set, and his eyes penetrate mine with a deep intensity that has my thighs shifting on my chair.

What is *happening*?

He leans forward. "I swear I'd sell my shares just to know what you're thinking right now."

"You'd make a killing as a phone sex operator." *Oh my god. Kill me now.*

He tilts his head back and laughs, his neck exposed. The sight has me pushing my embarrassment aside and licking my lips, all thoughts of professionalism and self-preservation gone as my mind envisions my tongue gliding along his throat.

"Funny, I could say the same thing about you and your sexy Southern drawl."

His words shock me enough that I blurt, "We'd have great phone sex."

The intensity is back when he reaches over and trails one finger across my brow and down my cheek. "Oh, Campbell. We'd have great sex, period."

Chase

Two birds, one stone, I thought when setting up this work dinner. See how the new social media plan was shaping up, spend more time with the intriguing Ms. King.

I hadn't thought that the one stone would turn to two, those being my balls, drawn up tight under my massive hard-on. But that's exactly what's happened tonight.

It all started in the hotel lobby, where I'd been waiting to pick her up. The elevator doors opened, and Campbell stepped out wearing that blue dress.

Asymmetrical, or something. That's what Susan said about the dress. At the time I didn't pay much attention. Occupied with sending someone down to bring up a selection of shoes for Campbell, I missed her trying it on. Now I'm thinking that the way the dress's hemline starts right below one knee and travels up and across to her other leg mid-thigh is one of the five things I'm most thankful for at the moment.

One through four being the tabletop that hides my dick's perpetual salute to all things asymmetrical.

I probably would've been able to control little Chase (although between you and me, there is nothing little about him, wink wink), seeing as the tabletop also hid Campbell's sinful legs, freckled from the Texas sun and just as shapely as any Victoria's Secret model's.

But then she had to speak, and damn if her mind isn't twice as hot as her body.

I've had glimpses of it throughout our time together. A comment here, a perceptive remark there. Even how she handled herself in front of my jerk father. Campbell isn't one to sit back and let things happen. She saw potential in Alice and snapped her up. She realized Stan was a dick and called him on it. And tonight, she was in full business mode, leading her marketing team while getting me up to speed on the on-point social media strategy they've built in the limited time they've been here and the suggestion for a spokesperson. Someone to direct an already established fan base Moore's way.

My dick and I are seriously impressed.

I told myself to keep her talking business. That I could keep it professional. That I wouldn't cross the line. I reluctantly thought of Thomas. Stan and his threats against Liz.

Normally, the echo of Stan's voice in my head would have my Superman hard-on softer than Mike the Sphynx's hairless ball sack. But not tonight.

It's like Campbell King is its freaking kryptonite.

Because then she mentioned phone sex. And that was after I caught her humming "All Shook Up" again.

"Come home with me, Campbell." The command bursts from my subconscious, damn the consequences.

She licks her lips again, and I'm so sure she's going to say yes my dick is near vibrating in anticipation.

"I…" She blinks hard, then straightens in her seat. "No. I—I'm sorry, but I…" She clears her throat and reaches for her purse that's hanging on the arm of her chair. "Just no." Slowly, she stands, and I follow her up, even though it's going to be painfully obvious how much I wanted her answer to be yes. I grab a napkin on my way up, holding it strategically so as to save face.

"I'm sorry if I made you uncomfortable." Frustrated at myself, I run my hand through my hair with my free hand. "I thought this wasn't one-sided. I mean, ever since you burned my chest with coffee—"

"You turned around too fast!"

I laugh. "Okay, so ever since I turned around too fast and you burned my chest with coffee…"

She crosses her arms over her chest. "Humph." She's adorable.

"I've felt…" My mind blanks, trying to put into words exactly how I've felt.

"Something," she whispers.

I almost don't hear it, but I do, and man does that one word fill me with exactly that—something. Something powerful that I can't quite name. Need? Hope?

Campbell steps back from the table, hooking her purse strap over her shoulder. "Thank you, Mr. Moore. It was a wonderful dinner, and my team and I very much enjoyed your company and insight."

I incline my head, letting my eyes enjoy the sight of her standing, the hem of her dress swaying into place. "I'll have your driver come around." I drop the napkin so I can reach for my phone.

"Oh, no need, really." She takes a few steps backward, toward the restaurant's entrance.

I'm about to let her escape, to let tonight's heavy flirtation and innuendo be a one-off, to not be a pushy douchebag. Until she looks down. At my dick.

In itself, looking isn't a big deal, seeing as my dick is desperately trying to break free from my thin, cashmere-wool blend slacks. I'm sure it looks like I'm sporting a lead pipe in my pants (which I basically am). But it's what she does when she looks. Her eyes widen, her chest swells, and her mouth parts. Her devilishly sexy tongue darts out, licking her pouty bottom lip before her front teeth bite down on it. As if she's trying to contain herself, contain the desire coursing through her body.

The best part? She doesn't look away. We stand for a moment, me watching her staring at my rocking hard-on.

Then this smart, sexy, stunningly beautiful woman sighs and presses her legs together, which due to the thank-the-fucking-lord short, asymmetrical dress she's wearing, I can clearly see.

"Come home with me, Campbell," I can't help but repeat, hating the desperation in my voice. I've never, not once in my life, been desperate. But then again, I've never met Campbell King before.

It takes a moment. A delicious moment where she isn't able to drag her gaze from my dick. But then her eyes are on mine, and what she sees there she must like, at least as much as what's in my pants, because she says one word. One word that is about to change everything.

"Yes."

10

BELL

This is foolish. So foolish.

But even as I repeat that to myself over and over again, I still place my hand in the one Chase offers me, leading us out of the restaurant. I still let him steer me into the elevator and allow his arms to cage me against the wall as it descends.

"Kiss me," he says.

For a moment I wonder why he doesn't just kiss me. Take me the way he wants. As evidenced by the massive erection he's pointing in my direction.

"But only if you want to. I don't want you to feel pressured."

And then I realize, he doesn't want me to simply let this happen between us. Or feel like I have to. He may have initiated the first move, the verbal invitation, but contact, physical contact, that'll be up to me. And damn if him giving me the reins doesn't make my need for him that much sweeter.

And I do want it. Him. Badly. Badly enough to call myself ten times the fool and not care. Badly enough that I raise my arms, dragging them up the sides of his body until my palms cradle his face and I lift on my tiptoes to bring my mouth to his.

Both of us groan on contact. Sweet, delicious contact. We devour each other, our tongues tasting, our breath mingling. It's the hottest kiss in the history of the world. I'm not even being dramatic.

But I need more.

I step forward, aligning my body against his, and press.

For a moment, it relieves the ache, until it makes it worse. I feel like an addict who's been given a taste but who wants the whole hit. I raise one leg and hook it around his hip, my hands grabbing his shoulders. This gives me the leverage I need to grind. And I do; I grind *hard*.

I'm grinding on Chase Moore, the owner of Moore's, my new client. Specifically, I am grinding my soaked center across his thick, hard length in the elevator of his building. In the back of my mind, behind the fog of sexual insanity, I'm pretty sure I grasp how wrong this is. How stupid. But when my clit rubs over the length of his hard-on, I just don't give a damn.

I'm so very tired of caring. Of holding myself back. Of masking key aspects of myself behind business verbiage and stoic expressions. I want to *feel*.

So I do. I feel his dick gliding across my clit with every circle of my hips. I feel the strength of his shoulders beneath my hands, and I feel the warmth spreading through my veins telling me that I am embarrassingly close to orgasm from simply dry humping in an elevator.

"Fuuuuck, Campbell," Chase says, pulling his mouth away from mine to trail hot kisses down my throat.

Yes, right there. Kiss me there.

He grunts and kisses my pulse point harder, and I realize I spoke out loud.

His teeth nip under my ear as I swivel my clit once more over his hard-on. That's all it takes.

"I'm coming, oh fuck, I'm coming..." I chant, my muscles seizing. He takes over, dry humping back, pressing his length over me as wave after wave hits me, prolonging my orgasm until my leg gives out. His arms wrap around me, holding me up.

It's then that I realize I've been the one moving, humping, grinding, in essence, swiveling my hips like Elvis in Vegas, while his hands remained braced on either side of me, until now.

Embarrassment overrides the warmth of my orgasm. I just got myself off on my new client's crotch, in his elevator.

Pulling back, I lower the leg hooked around his hip to the ground and find the courage to look him in the eye. And immediately wish I hadn't. We're both breathing hard, but while I'm sure I at least look satisfied, Chase's mouth is pressed flat, and little lines of tension crease the sides of his eyes.

"I'm sorry." My voice like a whisper.

His brows pinch, a look of confusion sliding over his face. "Baby." The endearment catches in my heart. He slides one finger down the line of my jaw, stopping at the corner of my mouth. "Why in the world are you apologizing?"

"I—"

The elevator dings, and the doors glide open. Down the hall, Raymond's eyes catch mine as he looks over Ben and Chris's shoulders. Quickly, I disengage from Chase and duck under his arm still caging me in. I run my hands over my hair and smooth down my dress. By the time Ben and Chris turn around, I look somewhat presentable as I exit the elevator, though I'm walking toward them on shaky legs.

"What are you two still doing here?" My voice sounds a bit too cheerful. A bit too loud. Hopefully Ben and Chris don't notice. I refuse to meet Raymond's eyes, not wanting to see any censure from the conservative floor manager whom I'd taken an instant liking to.

"We were on our way out and met up with Raymond here." Ben pats Raymond on the shoulder. "This guy is great. We should totally make him the face of Moore's. What do you think?"

"I think Raymond might quit." Chase smiles at Raymond's stoic expression. "Not exactly your thing, is it, Raymond?"

I glance back at Chase, whose countenance seems much more relaxed than before as he strolls toward us. He's taken off his suit jacket and has it draped over his arm, in front of his crotch. Knowing the reason why has my ears heating.

Raymond inclines his head. "Indeed, Mr. Moore."

"Indeed," Chris repeats, chuckling. "Are you sure, man? You are the definition of what Moore's should be presenting to the public." He looks Raymond up and down as the older gentleman lifts one eyebrow at Chris's inspection, managing to look both superior and acquiescent at once.

I step in. "I like the thought process, guys. But if we do decide a poster boy is the way to go, I'd like one a bit more willing. Don't want to make any of the store's long-standing and essential employees uncomfortable."

Like I am right now.

"You're right, as usual, boss." Ben sticks his hand out to Raymond. "Thanks for the insider's insight, as it were, man. It's been a pleasure meeting you."

Raymond pauses before relinquishing his own hand to be pumped up and down enthusiastically by the young marketing strategist. "The pleasure is mine, sir." He subjects himself to another handshake from Chris before turning toward Chase. "Anything I can do before I leave, Mr. Moore?"

Chase lets out a long-suffering sigh. "Chase, Raymond. Call me Chase." He glances at his watch. "And no, for god's sake, man, you're here way too late. I told you not to stay while we had dinner. Go home."

"As you wish." Raymond inclines his head to the guys once more and surprises me by taking my hand and bowing over it slightly. "Good evening, Miss Bell," he says, placing a chaste kiss on the back of my hand. The old-fashioned gesture is delightful, but even more so is the wink that follows.

A saucy wink from the staid, straitlaced floor manager. I can't help but smile even as my face heats. "Goodnight, Raymond. And thank you." One more nod in my direction and Raymond turns smartly on his high-shined brogues and strides away.

Chris sighs. "You sure we can't use him? He's perfect."

I laugh. "I'm sure, Chris."

"Well, now that you two have finished your business, wanna share that car?" Ben asks me.

It takes me a minute to realize he isn't referring to the business in the elevator, but when I do, I jump at the chance. Call me a coward, but I see my way out, and I'm going to take it. "Sure. That would be great." I take a quick look in Chase's direction, unable to meet his eyes. "Thank you for dinner."

Chase's charm is gone, in its place a strained annoyance, and I know it's directed at me. Taking a cue from Raymond, he inclines his head. "No, thank *you*, Campbell."

I leave him there, standing with his arms and jacket still in front, his posture rigid. I can feel him watching as I stride out of Moore's, trying very hard not to waver on my new Jimmy Choos.

* * *

Chase

I'm trying very hard to remain unaffected. I mean, other than the unyielding hard-on I'm packing. True, getting caught dry humping by our employees isn't the best way to make a good impression, but we're adults, damn it. And I'm pretty sure only Raymond saw.

Remind me never to play poker with him.

Back in that elevator, I had to keep my fists clenched against the cold metal wall to keep myself from shooting off in my Tom Ford slacks. If I'd caved and touched her, my orgasm would've been a foregone conclusion.

That is one stain I'd rather not have to explain to my dry-cleaner.

But why did she say sorry? That I don't understand. She should've said you're welcome, because I may still be standing here like I'm about to set up camp with the tent I'm pitching in my pants, but that was by far the hottest moment of my life, and no one was even naked.

Someone coughs.

I blink, coming out of the trance I've been in for the past few minutes, staring at the door Campbell just exited. It occurs to me that I've been doing that a lot lately.

The night security guard, Jeff, eyes me warily. Great, now my employees think I'm a pervert, staring after women while sporting a cock-stand.

Shaking my head in disgust, I head toward the side entrance and the employee parking area. As I drive home, I barely register the city passing by, my head filled with waves of auburn hair and sparkling brown eyes. Luckily, I'm in one of those ninja modes where I can't remember the ride from work into my parking garage, but somehow I got there safely. Well done me.

Up the elevator and through the door to my bachelor pad I go.

I drop onto my sofa and contemplate the last few days of my life and how everything has changed.

What is it about Campbell King? Why does it feel as if my life has been rebooted, far more so than when my brother showed his douchey colors and I took over the helm of our family's legacy?

Sister Sledge's "We Are Family" sounds from my pants pocket. I fish out my phone and answer. "Hey, sis. What's up?" Guilt creeps in, knowing my time with Campbell is exactly what my father would use against Liz.

"Ooooo, you are in trou-ble!" Liz sings into my ear.

"Great. What now?" I prop my legs up on my coffee table. It can't be that bad if she's using a sing-song voice.

"I'm really not sure, actually. Obviously, Dad ranted and raved before he set out to ambush you at work the other day. But when he came home, he was pleased. And we both know a pleased Stan does not bode well."

I frown. "What are you doing at their house?" Liz has her own apartment while she finishes grad school. But whereas I stayed gone after I left, Liz often spends her weekends at home. Stan's words about Liz being devastated if cut off echo in my mind.

"Mom and I are going to a charity lunch tomorrow. I finally got her to branch out and donate to the children's art project. Dad, of course, said it was nonsense, but I think it's important that underprivileged kids have access to art." Her passion comes through in her voice, and I smile. "Plus, it's a great opportunity to spy on Dad for you. Show some appreciation for my sacrifice, why don't you?"

I really freaking love my sister. "I'll buy you a pony."

She laughs, which has me thinking of Campbell. They both have first-rate laughs.

"No need for a pony, bro. But you could spare a wad of cash for the children's art project as well."

"That is more than doable."

"Sweet." She pauses, and when she speaks again, the humor is missing from her voice. "Just know that even though Dad is happy, he isn't."

"When is he ever?"

"That's just it." It's her turn to sigh. "I just... don't you ever want to fix things? Have us be a normal, happy family?"

Damn it. I close my eyes and sigh. "You know that won't happen, Liz. It would take more than just us wanting that. We can't change him."

"Yeah, I guess." Another pause. "Maybe instead of the check for the children's charity you could do me a favor and try to get Thomas out to dinner sometime? Now that he isn't heir apparent, maybe he'll be less of a douche."

Liz's eternal optimism is something I cherish about her. I do. But sometimes even she doesn't know a lost cause, even when it grew up with her. So I do the only thing I can think of—I answer her without answering her. "You would keep my money from the children just so you could go to dinner?" I deepen my voice and scold, "For shame, Liz. For shame."

She giggles, as I hoped. "I was actually hoping you'd spoil me like you usually do and give the charity their check *and* go make the dinner happen."

"You can consider the check in the mail."

She doesn't bring up Thomas and dinner again, thankfully.

After filling me in on school, friends, and her dating life (at which I enjoy making fun of the millennial, tight-jeans-wearing hipsters she dates), Liz says goodbye, and we hang up.

Before I can even put my phone down, it lights up again, blaring the standard phone setting ringtone. *Thomas.* First the office and now my personal number. Which I don't recall ever giving him. The fact that he doesn't have his own ringtone shows how little I think of him. For a second, I think of Liz and her belief that one day, we'll all get along. That maybe Thomas and I can one day look back on all the animosity of our childhood and laugh.

Then I get real and silence the call.

As if sensing my morose mood, Mike the Sphynx jumps onto my lap, his sharp claws making sure my dick is incapable of sprouting wood anytime soon.

"Fuck," I gasp as he settles down, his wrinkly skin covered in one of the cat shirts I got him. Buffalo plaid flannel. Thought I'd try to butch him up a bit, the poor dude. I'd planned on getting him studded leather but decided that would scream more Village People than badass. Plus, flannel is warmer for the little bag of skin.

My head falls back on the top of the couch, and I close my eyes. The day started with such promise. And yet here I am, on my couch, alone, with an injured dick, petting my hairless pussy.

Awesome.

11

BELL

If you do something as ill-advised as getting yourself off on your new client's trousers, you'd think you'd have a hard time sleeping.

Not me.

I woke up refreshed and satisfied before embarrassment and shame brought me back to reality. The combined feelings brought on a sense of déjà vu.

I pushed those feelings down, ordered room service, and worked remotely from my hotel room like a coward. I also put the Do Not Disturb sign on my door and called the front desk to have them send all my calls to voicemail.

I was mad at myself. I knew better. A woman makes one misstep, opens herself up for any ridicule, and she loses all credibility in business. It isn't fair. It isn't right. But it is what it is. My past is proof of that. A past that I thought I'd put behind me.

But here is the funny thing about the past—it doesn't like to stay buried.

This is made clear two days after the elevator incident when I walk into the sixth-floor boardroom at Moore's ready for the meeting between the current marketing firm and my team.

Chase warned me that he'd ousted some of the 'old regime' as he put it, when he took over operations from his father. He also mentioned that there are still some left who aren't thrilled with the young Moore's new way of running things. Like the marketing firm still under contract.

I was prepared for that. I've been through this before, with marketing companies that never expanded their knowledge toward new online forums and social media sites. Companies still stuck focusing on paper ads and television commercials alone.

I spent the last two days avoiding Chase while honing my team's plan, designing ad mock-ups to entice age demographics Moore's is currently failing, and planning social media feed image bursts with the help of Alice's floor display ideas. I know the proposal inside and out, prepared for any questions thrown at me or my team.

What I'm not prepared for is my past to come crashing so thoroughly into my present and future.

"I know you," a beautiful but severe-looking woman says when I step up to the long, oval table.

I know her too. I pause, taking in the familiar blond hair that probably costs hundreds of dollars a month in upkeep, the classic French-tipped fingers steepled in front of her, and the expensive mahogany leather attaché case embossed with her initials placed in the middle of the table, encroaching on everyone's space.

I catch myself humming "Devil in Disguise," disguising the noise by clearing my throat. "Yes, you do," is all I say, giving myself a moment to come to terms with this unwelcome surprise. I've researched Warren and Baron. Their clients, both past and present. Their outdated strategies. But I hadn't thought to ask for a list of names on the team assigned to the Moore's campaign. Because if I'd seen the name Denise Hampson anywhere, I would have prepared.

I take a seat next to Alice, who's looking equal parts eager and nauseous. Kind of how I'm feeling after seeing Denise, though hopefully I'm doing a better job of hiding it.

Chris is on the other side of me going over our presentation on his laptop, with Ben leaning in on his other side.

I'm thankful I took care with my appearance today, wearing a suit I brought from Texas and not one of the newly acquired outfits from Moore's. It's more masculine in style—a hunter green fitted, double-breasted jacket and flat front slacks. The trousers have a shorter hem, showcasing my lone pair of Manolo Blahniks. The shoes I wear on big occasions to make me feel strong.

Men have power ties. Women? Power shoes.

Chase comes in, and I turn my attention to him. *Son of a gun*, he looks fine.

He glances around the room, his eyes pausing a bit longer on me than others. I take a deep breath and try to remain unaffected.

"Okay, it seems everyone is here. Great. Let's get right to it." Chase doesn't sit but stands at the head of the table, looking toward the men and women across from me. "As you know, I've taken over the day-to-day operations of Moore's, having been given complete control by the majority of the shareholders. And you've probably heard that I've made some extensive changes as to how the company is run." He tips his head in my direction. "Denise Hampson, this is Campbell—"

"Dougherty," Denise fills in, using a name I haven't gone by in eight years. I can see her brain finally working out how she knows me. Her slick, red lips twitch into a smirk.

Last time I saw Denise Hampson was eight years ago at Douglas Marketing, the marketing firm I worked at directly after college. She was my cube-mate and colleague—the one who took credit for all my work, then accused me of sleeping with clients. I sat in front of our boss in silence, too blindsided to defend myself. This time I will not be silent.

"It's King, actually. Campbell King," I say, staring her down, giving her nothing. She blinks, eyeing my bare ring finger, my correction confusing her.

"Yes," Chase continues, with a slight frown pinching his brows, "of King Marketing. Ms. King will be developing a separate marketing department for Moore's and overseeing what you've been doing for Moore's through Warren and Baron as well as the new direction we'll be taking on our own."

There's a pregnant pause, one in which Chase simply lets Denise and her cronies marinate on what he just said. "King Marketing's main focus will be building up Moore's social media marketing, which has been sorely lacking. Ms. King and her team" —he smiles and nods to Alice, who flushes— "will be working with you to guide us into this next step. They will act as both consulting and marketing firm."

I have to give it to old Denise; she still has a great resting bitch face. "I see." A small tic by her left eye starts as she looks at Chase. When she finally deigns to look at me again, the tic stops as she narrows her eyes.

Well, shit. Here we go.

"I was at Douglas Marketing with Miss Dougherty." She pauses, trying and failing to look apologetic. "I'm sorry, I mean Ms. *King* here, a few years ago." There's a gleam in her eyes as if she's enjoying remembering our brief association all those years ago. "And though I didn't have the pleasure that some of my colleagues and our firm's clients had by working with her... *one-on-one*, I heard she is *very* creative in what she does."

People around the table are definitely picking up a weird vibe. Brows are furrowed, heads are tilted, trying to decipher the innuendo Denise is throwing around. For once, I'm not betrayed by my fair skin, and my face remains cool. Probably because whatever embarrassment I thought I'd face at Denise's words isn't there. Instead, cold rage fills me.

How dare she? How dare she show no remorse for her actions all those years ago? How dare she have the audacity to insinuate less than admirable things about my work? Just how fucking dare she.

"She is," Chase says. And when I look at him, I'm surprised to see his usual affable demeanor gone, his eyes hard and focused on Denise. I've never seen him so tense. "Ms. King is so creative that in the past week, since I first contacted her, she and her team have already put together a digital presentation, complete with financial gain predictions for the new modes of marketing for Moore's. Something that Moore's has failed to see from Warren and Baron even though they were contracted over a year ago."

They say you should rise above, take the higher road, not get pleasure from your enemy's failings.

To hell with that.

I smile widely and brightly at Denise, her poker face slipping as her red lips pucker like a spasming asshole.

Picking up the boardroom projector's remote from the table, I lean back in my chair and cross my legs. "On that note, I think we should begin the presentation. I'll get everyone up to speed," I say to the room. I look back at Denise. "It'll be my *pleasure.*"

* * *

Chase

Campbell's voice resonates clearly through the room as she flips through the slides and goes into the details of her marketing plan. Funny, her voice doesn't sound so Southern now. Her distinct twang is nearly undetectable, and I wonder if that's a conscious thing. There is obviously some bad juju between Campbell and Denise.

Not that I blame her. Since taking over, I've detested every moment working with the woman. It isn't just her incompetence, which makes me wonder how she's stayed so long on such a high-profile account. Her whole demeanor grates on my nerves. Both as a business associate and as a person. As I said to the table, Warren and Baron has been doing the bare minimum for Moore's. That, in addition to every unwanted advance Denise—a *married* woman—has thrown my way, would have had Warren and Baron fired in a heartbeat if it hadn't been for the damn contract.

I'm well versed in King Marketing's plan at this point, so I pretend to watch Campbell give her presentation, though I'm really just looking her over. Something I've been trying not to do since I walked in here today. I even arrived a bit late, striding in and immediately starting the meeting just to keep my eyes (and my dick) from lingering on her too long.

It's a good thing I waited, as she looks fine. Damn fine. Between her red hair and her green suit, Campbell looks like Christmas in spring, and I'd very much like to unwrap her while she tells me what a good boy I've been.

Fuck. This is not going to end well for me.

Denise interrupts Campbell mid-sentence. "It's nice of you to put this little show together, Campbell. But Warren and Baron has been handling the marketing at Moore's for years, and with our extensive experience, I'm sure Mr. Moore"—she glances at me—"*senior* will be more comfortable with what my team and I have already put together. This is New York, after all, not Kansas. Moore's needs—"

Before I can jump in and tell Denise exactly where her and her team can stick their unwanted and unasked-for presentation, and probably cost Moore's a mint by dissolving the contract with Warren and Baron early, Campbell steps in.

"What exactly does Moore's need, Denise? More outdated ads? Lackluster website interfacing? Are y'all at Warren and Baron content to sit back and watch Moore's get buried beneath your limited, traditional strategy while it sinks further into the red?" The more she talks, the heavier her accent falls, and my mind immediately goes to what she'd sound like all worked up in bed.

Focus, Chase.

"Because if that's what you think Moore's needs, then yes, by all means continue with your antiquated marketing plan," Campbell continues. "Maybe that's what the senior Mr. Moore wants, as he is, after all, closer to your generation."

Denise gasps, and Ben and Chris smile into their laptops.

"But as you can see"—Campbell looks dramatically around the room— "he isn't here." She levels Denise with a look that makes me think she wants to cut a bitch. "If you want to pretend to be a man and have a measuring contest, Denise, by all means, let's. But just remember, I'm not from Kansas, I'm from Texas. And everything's bigger there."

I stifle the laugh that bursts out of my chest, coughing, then pounding on my chest with my fist. My theatrics are not at all convincing, going by Denise's death glare. Campbell can take care of herself. And that is hot as fuck. Her eyes are flashing, her chest heaves slightly, and the focused, laser-like stare she has going on does things to my nether regions that I wasn't sure could happen after Mike's claws-out pounce two nights ago.

Before Denise can bluster, which I'm sure she's about to do

given the indentations her talons are making on the boardroom table and the bulge in her eyes, I step in. "There seems to be some misunderstanding." Everyone swings their attention to me, though it takes Campbell and Denise a moment to stop eye-murdering each other. "*I* am in charge. Not my father, not my brother. Me." I narrow my eyes in Denise's direction. "If anyone thinks their past relationship with my father has any sway, they couldn't be more wrong." She scowls at this, and it's not an attractive look. Seriously, the woman's lips pinch so hard creases deepen all over her face. "After me, the next in line in this room is Ms. King and her team when it comes to all things marketing. The contract between Moore's and W&B does not preclude us from hiring another firm to consult and oversee marketing operations." I stare Denise down. "If you have a problem with that, I'll let my lawyers know you're under breach of contract."

Silence fills the room. Denise is fighting to relax her posture, and her associates look embarrassed by her outburst, but no one gainsays me.

Campbell clears her throat. "In the next slide you'll see…"

I smile as Campbell picks up right where she left off before being interrupted. Her features are schooled into polite indifference as she informs the other marketing team exactly what they'll be doing in the upcoming months. She's poised, aloof, and utterly professional. It only makes me want to fuck her more.

Denise snorts at something Campbell says, drawing my eyes back in her direction. Something isn't right there. It's more than a marketing turf war, but I'm not sure what. But the same instinct that told me Gwen Hayes would be the one to pop my cherry in eighth grade, and that women would not only welcome the opportunity to rate dick pics but pay for the chance, is now telling me Denise isn't done causing problems.

* * *

Everyone but Denise nods and makes nice with Campbell and her team before leaving.

I think the entire room would agree that Denise is acting like she has a big old stick up her backside.

"This is your new email. I want you to come up with a strong password. It's better if it has letters, numbers, symbols, and a mix of capitals and lower cases," Campbell says to Alice, who nods. "Now pay attention, because what I'm about to tell you is for your own good as well as my company's, okay?" Another nod from Alice. Campbell reaches out for Alice's hand and makes sure to look directly into her eyes. "Never, not ever, give your password to anyone else, do you understand?" Campbell shakes Alice's hand when the younger woman simply gives another nod. "I'm serious, Alice. No one. If you have trouble remembering, or something happens to the system, Moore's has a very reliable tech guy who will give you a temporary password, but then you immediately change it to something else no one knows."

Sensing Campbell's sincerity, Alice finally speaks up. "Yes, Ms. King. I promise."

Campbell pats Alice's hand. "That's good, Alice. But call me Bell. You'll also have a sign-in code to all work computers that's different from your password. You're only to use work computers for work. No personal computers allowed. Do you understand?"

Alice perks up. "I get a computer?"

Campbell smiles. "Yes, and a new smart phone."

"Holy crap." Alice claps a hand over her mouth and turns pink as Campbell's husky laugh tumbles out.

Frowning, I move to the other side of the room while Campbell continues lecturing Alice on work phone codes as well as various security protocols and procedures.

Ben and Chris have decided to spread out and use the far back of the boardroom for a marketing brainstorm session. They're arguing over font choices when I sit beside them.

"Is security that much of an issue in marketing?" I ask them. "Do other companies really try to hack your system?" I just can't understand the sense of urgency Campbell had when explaining tech precautionary measures to Alice.

"Oh, that's not for other companies." Ben looks down at his laptop again. "It's really for the personal protection of employees."

Chris joins in, glancing at Campbell and Alice across the room before lowering his voice. "Story goes that when Bell was starting out, she got set up and fired for something she didn't do. Someone logged on as her or something. The company didn't have individual sign-ins or anything." He shakes his head. "Now she's fanatical about security. Makes sure everyone has their own personal passcode to log in, so all work is traced back to the computer's user log-in with date and time stamps and stuff. It's the only thing I've ever known Bell to get pissed about if she finds that someone didn't follow the rules."

"Good thing too," Ben jumps back in. "A few months ago, her assistant tried to steal company information and pass it off as his own. Actually tried to set up his own business on the back of Bell's work." He snickers. "Moron."

"She shut him down quick though, didn't she?" Chris must've been addressing Ben because they both laugh at some private joke, their shoulders bouncing.

"You boys done giggling over gossip? I might need you to do some actual work for a change." Campbell speaks from across the room, her brow and smile quirked up to one side, clearly amused at catching us whispering and laughing like kids.

"Yes, ma'am," Chris says with another laugh, causing Campbell to roll her eyes. Chris sports a smirk while hunkering down once more over the laptop.

I store away the knowledge I've just learned with the rest of what I've gathered. But it seems with each new piece of information I acquire, the puzzle of Campbell King just gets bigger, not clearer.

12

BELL

I deserve a drink.

Following the first meeting with Warren and Baron, I arranged for all upcoming discussions involving Denise to be handled by Chris. I had to make him promise to stay vigilant when it comes to his work and security, probably feeding the rumor mill I know is already running. He wasn't thrilled to be picked for the job, but hey, I'm the boss; I can do what I want.

Except Chase Moore. I cannot do him. Well, any more than I did in the elevator.

At first, seeing Denise had seriously doused my libido with the equivalent of glacial waters. However, Chase revved my sex drive up so much that after Denise stormed out, one look at him and I thawed out significantly. Luckily, by the time I reached my sexual boiling point again, I had Warren and Baron up to speed and the new tasks distributed amongst them and my team.

So I hightailed it back to Texas for a week under the guise of needing to get back to fix another client's last-minute problem.

Now I'm back in the city that never sleeps, and even though it's been a while since I last had physical contact with Chase, just thinking of it has me crossing my legs with a shiver.

Maybe I should've stayed in Texas a little longer. At least until Sunday night. Instead I came back Friday morning at Alice's request. I haven't been a very good mentor, leaving her to the wolves of Warren and Baron with just Chris and Ben as buffer. Flying in this morning seemed like a wonderful idea at the time. After all, I had a week to shore up my defenses against the sexy-as-hell Chase Moore.

I was confident. And also very, very stupid.

I didn't tell Chase I was flying in early. In fact, I've been very brief and stingy with my emails to him, choosing to copy him on group emails rather than email him directly. I thought I'd fly under the radar, as it were. Meet Alice for lunch, go over her goals and tasks, and have two and a half days to enjoy the city I still love before facing the man I dry humped in an elevator.

Except after lunch, Chris, Ben, and Chase sauntered in for an impromptu meeting. I honestly don't know why Chase was even there—he barely said two words. And I should know, as I spent the entire time staring at his mouth while fighting the urge to mount him like an animal.

I totally deserve a drink. Or a few.

Definitely a few.

I can't forget Moore's is temporary. Chase is temporary. As much as the sounds, sights, and even smells of the city calm me, make me feel right with the world in a way that the humid heat of Houston never has, I can't forget this isn't home anymore. And why it isn't.

I'm perched on my stool, legs swinging back and forth. Alice recommended this bar when I mentioned I wanted to get a drink. Angel's Share is a speakeasy that you get to by entering a hidden Japanese restaurant in the East Village. Above the ornate bar is a creepy-cool mural. It's like a macabre twist on those cherub frescos from the Renaissance with passed-out angels and devil-horned babies. Otherwise, the place reminds me of something straight out of the 1920s, when speakeasies were actually needed. Dim lighting, fancy drinks, and smooth jazz.

The whole idea is pretty cool, and my mind is busy running scenarios on how well a place like this might work at Moore's. Maybe as part of Winston's, with a separate entrance for later hours. A bar that serves fancy drinks from the era that Moore's was founded in. The social media scene would love it.

Suck on that idea, Denise.

I take another sip, toasting my awesome idea, while my taste buds enjoy the sweet tang of an Angel's Share Flirtibird. It's a cocktail of yucca juice, agave nectar, and shochu, a Japanese barley-based drink that reminds me of whiskey. Usually I'm a straight-up kind of gal, but with where my mind has been these past few days with Chase, a Flirtibird sounded apt.

"Howdy, ma'am." The voice comes from behind me. A sexy voice with a deep timbre that I know too well. I let the vibrations of that voice flow through my body before slowly spinning my bar stool around.

Deep blue eyes meet mine. He's wearing a T-shirt, blue jeans, and a smile. One of his charmer smiles that he tops with a wink.

"Fuck," I whisper, as I lick the plum salt from the rim of my cocktail off my lips. His smile fades and eyes darken at the sight of my tongue. Knowing I must have the same sort of effect on him as he does on me makes me want to be reckless. Makes me want to fist his T-shirt and haul him against me in front of God and the creepy-ass devil baby mural. With just one look, my resolve crumbles, and my survival instincts scream at me that I will die if I don't get Chase between my legs, and fast.

"Hi! You must be Campbell!" A bright, cheerful voice snaps me out of my illicit daydream.

To Chase's right is a young woman, currently bouncing on the balls of her feet and sticking out her hand for me to shake.

"Um, hello." I put my hand in hers only to have it pumped enthusiastically.

"I've heard so much about you. I'm so glad you could meet us for drinks."

"Drinks?" My brain doesn't seem able to compute what's happening, my eyes locking on this woman's arm threaded through Chase's. My first thought? I could take her. My second? He talks about me? The third? What *the fuck* had he been doing letting me kiss him in an elevator when he has a girlfriend?

"Yes, *my sister* Liz here, has been quite interested in meeting you." Chase's knowing smile says he read my thoughts.

Jerk.

I plaster on a smile, now recognizing her from the family picture on Chase's desk. "Then I am delighted to meet you." I think back on what she said. "You were expecting me?"

Chase butts in. "I may have asked Alice about your evening plans."

Liz scoffs. "You mean you called Campbell's hotel room and when she didn't answer you drove there and knocked on her door. And when she didn't answer *that*, you called Alice and demanded to know where she was." Chase shoots his sister a look. She glances to the side, mumbling, "Just saying."

I'm not sure what to say here. I'm an only child, so the antics between siblings confuse me. Is Liz being truthful, or just messing with her brother? I decide not to touch on this.

"Why don't we get a table?" Chase gestures behind him to the lone vacant four-top in the bar.

Not wanting to be rude, especially in the face of a bubbly youth like Liz, I hop down from my seat. But before I get very far, Liz grabs my arm.

"Oh my god, your boots! Amaze-balls," she says, looking down.

Thinking I'd be on my own tonight, I'd simply worn jeans, a tank, and my boots. They were a thank-you present from Cavendish's when I got their profits up and store expansion going. Cognac-colored leather, inlays of red and black birds along with white flowers and green leaves. The vintage boots were hand-tooled with a snipped toe and cost more than my new Jimmy Choos.

Though I love the city, I adore my cowboy boots. Some things you just can't change about a Southern girl.

I stick out my heel to give her a better look at the intricate stitching. "Thank you. They were a gift from a client after a job well done."

"I'll have to think of something equally as cool then, for what you're doing for Moore's," Chase says, guiding us toward the table.

"Slow your roll, cowboy," I tease, sliding into my seat, cocktail in hand. "You already had your *team* put together a welcome package." I squint in an overexaggerated glare in his direction before shrugging. "And, besides, I haven't done much yet."

"But you will," Liz pipes up. "Chase told me all your plans. I think it's just what the family store needs."

Calling the extravagance of Moore's a family store has me smiling. As does Liz. She's bouncy. There's no other word for it as she literally bounces on the seat of her chair. Her long blond hair is up in a messy bun, the escaped strands swaying with each bounce. She has on a cute cotton sundress with sandals and no makeup. All of it seems very casual, but I can see the quality of the clothes. And I may have seen those sandals in *InStyle* magazine captioned with a price tag of eight hundred and fifty bucks.

"I'm at a distinct disadvantage then," I tell her. "You know everything about me, and all I know is that your name is Liz and you have the unfortunate reality of being Chase Moore's sister." I throw my own wink at Chase, who blinks in surprise. *Take that, pretty boy.* "Tell me all about yourself, Liz."

I let the young woman's words wash over me as she explains about her graduate degree in art history and her interest in abstract painting, at the same time sneaking looks at Chase out of my peripheral vision while pretending to studiously ignore him.

What can I say? I'm good at multitasking.

"You'll have to come by Moore's and tell me if you have any ideas for the displays. You're a shareholder, and with your background in art, I'm sure you'd have great insight. I recently acquired a display dresser, but she's new at it. She has a great eye, though."

Chase laughs. "Yes, my former shoe salesman, Alice."

"Sales*woman*, brother. Let's not be sexist, now."

"Heaven forbid." Chase holds up his hands in surrender.

I envy their easy camaraderie.

The next hour sails by smoothly, with Liz getting a kick out of my Porn 'stache lawyer story, though Chase stays conspicuously quiet. Liz promises to come by the store next week, and Chase pays the bill. I try to fight him on it, for like a second before giving up with an eye roll in his direction.

Liz touches my arm, directing my attention away from her smooth-talking brother. "What is it that you're humming?"

"I'm humming?"

Chase snorts. "Yes. You do it all the time."

"I do?" Shoot. I know I do. I just hadn't realized how noticeable it was.

"Was that an Elvis song too?" His simple question tells me he's been paying attention to my ridiculous quirk, and I can't help but feel happy about that.

"Um, yes. It's 'Little Sister.'"

Chase and Liz laugh while my face heats.

"I don't know that one," Chase says.

"You know a lot of Elvis?" Liz nudges her brother. "I mean, I knew you were old, but not that old."

"Hey, now," I interrupt, unable to let any slight to the King go. "Elvis is a classic. A legend. Anyone who has any taste in music knows Elvis."

Liz looks back and forth between Chase and me, an amused look on her face. "I like her," she directs toward her brother, ignoring my previous indignation at her lack of respect toward the King.

Even so, my heart warms at her words, because I find myself liking her too. But then the treacherous muscle skips a beat when Chase nods in agreement, murmuring, "Me too."

Quiet descends for a moment until Liz saves us from awkwardness, getting us back on track. "I haven't been to the store in ages. I used to go with my mom, but..." She shrugs. "It's been a while, what with me at school and her with her charities. Now I just have Susan pull clothes for me." She motions me forward and leans in, whispering, "Don't tell anyone, but I really hate shopping."

I lean back, blowing out a breath. "I don't know. A secret like that coming from the heiress of a shopping magnate..." I look at Chase, smiling. "Does your father know about this?"

The levity I'd been going for falls flat as their smiles disappear. I could kick myself for forgetting that their father is actually a world-class dick.

I'm about to apologize when Liz quickly rebounds with a laugh. "Nothing to worry about. My lackluster shopping skills are just a drop in the bucket for paternal disappointments."

I laugh with her, but just like hers, it's forced.

"Speaking of, I'm pretty sure Stan cooled down a bit when he saw the recent numbers," Liz tells Chase. "Maybe you'll be saved from a face-to-face with Daddy after all."

"Another one?" I suppress a shudder. I don't know how Chase can deal with that man, father or not. "How often does he come to the store?"

"What do you mean, *another one*?" Liz shoots her brother a look. "You mean Bell was there when he stormed the store a week or two ago?" She pouts and punches him lightly on the arm. "Why didn't you tell me?"

Once again, I've put my expensively booted foot in it.

Chase lets out a long-suffering breath.

"Sorry, I didn't mean to upset you," I say to Liz before Chase can answer. "Your father just... introduced himself, is all."

Before Liz can do more than roll her eyes, Chase butts in. "Don't worry about it, Lizzy. Focus on your degree."

She slaps his shoulder. "Ugh, don't call me Lizzy."

They continue squawking at each other in that familiar, loving way I've always imagined siblings having. It's obvious how much he cares for his sister. One more layer to Chase I find attractive.

And now that the downturn of the conversation after I'd brought up Stan has passed, I should quit before I step in the metaphorical cow patty again.

Clearing my throat, I grab their attention. "Thanks so much for the drinks," I say to Chase. "And for the lovely company," I direct at Liz. My chair scrapes over the wood floor as I rise. "But I should be off."

Chase jumps up. "I'll take you back to the hotel."

I open my mouth to argue, since his suggestion has danger written all over it, but Liz beats me to it. "Great! That actually makes me feel better," she says, also standing. "I'm meeting a friend here in about five minutes, and I didn't want to be rude."

She gathers her large sack purse from the back of the chair. "You two go on. I'll just wait for my friend at the bar."

A weird, nonverbal communication happens between Chase and Liz. I stand there awkwardly in my boots trying to think of a way out of the ride. Nothing comes to mind.

I'm not sure if my lack of ideas stems from my brain freezing on me or from my subconscious wanting to find out if Chase gives as good a car ride as he does elevator rides.

My subconscious is a slut.

13

CHASE

My sister truly does deserve a pony. I know Liz isn't meeting any of her friends. But she took one for team Chase. The look she sent me basically told me I owe her. Again.

A stab of panic hits me when I think of what's at stake for Liz if I somehow screw up at Moore's.

But I won't. I can't.

"So great meeting you, Bell." Liz steps forward and hugs Campbell. When she steps back, my sister looks slyly at me before saying to Campbell, "Don't let my brother get away with any crap." Then she blows me a kiss and walks to the bar, a bounce in her step.

"Your sister is kind of cool," Campbell says, still looking after Liz's retreat.

"You have no idea." I rub my chest, trying to ease the panic.

"She must take after your mother."

I burst out laughing, the panic leaving and only humor remaining. Stan may consider Campbell a pathway toward failure, but obviously his opinion is just as outdated as he is.

"Let's get out of here." I thread my fingers through hers and lead us out of the speakeasy. Campbell frowns at our clasped hands, and I think I may have overstepped. But then, as if a switch flipped somewhere inside, her frown disappears, and her fingers tighten around mine.

We grin at each other before maneuvering out the secret door and down the stairs. It hits me that I've never been happier than when Campbell is near. She has a way of exaggerating the good and dimming the bad. Part of me wonders if that shouldn't scare me a bit, but I can't drum up any fucks to give.

Instead, I concentrate on the victory of her hand in mine. With Campbell, I'm sure holding hands is just one battle of many I'll need to win before the war is over.

After all, love *is* a battlefield.

* * *

"My hotel is that way," Campbell says, jerking her thumb to the left while I turn my car right.

"Yep. It is." I look straight ahead, changing gears.

I can actually feel her eyes narrow. "Is that a 'yep' as in *I-momentarily-forgot-and-I'm-about-to-turn-around*, or 'yep' as in *I-never-intended-to-take-you-to-your-hotel*?"

I ease around the city's traffic, loving her annoyed tone. "It's more a *we're-gonna-finish-what-we-started-in-the-elevator* kind of yep." Out of the corner of my eye, I see her mouth drop open in a perfect O. I groan. "Goddamn it, Bell." I brake hard at an upcoming traffic jam and turn to her, my eyes narrowing on her open mouth.

Reaching out, I rub my thumb over her bottom lip. "I know you've been hiding from me since Winston's." She stiffens at my words but doesn't refute them. "You don't have to be afraid. I'm serious when I say I'll turn around if you tell me to. I'll drive you to your hotel and watch as you walk into the lobby. Alone. I won't push anymore. And saying no won't interfere with work." I rub her lip again, holding her gaze with my own. "I'm not that guy."

I can almost hear the thoughts whirling through her mind as she sits there silently, leaning in a fraction to my touch. "I don't mean to kidnap you, it's just that..." I rake my hand through my hair, trying to find the words. Meeting my eyes, she looks turned on but unsure and a little lost. Just when I feel rejection and defeat stir in my chest and I'm about to turn the car around, her tongue slides out, the tip tickling the pad of my thumb. My fingers, resting on the side of her face, bite into her skin at the contact.

"Fuck, Bell." I pull her toward me hard and fast. Our mouths collide, and it isn't pretty. It's teeth and lips and grunting, and it's hot as hell. It's over a week's worth of wanting forced into a kiss. Her hand reaches down and palms me through my jeans, the zipper biting into my dick. But that's okay, I need it. Without that sharp dose of pain, I would've already come in my pants just from the need rolling off of Campbell in waves.

My knee knocks hard into the gear shift, and the seat belt cinches me back when I try to lean further into her. Soon the sound of honking horns snaps me out of our ravenous sex fog. The traffic jam has cleared, and New Yorkers aren't patient with idle drivers.

Quickly, I pull back, shift gears, and shoot down the road, making a hard right into my building's parking garage. No valet tonight. I don't think either of us want so much as the doorman seeing the condition we're in. Thanking all the unsolicited dick pics that allowed me to purchase my own parking spot, I throw the car in park, unclip my belt, and reach for Campbell. She stops me with a hand on my chest and a seductive smile. Slowly she drags her hand down my chest and starts unbuckling my belt.

"It's okay, baby, we can go up—"

"Shhh," she says, not looking up from my hard-on straining at the denim fabric. I can hear the smirk in her voice when she says, "I'd rather go down. It's your turn, after all." My dick pops free once she lowers the zipper and that delectable pillow-soft mouth of hers widens, along with her eyes.

"You sure this is just nine inches?"

"Uh, well..." A nervous laugh escapes me, only to turn into a groan when Campbell licks her lips.

Any fight I had about doing this in the car is gone, especially when her thumb circles the top of my dick, spreading the bead of moisture over the sensitive tip.

Leisurely, as if she can't tell I'm about to start thrusting my dick in her hand for some small amount of relief, she lowers her head. A hiss escapes my clenched jaw at the first touch of her lips against my cock. At odds with the emotions raging beneath my skin, I gently place my hands on her head, sifting my fingers through her hair, needing more connection to this woman.

"Mmm-mmm," she hums, the tingle of her voice traveling down my cock to the base of my balls.

I fight the urge to thrust, but my ass can't help clenching in time to her movements as she begins to bob, her hand encircling what she can't fit into her mouth.

She starts off gently, light tugs with every suck on my dick. But soon her pulls are harder, deeper, causing my eyes to roll back in my head while I let the sensations wash over me. Fuck me, I've never had better in my life.

It isn't because she's giving me head in the car where anyone passing by might see us. It isn't even her skills, necessarily, although, wow, just wow. It's her. *Campbell*. Her intellect, her sass, her goddamn cowboy boots with birds on them. In just a few short weeks, she's fucking ruined me, and I—

"Fuck, I'm coming." I try to pull her up, but she fights the grip I have on her hair, sucking harder, going deeper. The sounds I make aren't human as I shoot my orgasm down her throat.

An hour passes.

Okay, maybe a minute.

Lazily, my brain comes back to functioning order, and I open my eyes. I shift my head on the headrest to look at the woman who is slowly breaking me down in the best possible way. Her brown eyes look black in the dim light of the parking garage, large pools of midnight. Her bottom lip is being worried by her teeth, so I raise my hand to once again rub my thumb over it. The contact has my dick twitching, even as it lays worn out on my thigh.

The dude better get his shit together; we aren't done yet. Not by a long shot.

Headlights illuminate the car for a brief moment as someone drives past my parking space. Campbell ducks her head, and I'd be willing to bet my shares in Moore's that her fair skin is pink right now.

Knowing she must be uncomfortable, I lift my hips and tuck myself back into my jeans and get out of the car. I'm slower than normal, my muscles sluggish from an epic orgasm. By the time I round the back to open Campbell's door, she's already out, standing next to it.

Not meeting my eyes, she says, "I can just get a cab from here."

Oh no. This will not do.

I tilt her face up to mine by her chin. "Hey, boss lady, none of that. I've got plans on how to return the favor."

"Having trouble counting, are we?" she asks, laughing nervously. "One for you and one for me. No return needed." She may be meeting my eyes, but I can still sense a distance. A distance I don't like.

Dropping my hands from her face, I lean into her and trace my lips up her neck. "I may not be from the South, but I still like to consider myself a gentleman," I whisper into the shell of her ear. "I'm pretty sure the going market rate is *at least* two female to every one male orgasm." I gently bite her earlobe, making her gasp before sucking the hurt away and moving toward her mouth. "And a Moore always pays his debts."

Tenderly, I touch my mouth to hers. It's completely different from any of our previous kisses. I want her to know there is more to this than sex. More than just scratching an itch or notching our respective bedposts. I want to woo her, charm her, *romance* her. I pull back to tell her that, but I'm momentarily transfixed by the ardent look on her face, her eyes still closed, savoring our kiss.

Before her eyes open, a slow grin lifts the corners of her mouth, making me all that more dumbfounded by her beauty.

"Okay then, boss man. Let's go get you out of debt." She steps around me and saunters over to the elevator, expecting me to follow.

I do, but not because she expects it. She doesn't understand —*hell*, I don't even understand. But I don't need to make sense of everything going on between us to know I'd follow her anywhere.

* * *

Bell

Focusing on the shiny elevator doors, I put one booted foot in front of the other and try to calm down.

Road head? What am I, eighteen?

In the moment it felt right, but in the light of oncoming head-lights, I panicked.

I mean, I guess technically we were parked, but still. And nine inches? The ache in my jaw says differently.

Too quickly, my boots take me to the elevator door. I wait for Chase to catch up, refusing to look back at him. Still revved up from sucking him off like a prizewinning Hoover, I don't trust myself not to ride him like a stallion at a Wild West show. Jesus, listen to me. I'm so turned on I'm mixing up metaphors.

I've been fighting the need to jump his bones since that first phone call. Since I dosed him with hot coffee. Don't even get me started on the state of my newly purchased panties while he watched me play dress up. True, I had some setbacks. Dinner. The elevator…

But I'd regrouped!

I flew halfway across the country and avoided all phone-sex-voiced phone calls, for heaven's sake. Distance. Time. Both things that should've lessened an overwhelming, no-good, should-know-better desire for Chase Moore.

It didn't.

And then I had to watch him affectionately tease his little sister before he sweetly held my hand on our walk to his car.

There's only so much a girl can take.

Speaking of… His body heat invades my personal space as he leans forward and swipes a card to open the elevator doors. As we cross the threshold, he swipes his card again before pushing the button for the top floor. Then he slips his hand into mine.

I've never been one for public displays of affection, not even simple ones like holding hands. But for some reason, his hand in mine calms me. The feel of Chase's skin, even just the smooth glide of his palm on mine, brings a smile to my face that I don't entirely understand.

There are a lot of things I don't understand about my body's reactions when it comes to Chase Moore. But I'm tired of fighting it, tired of expending so much energy avoiding and trying to rationalize my irrational behavior. It's time for a little less conversation and a little more you-know-what.

"Are you humming Elvis again?"

Blinking, I focus my attention on Chase's amused grin. "Uh..." Oh dear lord. I *was* humming the King again. My face heats when I realize just which song I'd been humming.

Chase laughs, pulling me to him with our connected hands. Now we're more than just palm to palm, we're front to front, all his good bits against mine. The elevator door chimes and slides open. I don't look away, still caught in Chase's smiling gaze.

"You needing a little more action?" His voice husky, he leans down and gives me a light kiss on the tip of my nose. "I think you're on to something, Bell." He sings a little of the song, his phone-sex-operator voice ten times more powerful when put to a melody. But what he does next seals the deal. Changes the tone from sweet to sexy in one move.

He winks at me.

That freaking wink.

Game. Fucking. On.

Before Chase knows what hit him, I push him out of the elevator and climb him like a tree. Just think of me as the lumberjack to his hardwood. TIM-fucking-BER!

My legs wrap around his waist, and my cowboy boots hook behind his back. I shove my hands in his hair, using my leverage to devour his mouth.

I keep kissing, barely breathing, while somewhere in my mind I process Chase's struggle to stay standing. I don't care. I'm determined to make him crazy, to burrow my way under his skin just like he has mine.

Maybe we can exorcise each other out of our minds through our bodies. And if not, by the feel of him in my mouth earlier, I know that what is about to happen next will at least feel fucking fantastic.

We whirl through the foyer like a tornado through Oklahoma. Keys fall, lamps crash, a cat hisses...

Wait, what?

"Mike, fuck!" Chase's foot catches, and he careens over something that sounds like a pissed-off tiger. Suddenly we're airborne. I feel Chase trying to throw me forward, and I appreciate his efforts when my ass lands on some sort of cushioned furniture. But any appreciation evaporates when something hard crashes on my head.

"What the—?"

"Fuck. Campbell. Are you okay?"

There is a beat of silence as we both assess the situation.

Chase is stretched out on his stomach in front of me, his arms out. I'm sitting, legs akimbo, in a large, overstuffed armchair, and there's a picture frame on my lap. Still stunned from the knock to my head, I turn over the frame and stare at the photograph mounted behind cracked glass.

"It's a dick." I blink a few times to make sure I'm not seeing things. Maybe I have a concussion.

Chase chuckles as he pushes up from the floor. "Uh, yeah. It is."

I look up at him, still not making sense of it. "Why do you have a framed picture of a dick on your wall?" And not just any dick. This one is huge and hard and very veiny.

He steps over to the side of the chair I'm on and runs his hands over my head, checking for a bump or cut, I guess. Finding the former, but not the latter, he crouches down in front of me, his hands on my thighs. "My sister gave it to me."

"Your sister gave you a picture of a dick?" Definitely a concussion.

He lifts one hand and runs it through his hair. "Yeah," he chuckles. "She did."

Before I can think of another question that would somehow make sense of the fact that his sister sends him dick pictures and he has them framed and hung on his wall, a beige bag of rocks jumps on the large picture on my lap.

"Meow."

Oh, excuse me, I misspoke. It's a cat. A scrawny, hairless cat.

The tag on his collar swings back and forth before settling against his smooth chest.

"Mike Hunt," I read out loud. Then my eyes widen at what I just said. "You named your cat Mike... Hunt." Sheesh, even with the pause it still sounds perverse.

Chase is eyeing me strangely, like a kid who poked at a hornets' nest and is waiting for the sting.

I glance down at the unfortunate dick picture that the hairless pussy is perched on.

"Mike Hunt is on your dick," I deadpan.

And then I bust out laughing.

14

CHASE

Laughter.

I can deal with Campbell's laughter.

Especially seeing as I unceremoniously threw her across the room, causing a large picture frame to crack down on her skull and all. Not to mention my unconventional wall art and odd-looking pet. All in all, laughter does seem the best I can hope for.

After a moment, Campbell's breath evens out. "Okay. First things first." She wipes the tears under her eyes, then slides her hands down the edges of the frame on her lap. "Why did your sister give you a picture of a dick, and why did you feel the need to hang it on your wall? Artfully framed, no less."

"Ever heard of Pick a Dick?" I lift Mike off her and grab the frame.

"Excuse me?"

I chuckle. "It's an app that lets women post all the unsolicited dick pictures they get. Then other subscribers can score the dicks from one to ten."

"Oh yeah, I've heard about that. My lawyer Leslie mentioned it. Said giving zero scores to the pictures guys sent her on some dating app was better justice than a lawsuit." She glances at the picture, eyebrows arching. "And that's your picture?"

"Uh, no." I flip the frame over and lean it against the wall. "That was the first picture ever posted on the site. It's a dick picture that some asshole sent my sister. It's actually what inspired me to create the application."

"Wait." She sits forward in her seat. "*You* created that app?" Her auburn hair ripples as she shakes her head from side to side. "How did I not know this?"

"I may have created it, but I didn't own it for long."

She gives me a look. "Why not? All the research I did before taking on the Moore's account showed you to be a savvy business-man. Doesn't make sense to let go of an app like that too soon. It's still really popular."

I shrug, not really wanting to get into the why. Getting beaned in the head by a dick and then sat on by a hairless pussy is enough for one night. "Anyway, yeah, I'm the creator. Thought it would be a good way for women to even the score. Especially after that stupid Hot or Not app."

"Wow."

"That's why my sister gave me the picture. She said it was like when people frame the first dollar their store makes."

She laughs. "I love your sister."

Her sincerity makes me smile.

"Okay, well, that's the dick pic explained." Her eyes wander down to Mike, now licking his smooth ball sack on the floor by her feet. "Now what about the... cat?"

As if knowing we were talking about him, Mike pauses mid lick and jumps back up on Campbell's lap, his bony legs balancing on her thighs. Both tilt their heads and regard the other quizzically. It's hilarious.

"He's a hairless cat. A sphynx. Good for people with allergies." I reach down and scratch behind Mike's ears. It's like touching raw chicken.

"You have allergies?" Tentatively, Campbell brings her hand to Mike's back. When he starts to purr, she lightly pets him.

"Uh, no. But that isn't exactly a requirement to own a sphynx." Once again, I avoid mentioning my ex. Bell runs hot and cold, and I don't want to give her any excuse to freeze me out after we've come so far.

If you count elevator and car rides far.

"Hmmm." She quirks her eyebrow at me while a sexy smirk twitches her lips. "And the name?"

Feeling like a kid caught with a porn mag, I smile sheepishly at the floor. "Well, I mean, if I'm going to own a hairless pussy, he might as well own the name."

Mike leans into her touch and purrs louder, and Bell's smirk turns adoring. The damn bastard may be a pussy, but he's also my number one cock block at the moment.

"He's so soft." She leans her whole body forward, cuddling into him. Mike wastes no time in nuzzling her chest. "Such a sweet boy, aren't you?"

The damn cat looks back at me while she pets him. I swear the hairless bastard is smiling at me.

Fucker.

"I had a pet once." Bell sounds slightly sad. "A dog." She continues cuddling Mike. "Since then, I've always considered myself a dog person, but Mike's kind of great, isn't he?"

She's cradling him in her arms now, like a baby. Like a saggy-skinned, ugly-as-fuck baby. But the soft smile on Campbell's lips keeps me from being too jealous.

"Just the one dog?" I think back to the number of strays my sister brought home to us over the years. As long as the animals stayed in the kids' wing of the house and my parents didn't have to deal with them, they didn't much care what pets we had.

"Yeah. His name was Elvis." She continues to talk while looking down at Mike. "He was awesome."

"Elvis? You're kidding me." Although that would explain her affinity for his songs.

A light chuckle bats back the sadness in her voice. "Nope. Mom and I always loved Elvis Presley. It was kind of our thing." The sadness returns. "I got puppy Elvis when I was nine. But when I went to college, I wasn't allowed to take him with me. Had to leave him at home." She hugs Mike to her chest. "He died while I was away."

I picture a younger version of the woman in front of me, heartbroken and far away from home. The vision makes me angry, though I'm not sure why. "That sucks."

"Yeah. It did. But it was a long time ago." Mike licks her cheeks, and she smiles, giving him an Eskimo kiss.

"And now?" I ask, wondering at this softer side of Campbell. "Why not get a pet now?"

She shrugs. "I don't know. I spend my time between a small apartment in Houston and my parents' old house outside of a small town in the country. Plus with how much I work and travel, I don't think I'd be a good pet owner."

From the motor humming in Mike's chest at the moment, I'd disagree with that. Who'd have thought Campbell was a natural-born cuddler? It would've been nice if it had been me and not my two-faced sphynx wedged between her boobs right now. "Hmmm."

The usual pinch of concentration between her brows has smoothed out as she pets the bag of bones in her lap.

"So your parents still in Houston?"

"No." Her voice is soft. "They passed away a while ago."

Great. First I got her to bring up her dead dog and now her

parents. Smooth, man, real smooth. "I'm sorry, I didn't mean to be such a Debbie Downer."

"It's okay." A shadow darkens her eyes for a moment. Mike shifts and licks her face again, lighting her up with a smile.

Fine. The cat can stay.

"I'm sorry," I repeat, not knowing what else to say. "About your parents, I mean." Having both parents pass couldn't have been easy.

"Really. It's okay." She looks up at me, her expression sincere. "It's been eight years. And though I still miss them, I was lucky to have such great parents. They loved me. So much. When I got the scholarship to Columbia, I didn't want to leave Texas. To leave them. Then one day I came home to find all my bags packed with a plane ticket on top, like a cherry on a sundae." She looks back to Mike. "That was a big deal for them, that plane ticket. I was their only kid, but not only that, we didn't have a lot of money. But they didn't want me to pass up my dream of New York."

"They sound great." And so different from my own.

Her eyes focus on the distance, and I imagine her thinking of her parents. A small smile plays at her lips. "Yeah. They were. They were older when they had me, so they might not have been chasing me around playing tag or rushing me from activity to activity, but they did the important stuff. They taught me right from wrong. The importance of hard work. To learn from my mistakes." She stiffens, straightening in the chair, causing Mike to jump down. "You know, I should really go. It's getting late."

I wonder how she doesn't give herself emotional whiplash.

When she gets up from the chair, I settle my hands on her shoulders. "Okay, what just happened?"

She doesn't meet my eyes. "Nothing, I just..." She blows out a long breath. "Look, you know this isn't a good idea. We *work* together."

She's right. I know she's right. But it doesn't make me do the smart thing and step back. Maybe I'm spoiled and used to getting my way. Maybe I have too much confidence for my own good. Or maybe something inside me just knows that Campbell is different. *We* could be different. More than a hookup. More than just two people thrown together by proximity and opportunity. Just... *more.*

"Look. I like you. You're..." God, I feel like a fucking adolescent as I struggle to find the words that will convey how I feel without scaring her, or me, with their intensity. "Unlike anyone I've ever met, and I need... well, fuck, I don't know exactly what I need, but I know that *we* need to stop being a couple of bitches and actually do something about this." I drop one hand from her shoulder to motion between us.

"Bitches?" She chuckles before getting serious again. "We work together," she repeats. "I mean, technically, I work *for* you, even though I have my own company."

"Are you worried what people will think?" I'm not stupid; I know the world is unfair to women. That's why I invented my dick app in the first place, after all. But maybe I'm the only one with feelings strong enough to think that, together, we won't let it matter.

"I hate saying this, because it's unfair and a cliché, but it's true. It's *different* for men than it is for women. If anyone knew that we" —she flails her hands about— "you know, or even if they thought we did, I'd be the one facing rumors and innuendo. Not you."

She's right. I don't want her to be right, but she is. "I would *never* say anything if you didn't want me to."

The pinch is back between her brows, like she's thinking. I trail one finger between her eyes and down her nose, smoothing out the frown.

"Look, it's Friday. We have nowhere to be and nothing to do for the next two days. Unless you're jetting back to Houston again?"

She smiles. "No. I'd actually planned to stay the weekend."

"Good." I step closer, and her head tilts up to keep eye contact. "Give me two days. Fuck, give *us* two days. No work, no co-workers. Just two people who like each other wanting to spend more time together."

The silence stretches out between us, and I would give my right nut to know what's going through her mind right now. I've always liked lefty better anyway.

Finally, she releases a long, slow breath, tickling the underside of my jaw. "Okay." She leans forward and kisses the hollow of my throat. "Two days."

My shoulders sag forward, and I touch my forehead to hers. "Two days," I repeat, letting relief wash over me. I'm not sure what I would've done if she hadn't agreed.

She pulls back. "I should probably get going then."

"I'm sorry, what?" Emotional whiplash is a thing. True story.

"You said two *days*, right?" She asks this with a calm demeanor. No trace of the uncertainty or lust from a moment ago.

"Uh, yes."

"Okay. Then I'll head back to the hotel tonight, and you can pick me up in the morning. We'll have Saturday and Sunday."

"Yep. Good idea." I hate this idea.

Campbell gives me a wide smile.

My dick is crying right now.

It isn't that I'm after a quick fuck. I mean, yes, *obviously* I'm attracted to her body. Hence the dick tears. However, I became enslaved to the whole idea of Campbell and me the moment hot coffee burned my nipples. And even more so once she opened her mouth. When she showed me how smart, funny, and kind she is. Damn it, I sound like a Hallmark card. Whatever. I want her. *All* of her. So if not sleeping with her tonight, or even the entire two days she's granted me, is what it takes, then I can handle it. I mean, I've had blue balls for weeks. It's become my norm.

"Okay, I'll drive you back to the hotel and then I'll pick you up for breakfast. Not brunch. Breakfast." I reach out and cup her cheek, smiling at her. "If I've only got two days, I'm making the most of them."

Still smiling, she nods.

I drop my hand and pace a little. "Pack a bag if you need to 'cause you won't get back to the hotel until tomorrow night. It'll be an all-day date." I look up at the ceiling, thinking. "You like sports? Theater? I can see if I can scrounge up some tickets if you like. Maybe a picnic in the park, that's a good time. Shit." I run my hand through my hair. "Okay, give me the night, I'm sure I can come up with something to make the most of our time."

"You need the night?"

"Yeah, that'll give me time to plan. But I'll let you know before tomorrow, so you have some sort of idea of what we're... what are you doing?"

Campbell's halfway down the hallway toward my bedroom before she stops and looks over her shoulder. "You said you needed the night."

"Uh, yeah?"

"So I'm giving you the night." She tilts her head to the side, just like she had when looking at Mike. "Unless you don't want me to stay?" Her lips twitch.

"Stay the night?" What is happening? I've lost control of the situation. Again.

"Yes," she says, nodding slowly, like I'm short on the uptake. I am. I definitely am. I swear she is the only one who can do this to me. I sort of love it.

"But I thought you wanted to start tomorrow," I point out.

"I did. But then you made a valid comment about two days not being a lot of time and needing the night." Her fingers trace over her collarbone as she talks. Back and forth.

"Uh-huh. Yes. Valid." My eyes are glued to her fingers as they slowly trail down her chest, between her breasts.

"And if you think I'm going to let you plan my whole day tomorrow without any input, you're crazy, Mr. Moore." Her fingertips rest at the button of her jeans.

My dick has stopped crying and is currently praying that this is leading where he thinks it's leading.

"So," she continues, circling the button, "if I stay, we can plan our date and spend more time together. Much more efficient use of time, don't you think?"

"Yes. Efficient." I nod. "I definitely think that." I nod again. "Efficiency is good."

She turns and continues her walk to my bedroom.

"Wait."

One eyebrow arches when she looks at me over her shoulder. "Yes?" Her tone is seductively lazy.

My dick salutes her.

I take a breath and hold out my hands. "I just want to make sure I have this straight."

She turns to face me again. "Okay."

"You are spending the night."

One side of her mouth curls. "Yes."

"We're having sex."

A full-blown smile. "Yes."

"And tomorrow we are spending the whole day together. *Two* whole days together."

She opens her mouth, but I cut her off. "*And* two nights."

"Yes." She chuckles softy. "Two days and two nights."

"Okay then." Before she can put me or my dick through any more emotional whiplash, I take two steps and haul her up into my arms, smiling when she immediately locks her legs around my waist like before.

"Then I better make them count." I make sure Mike is on the couch (which he is, licking himself, no less) before carrying her to my bedroom.

"Oh, I'm counting all right," she whispers, her hot breath moving up my neck. "And at last count, I'm still down by one."

I lay her on my bed, letting my weight settle against her while she hums "A Little Less Conversation." My lips vibrate against her neck, and I smile, promising myself then and there to give her all the action she can handle.

* * *

* * *

Two days, he said.

His lips continue their journey down my neck, across my collarbone.

Two days of *this*.

I asked for him to back off. To let me go back to the hotel. To start tomorrow. And he did. Without question (though with a hilarious look of disappointment).

But when I watched as he sorted through various types of 'dates' he could set up for us over the weekend, I wavered. He was so agitated, like the fate of the world depended on him getting these two days right. And everything about him in that moment led me here. To his bedroom. His mouth moving down my body.

Two days.

My mind wanders to the consequences of this night. Monday morning at the office? Our contract? My heart? One sharp nip of his teeth beneath my collarbone and I'm back in the moment.

Consequences? What consequences?

"Bell... fuck, you feel so good." He slides down my body, his hands curving under my hips, his fingers curling into my back jean pockets. "I have to taste you."

I'm not about to say no to that.

Quickly, I unbutton my jeans and toe off my boots all at once. His hands take over, grabbing my waistband and stripping my jeans off my legs, turning them inside out. Sitting up, I grab my tank with both hands and rip it up and off my body. I'm about to reach back and undo my bra clasp, but his hand on my thigh stops me.

I look up from his large, strong hand, resting on my pale skin, into his eyes. I'm used to his wink, his smirk, his slightly arched brow. Any of those expressions are panty-melting. But now, with no distractions, without the back-and-forth indecision of us, Chase's eyes are serious. There is a deepness to them he doesn't usually reveal. Though fully clothed, Chase Moore is stripped bare in this moment. I see his desire, but also his pain. He's wounded. Like me. And though that shakes me, makes me want to start stacking bricks between us, it also makes me want him more.

He's so much braver than I am.

"You're so goddamn perfect. You know that, don't you?" His voice is soft, hypnotic, floating above the restless noise of the city in the background. "Everything about you, I want. *Everything.*" His hand on my thigh tightens at that last word, the intensity palpable.

I'm not sure I have it in me to give him everything. But I'll give him two days.

I continue to strip off my bra, freeing the heavy weight of my breasts from their confinement. I toss the lace aside, never breaking eye contact with Chase. When I touch the waistband of my panties, his hands cover mine. Dropping to his knees, he leans forward, my legs spread farther apart to accommodate his broad shoulders. He gives me one more meaningful look before he dips his head, dragging his nose up my lace-covered center, inhaling deeply.

"Mmmmm... so good," he murmurs, kissing my clit through my panties once, twice, before finally pulling down the lace barrier.

I lift my hips, helping him, wanting him to devour me. Instead, his eyes lock between my legs. His tongue peeks out between his lips, as if imagining tasting my wetness. My desire. Moments pass and still he simply looks. Part of me thinks I should be embarrassed by his blatant scrutiny, and yet the larger part of me is more aroused by his interest, his intense focus. I'm about to give in and ask for his mouth when he finally leans forward, letting his tongue caress my sensitive flesh. Bottom to top, circling my clit in one hard, fast movement. He isn't fooling around. His tongue is firm against me, tasting me.

"Holy..." I lower my back to the bed and close my eyes, allowing him dominance over my body. His hands curl under my thighs then hook over my hipbones, holding me in place while he devours me.

This must be what it's like to lose your mind. My whole world, every thought and feeling, is centered on Chase's mouth moving against me. I'm desperate, my skin on fire, my stomach tightening.

He slides a finger in me while sucking on my clit. I'm close, so fucking close. A second finger follows, and he curls them ever so slightly, rubbing on the bundle of nerves there.

In a second, the languid, drugged-out feeling evaporates, and my muscles tighten. "Chase. Oh my god. Don't stop. Don't you fucking stop." I barely register that my fingers, once fisted in the sheets, are now locked into his hair and I've clamped my legs around him in a vise. How he's able to continue to—

"Fuck!" My back bows and every muscle in my body tenses as

the wash of heat courses through my body. "I'm coming, I'm coming, oh my god I'm coming..." My chant goes on and on as does my orgasm. And Chase is there, right there, teasing out the last sensations until my body drops limp and satiated against the sheets.

Slowly, I come back to myself, to the feeling of Chase kissing his way up my body. He's taking his time—laving my navel, dragging his teeth across my hip, kissing the underside of my breast. My hands find his hair again, tugging gently. He heeds my desire and raises his head to mine. I love his lips. Soft, sensual kisses coated with the tang of my release. My taste on his mouth is sexy and dirty and so right.

My god, sex has never been like this. But then again, it's never been Chase.

I want more.

"Please."

I feel his smile against my mouth. "Please what, baby?" His lips trail toward my ear. "Tell me what you want."

"This." I reach down and grab him roughly through his jeans. His groan vibrates against my ear.

He's still dressed while I'm naked and desperate.

I pull at his shirt, and he reaches back with one hand and yanks it over his head. Greedily, my hands roam his body. Smooth skin and toned muscles bunch as he shifts over me, the coarse fabric of his jeans finding my sensitive clit, making my back arch off the bed.

"Look at you. So beautiful," he says as if mesmerized, while once again dropping kisses down my body. He gives my pussy one last, lingering kiss before standing at the foot of the bed and undoing his belt.

He's insatiable. And for two days, he's *mine*.

Taking ownership, I push his hands away and finish with his

belt, hastily pushing his pants and boxer briefs down his legs. He toes off his shoes and steps out of his pants. Sliding off the bed and dropping to my knees, I take him deep. Much deeper than I could in the car.

"Goddamn." Chase groans, his feet faltering for a moment. He steadies himself as I continue to suck. I suck hard and frantically, wanting to give him something, something even close to what he's given me in our short time together.

It's his turn to anchor his hands in my hair as I worship his dick with my mouth, my hands stroking his ass, fondling his balls.

"Fuck, Bell. Wait." He steps back, and I release him with a pop. "Inside you," he says, cradling my face.

"Yes. I want that. My god I want that." I turn and crawl back onto the bed as he goes to the nightstand and gets a condom. I watch him stroke himself once while looking at me before rolling down the latex.

I face away from him on my knees, ass at the edge of the bed where he stands, looking at him over my shoulder. Waiting.

"Jesus, Bell." His palm glides over my ass. "You're either going to save me or be the death of me." Then he steps forward and thrusts inside, hitting my very core. He pounds his huge dick into me, fisting my hair for leverage as we fuck. With each thrust, he burns down my walls until it's just him and me and this incredible need we have between us.

Just when I feel panic start to rise in my chest, the need to withdraw emotionally and let this be what it needs to be—a good fuck —he reaches around and smacks my clit, sending me over into the most intense orgasm of my life.

Before my body collapses from the onslaught of sensation, Chase lifts my torso up, holding me against his chest while he continues to power up into me, prolonging the raging storm of pleasure washing over my body.

As the waves of my release ebb, Chase tenses against my ass, gripping my shoulders as his orgasm pulses inside me.

We collapse on the bed, our heavy breathing indistinguishable in the night. Minutes pass before my mind begins to piece back together. The bed jostles when Chase leaves for a moment, probably to take care of the condom. I don't move. I can't.

A minute later, he returns, gathers my still-limp body in his arms, and kisses my temple.

"Two days won't be enough, Bell."

I don't answer. The sounds of the city filter back into my consciousness. I become aware of Chase's body wrapped around me. The heat, the hard planes, the steady rhythm of his heart.

The panic that threatened me earlier has quieted. But not enough to silence my last thought before I drift off to sleep. *Two days is all I can give.*

15

BELL

Pretending to be asleep is exhausting. I passed out hard after round three last night. The oblivion of orgasm-induced, blissful sleep was wonderful. But as soon as the sounds of the city awoke, so did I, and now my mind won't stop spinning.

Eight years ago, my parents died. And in my grief, I agreed to give my co-worker, Denise, the finished project I had been working on so that I could go home for the funeral.

I came back to New York to find that she'd taken credit for my work. When I tried to speak up, Denise went in for the kill.

I'd been so stupid. So overcome with grief, and frankly, too naive to think someone would take advantage. Handing over the project gave Denise an excuse to use my computer, which she used to not only take credit for my work but to send ridiculously sexed-up emails to our clients from my email account. In light of this, my objection to her turning in my work as her own fell on deaf ears. With the complaints from clients pouring in, I was fired. Escorted from the building by security, my name blackened in the industry.

I get that this is different from what I was accused of years ago. I'm my own boss. No one is going to fire me from my own company. I mean, I could lose the Moore's contract, but I'd survive. King Marketing would survive. But it's still my reputation. A reputation I once had to repair by changing my last name when other marketing firms blackballed me once both the lies Denise spread about me and the pornographic emails were sent from my account.

Chase and I may both be interested, consenting adults, as last night's multiple orgasms helped prove, and neither of us is competing against each other at work, but it still *feels* dangerous.

Like it or not, a woman sleeping with someone she's working with/for/alongside is judged ten times more harshly than a man. Especially when that man is handsome and rich.

What's even scarier is that this time, it may not only be my professional reputation on the line. This time, my heart may be involved too. The heart is currently beating a mile a minute as I think of the various awkward scenarios that await me when this thing between Chase and me crashes and burns.

Scenario one: Chase is annoyed I'm still here in the morning. I leave and Monday morning is awkward. I quit, or more likely he fires me.

Scenario two: After our two days, he falls out of lust with me. I have to watch from afar as we work together over the next month or so while he dates other women. I quit, or more likely he fires me.

Scenario three: I won't extend our sleeping arrangement beyond the two agreed-upon days. His anger filters into our work. I quit, or more likely he fires me.

Scenario four: I—

"Morning."

Great. Chase is awake. And he knows I'm awake.

My pretending has been for naught.

I crack one eye open, enjoying the morning fantasy laid out

before me. Chase, on his back, hair on end, face shaded with scruff and eyes narrow from sleep.

He's never looked so good.

"Morning," I mumble, seeing as I probably have dragon breath.

His sleepy eyes light up as they travel over my face. On top of morning breath, I probably have pillow creases in my face, and let's not mention under-eye mascara smudges.

"Guess what?" he asks, his usual sexy voice ten times more affected when deepened by sleep.

"What?"

"I have the worst morning breath."

And just like that, I'm giggling, the tension I'd been building up inside eases, and all seems right with the morning.

"Do you often feign sleep in the morning?"

I give him a good eye roll. "Ha-ha."

The jerk just smiles broadly. "I bet you were tallying the latest orgasm count."

I snort.

"Reliving the best sex of your life. You know, the sex that took place just hours ago." He pats the mattress between us. "Right here."

"Best sex of my life, huh?"

He leans back with his hands behind his head. "Yep."

"Feeling a bit arrogant, are we?"

"Arrogant? Me?" He smirks. "Nah. Just confident."

"Uh-huh." I hug my pillow tighter, propping my chin on the edge. "I was actually thinking about pussy."

Chase curls up, coughing out a laugh. "What?"

"You know." I drop my voice, purring out the word. "Pussy."

"Pussy," he repeats, as if he can't believe what I'm saying.

"Yeah." I lean in closer. "Smooth, wet pussy."

His eyes track down my exposed back, over the sheet draped

off my ass. The smirk on his face slowly fades, while the sheet around his waist starts to rise.

"Mmm... pussy." I practically purr.

Chase licks his lips, and I bust out laughing.

"Wait. What? What's so funny?"

I continue to laugh, face in my pillow, but jerk a thumb in the direction of the doorway.

Where Mike Hunt is currently sitting, leg up, giving his privates a bath.

"Ugh. Mikey. What the fuck, dude?" He grabs one of his many pillows and tosses it at his cat. "Show some decorum."

I laugh until Chase rips away my pillow and smacks me in the ass with it. What follows is a kinky pillow fight between a man with morning breath and a raccoon-eyed woman, both naked and in full view of a wet, hairless pussy.

In the end, I added two more orgasms to my tally.

Not a bad way to start the day.

* * *

Chase

This morning rules.

Not even hairless Mike perving from the doorway while I was balls deep in Bell during morning nookie hour could dim this euphoric feeling.

The little man is eyeing me while we wait in the kitchen for Campbell. I've already fed the beast, but I probably owe the sad sack of skin a treat or two for being the precursor to a naked pillow fight.

I mean, come on. That's one for the record books. Men fantasize about panty-clad co-ed pillow fights, but to actually be in one, with a hot-ass naked woman? I win, dude. I win.

"You ready?"

Speaking of male fantasies...

"What?" She looks down, running a hand down my Tom Ford white dress shirt that she's wrapped around her body, held in place by one of my Louis Vuitton tan leather belts.

Being a descendant of luxury retail magnates, my clothes have always been fashionably on-point. But until this moment, they may as well have been rags.

And if I look too long at her gloriously exposed and freckled legs, capped off with those unique cowboy boots that are just so quintessentially Campbell, we will never leave this apartment. What little blood is still left in my big head is busy helping my mind conjure up sexy scenarios where those boots are propped up over my shoulders. That particular train of thought isn't helping my "little" head situation.

"Chase?"

I snap my jaw shut and try to blink away the fantasies. "Yes?"

She tilts her head to the side, her hair falling over one shoulder. "Everything okay?"

"Uh-huh."

"Then why are you looking at the floor?" There's a lilt in her voice, and I'd bet money it's from amusement.

I'd like to see how amused she'd be with a nine-inch pole in her panties.

Clearing my throat, I try to recover. "Just making sure Mike hasn't made any messes." As if sensing I've thrown him under the bus, Mike turns his bare ass to me and saunters away.

Giving Bell what I hope is a bored, unaffected look, I gesture to the elevator door. "Shall we?"

Not buying my excuse, or my look, Bell rolls her eyes, walking over to Mike. If the damn cat had hair, he'd be quirking a smug eyebrow at me right now.

"Be a good boy, Mikey," she coos, bending down to pet him. I swear, it's like she doesn't want to leave the apartment, waving her backside at me like that.

Mike purrs loudly, still looking in my direction.

Fucker.

But even with having to adjust myself while my girl pets my pussy, this morning is still tons of awesome. Because Bell is here. I have two whole days with this amazing woman. And though it's been a fight just to get her to agree to two days, I'm making the most of them.

The day only gets better when, without prompting, Bell slips her hand in mine before stepping into the elevator with me.

"So what's the plan, Stan?" she asks, leaning against me as I push the button for the lobby.

I cringe, making her laugh. "Oops, sorry."

"Yeah, how about we *not* bring my father up for the next two days?"

She squeezes my hand. "He is a bit of a mood killer, isn't he?"

"You could say that. Stan is like the anti-Viagra."

She laughs again, her breasts shaking against my arm. I groan.

Looking pointedly at the bulge in my jeans, she says, "Maybe you could use some anti-Viagra."

The elevator doors ping open, and Bell moves to exit. But I pull her back.

"My dick can't help it." I lean her back against the wall, bracketing her with my arms. "There's just something about you and elevators that makes him rise to the occasion."

"Rise to the occasion?" Soft laughter tickles my neck. "That's a horrible line, Mr. Moore."

Together, as if choreographed, my hands slide down the slick metal elevator wall to her ass as hers rise to cup my jaw while I dip my head toward hers.

"Mr. Moore?"

I pause, my lips barely touching Bell's, and sigh.

Turning my head to the left, I see Duke, the front desk concierge, holding the elevator door open for us. He's studiously looking out toward the lobby.

"Hello, Duke."

"Hello, Mr. Moore," he says, still looking away. "Lovely weather we're having today."

Bell giggles, pats my hard-on like she did Mikey just a minute ago, and grabs one of the hands still squeezing her ass. "Yes, Duke. Lovely weather. Great day for a walk in the city." She pulls me out of the elevator and into the blinding sun filtering through the lobby windows.

"Yes, ma'am."

She pauses mid-step. "No ma'ams, Duke. Just Bell."

"Bell?" Duke's bushy gray eyebrows come together, looking like a large, geriatric caterpillar.

She nods once. "Yes. Bell." She smiles and sticks her hand out. "Nice to meet you, Duke."

Clasping her hand in both of his, Duke smiles back. "Nice to meet you too, Bell."

And just like that, another one bites the dust of Bell's charm.

She tugs my hand and pulls me toward the doors. "Come on, slowpoke. It's been ages since I've gotten to walk around the city, and I couldn't have asked for a better day."

I wave the doorman back and hold the door open for her. "Or better company."

Bell snorts. "That has yet to be seen, Mr. Moore. What did you have on the agenda?"

A funeral dirge plays out, making both of us pause. Hurriedly, I fish out my phone from my pocket and silence the call.

"The funeral dirge? Who has the honor of that ringtone? The father-that-shall-not-be-named?"

I just smile and shake my head, not wanting to bring up the recently added ringtone for my brother.

I let go of her hand to cup her jaw, my thumbs caressing her cheekbones. "No one we need to worry about."

Then my arm is sliding around her shoulders at the same time her arm wraps around my waist.

The sun is shining, the breeze is cool, and I've got a hot girl wrapped around me.

Nothing can ruin this day.

16

CHASE

This day has gone to hell in a hand basket.

Do you know how many restaurants there are in New York City? Hell, even just in Manhattan?

No? Well, neither do I, except to say there are a shit-ton.

A shit-ton, people!

And yet, out of all the restaurants catering to the bougie, millennial brunch crowd—and, you know, me—my family somehow found me. Or I managed to find them.

I've taken Bell to brunch at Boucherie in the West Village. I know, a little much, but it's the best.

Now I'm thinking I should've gotten her an Egg McMuffin and called it a day.

"What's wrong?" Campbell's hand rests on my chest, her body given no choice but to curl into mine, what with my arm pulling her close. We're waiting behind a trio of young women at the hostess stand who are blocking Campbell's view of the restaurant, but not mine.

"Nothing. It's fine." And it is, for the moment. Between two topknots, I can just make out my brother who, unfortunately, is facing our way. "Maybe we should go someplace else."

"Really?" Bell blinks up at me. "But you were so excited when I said I'd never been here. You said you wanted to show me something new."

Our limited cover is blown when the hostess grabs three menus and herds the women to their table.

I turn my back on Thomas, trying to shield us from sight. "I know, but—"

"Chase?"

Fuck. I hang my head for a moment before surrendering to the inevitable and facing my brother. Thomas, eyebrows together, constant frown in place, is looking up from the table, fork and knife poised above his plate. My mother swivels in her seat toward Bell and me.

I try to smile, but I'm pretty sure it comes off as more of a grimace.

Thomas smiles his stupid, annoying, charming smile. "It *is* you."

He can't just wave or acknowledge my presence with a nod and move on, like he's done our whole lives. No. The bastard has to get up, take the time to place his napkin on his chair, push said chair in, then murmur a polite "excuse me" to our mother and walk over.

It's like he's doing a play-by-play of how to be a smarmy, obnoxious douche-hat.

"How are you?" His hand is out, and if I don't shake it, *I'll* look like the douche-hat.

Reluctantly, I release my hold on Campbell to shake his hand.

Brothers. Shaking hands. We are so damaged.

"Fine."

He glances at Campbell, then back to me. Internally, I sigh. Externally, I smile and make introductions.

"Campbell, this is Thomas Moore."

She glances back and forth, as if trying to figure out the dynamic. "Your brother," she states, like she's unsure given our demeanor. When I nod, she extends her hand in greeting. "I recognize you from the photo in Chase's office."

He shoots me a quizzical look. "Photo?"

Great. Don't want the bastard thinking I'm sentimental or anything. "Just leftover stuff from Stan."

"Oh."

He looks disappointed. Probably hoping to sniff out some weakness so he can convince me to sell the company.

"Mr. Moore?"

Thomas and I both turn to the hostess desk where a young woman holds two menus.

"Mr. *Chase* Moore?"

I take a slight step forward, making sure to grab Bell's hand.

The young woman smiles. "Your table is ready." She tilts her head in the opposite direction of Thomas's table, thank god. "If you'll just follow me."

"Sure—"

"That's not necessary," Thomas says, shifting his eyes to Campbell. "Sit with Mother and me. We just sat down ourselves. We'd be happy to dine with you both."

"That's okay, bro," I grind out. "Wouldn't want to interrupt family time."

This time Campbell is the one throwing me the questioning look.

"Chase," a familiar, feminine voice says.

Sighing, I face the lady. "Hello, Mother." I wrap my arm around Bell, tucking her close, not sure if the close contact is for her comfort or mine.

Please. We all know it's mine. I'm afraid of a woman in a classic

Chanel baby blue tweed suit. It's so stereotypical, it shouldn't still be fashionable, but it's Chanel and it's on my mother, so it is. She glances at Campbell, arching a thin brow. "Come. Join us." Then she turns on her expensive nude pumps and walks back to the table.

Awesome.

* * *

Bell

Awkward.

The word plays on repeat in my head. This is nothing like drinks with Liz. Drinks with Liz make this feel like a funeral for someone's secret baby daddy.

Chase's mother, Emily Moore, straightens her silverware and smooths the white linen tablecloth in front of her. For the third time in as many minutes.

Chase is staring at the salt and pepper shakers like they've mortally wounded him somehow and only the sight of their shattered glass remains could appease him. I've lost feeling in my fingers, since he's probably channeling that same determined Jedi-mind-fuck aggression into the death grip he has on my hand. Luckily, no one can see my dead, lifeless fingers as our linked hands remain between us, on the booth seat we're sharing.

"So..." Thomas clears his throat, finally breaking the silence. The terrible, awkward silence. "You haven't returned my calls."

Chase's fingers pulse harder on mine, then he lets go and shifts his focus to his brother. "I wonder why that is?"

Thomas sighs. It isn't a nice sigh. It's like a parent getting frustrated trying to teach a toddler how to use a spoon kind of sigh. "Listen, I know—"

"Hi there. My name is Stacey, and I'll be your server. Can I get you something to drink while you look over the menu?"

"Bloody Mary." I realize I'd basically shouted this when Chase's mother jumps in her seat. I lower my volume. "I'll have a Bloody Mary, please."

"Sure thing." Stacey jots my order down on her notepad. "Anyone else?"

"Water for me," Mrs. Moore says, her lips stretching into a tight smile.

"Same," Thomas murmurs.

I'm about to change my order to just water. I mean, if they want to do this whole awkward silence thing sober, I guess I can hang.

Then Chase speaks up. "Just water, Mom? That's new."

Mrs. Moore blinks, Thomas squints his eyes, Stacey raises her eyebrows at the whole angry vibe Chase is throwing off, and I just really want that Bloody Mary.

Chase's anger seems to evaporate when he addresses the waitress. "I'll have a Bloody Mary as well, Stacey." He smiles and winks after he says it, Chase Moore charm in full force. Stacey visibly relaxes, jots it down, and spins on her heel back to the kitchen.

"That was uncalled for," Thomas admonishes. And though I agree with him, I remind myself I'm on Team Chase. I also don't want to draw too much attention to myself. Chase introduced me as Campbell King but left it at that. I'd rather not have my two-day bubble burst by two shareholders of Moore's realizing I'm mixing pleasure with their business.

Plus, Thomas is really condescending. I hate that.

More silence. Oh my god. I can't take it anymore.

"I love your suit," I blurt out.

Chase stiffens beside me, while Thomas smiles and looks down at what is, admittedly, an immaculately cut suit, but I cut him off before he can speak. "Sorry, I meant your mom."

Chase coughs, but I know he's really trying to cover a laugh.

You know how some women have resting bitch face? Thomas has resting flagpole-up-his-ass face. Which is sad, as he's a good-looking guy. Perfectly styled dark hair, strong jaw, broad shoulders, tall, fit body. All the things women like to see ticked off on their list. In fact, before Chase, he would've ticked off all *my* boxes. But comparing him to Chase? No contest. For the past eight years, I've dated nothing but serious, straitlaced men, thinking their lack of charm somehow protected me from being fooled into trusting them too soon. It's hard to trust a robot. Or fall in love with one.

Shaking off the revelation, my eyes move to Mrs. Moore. "I meant your suit. The color is beautiful on you." And though I had just been trying to fill the void of awkward silence, the suit does look great on her. Mrs. Moore is one of those classic beauties. High cheekbones in a heart-shaped face, relatively unlined in that way some older, well-kept women have where you wonder if it's from good genes or a good surgeon. Ash blond hair that looks so natural, if it wasn't for her age, I'd swear it was the color she'd been born with, pulled back in a timeless French twist. No heavy makeup or garish lipstick, but rather a lovely palette of neutrals and a pale pink gloss.

Surprise flashes on her face before she speaks. "Thank you, Ms. King. That's very kind of you to say."

I wave my hand, the feeling of which has been fully restored, in the air. "Please, call me Bell."

A small smile curls her lips. "Bell. What a lovely nickname." She opens her mouth, closes it, then opens it again. "I think you should call me Em, then. It's been a while since anyone called me that, but I always did like it."

I can envision a younger, more lighthearted version of herself, someone just like her daughter Liz, answering to the name Em with a laugh. The mental picture has me smiling my first real smile since Chase and I joined their table.

"Em it is."

Thomas manages to look polite and disapproving at the same time. I'm starting to feel bad for the guy. It can't be that comfortable living with a huge stick up your butt. Chase looks confused, which is a step away from murderous, but still. I'm not going to ponder why Chase being upset makes me uncomfortable. Instead, I'll chalk my feelings up to me being angry and annoyed that Thomas is horning in on the two days I've given myself to simply enjoy being with Chase without shame or guilt.

I'm in marketing, I can spin things however I want. And right now, I want Chase to cheer the heck up.

Playing innocent, I bat my lashes at Thomas. "Are you Tom, then?"

Chase chokes on a laugh, his fist coming up to cover his mouth.

"No." Thomas's disapproval isn't as polite now.

"Tommy?"

"No." His nostrils flare, which for some reason, amuses me. And Chase, judging by the smile on his face.

"T-Moore? The Tom-bomb?"

"No." This said through clenched teeth.

I sigh at his inability to joke, but figure I've messed with him enough. I got what I wanted, anyway—Chase smiling. Heck, even Em seems amused.

"He always did insist on Thomas. Even as a child," she says, as if apologizing for her son.

"That *is* my name." Thomas bristles.

I bite my lip to keep from laughing, 'cause it's funny seeing a grown man actually bristle.

"If you'd wanted to call me Tom or Tommy then you should've put Tom or Tommy on my birth certificate."

Thomas's attitude hasn't changed, but at least Chase doesn't look so tense. I grab his hand again under the table, relieved when he doesn't re-establish his death grip.

"I don't know, brother," Chase drags out, his trademark smirk in place. "There's always T-money. Has a certain ring to it."

"Here are your drinks." Stacey places tall glasses garnished with celery, bacon, and blue cheese-stuffed olives in front of Chase and me, then refills everyone's water.

Chase takes a long pull on his Bloody Mary. "Damn, that's good."

"So good," I say after taking my own sip. Or gulp. Okay, I'd sucked down half the spicy drink, and I'm blinking fast so my watering eyes don't overflow.

"Best Bloody Marys in Manhattan," Stacey says with a smile, obviously choosing to ignore the tense atmosphere around our table. "Have you had a moment to look over the menu, or would you like more time?"

"We still need a minute," Thomas says.

With a nod, Stacey departs.

Great. If we prolong ordering anymore, this brunch is going to take forever. Not that it doesn't already feel that way. I nibble away on my tall drink's garnish. Between the bacon, celery, and olives, it hits most of the basic food groups and could maybe amount to brunch in a glass.

"Now, if you'll just *listen*." Thomas glares at his brother.

That quickly, the smile drops from Chase's face.

"I've been trying to inform you that Moore's—"

"Shut. Up."

My mouth drops at the murderous glare on Chase's face and the venom in his words.

Chase leans forward toward his brother. "You lost your right to *inform* me of anything having to do with Moore's when you dropped the failing family legacy on the dining room table and washed your hands of it weeks ago. You don't get to call me, expecting me to listen to whatever the fuck you think is important. You lost *that* right years ago when you couldn't be bothered with your second-rate younger brother and you shoved your head so far up Stan's ass you basically became his butt puppet."

This time I'm choking on a laugh. But really, *butt puppet*?

"Chase, dear," Em tries, reaching one of her hands out across the table for his.

Chase immediately sits back, hand out of reach. "No."

Em stills. The sadness in her eyes pulls at me, but Chase must be blind to it. Or immune.

"You don't get to dear me, *Em*. Besides not openly objecting to me taking over Moore's, which isn't exactly a ringing endorsement, by the way, you've never stood up for me over the years. So don't pretend that this serendipitous little meeting is anything other than a way to try to blindside me into falling into line with whatever the Golden Boy wants."

Golden Boy bristles again. I avoid eye contact with everyone and suck down the rest of my Bloody Mary. Unfortunately, I suck too hard. The loud, slurping noise of my straw on the bottom of the empty glass draws Thomas's angry attention to me.

"Stan did have one thing right, brother. You took over Moore's and got distracted by the first pretty woman in the place."

I still, the alcohol and spice unable to stop the cold feeling Thomas's words evoke.

He continues, "How is the marketing campaign going, *Bell*? King Marketing getting everything they need to pump life into Moore's? I do hope you're getting paid well for your endeavors. Above the counter, as well as *under* it."

Em gasps, looking wide-eyed at her older son. "Thomas…"

For a second, Thomas looks stricken. But I can't be sure

because I'm trying to remember how to breathe. Black dots form around my vision. This. *This* is what I was afraid of.

Just as I manage to inhale, Chase yanks me out of the booth, almost colliding into poor Stacey.

"Congratulations, Thomas," Chase says, reaching for his wallet. "You've finally become our father."

This time I do catch the look on Thomas's face. He looks downright ill.

"Here." Chase thrusts two hundred-dollar bills at our waitress. "I'm sorry for taking up your table. This should cover our drinks and your time."

Death grip back in place, he leads me out of the restaurant.

17

CHASE

As soon as I exit the peaceful tranquility of upscale dining, the cacophony of city noise hits me. Bell's hand in mine is the one thing keeping the feelings roiling inside me from imploding.

I'm halfway down the block before I realize Bell is tugging on my hand for me to stop.

"What the heck *was* that back there?" she pants after I make a sudden stop.

A fast-walking New Yorker bumps into her, and I turn to shield her, drawing her closer to the building and out of the way of pedestrian traffic.

I try to steady my own breath, which is also heaving. From exertion, anger, hurt. Who knows? "That," I say, jerking my head behind us, "was an ambush, apparently."

"An ambush?" Bell's small smile falters, then fades when she realizes I'm serious. "You really think Thomas and Em planned that?" When I don't answer, she scoffs. "How would they even know where you were, Chase? That's crazy."

Her coming to their defense irritates the shit out of me. As does her logic. She doesn't know my family's history. Doesn't know them. Should never have even met them.

"Oh, I'm sure Thomas and your new best friend *Em* could've found a way." I can't help but sneer.

Bell takes a step back, pulling her hand free from mine. "Wait, are you mad at *me*? How did I become the bad guy here?"

My hand flexes with the loss. I take a deep breath, trying to recover from her withdrawal. I don't like how quickly I calm at her touch. But I hate her physical retreat from it even more.

"I just sat through one of the most uncomfortable brunches in the history of brunches, which never even made it to actual food being served, and finished with your brother insinuating that I was some sort of prostitute-marketing-exec, which is the very reason I didn't even want to start something with you, and *you're* mad at *me*?"

Fuck. "No. No. Of course not." I run a hand through my hair, trying to calm down. "Sorry, I'm just… it's just… my brother and I don't get along."

"Really? I couldn't tell." Sarcasm heightens her Southern accent, and she plants her hands on her hips. When I keep silent, she quirks a brow, daring me not to explain.

I clear my throat. "In fact, I don't really get along with my family in general."

She lets out an exasperated breath. "What about Liz? You seemed to get along with her just fine last night."

Remembering the bar last night and the laughter between Bell and Liz settles the churning in my chest. "Okay, so I only get along with Liz."

She cocks her head to the side in that adorable way she has when she's trying to figure things out.

"Does Liz feel this way about the rest of your family?"

"Ah, no, actually." It's just me that's the outcast. Me who can't measure up. "Besides my father, who mostly just ignores her, Liz is on good terms with our mother and brother." I pause as I remember Liz calling Thomas a douche. "I think. I've never really asked her. We don't really bring them up when we hang out."

"I see."

I bet she does. She's too smart, too quick to not see how I'm the misfit in the family. The last choice to run the company. The one who flies off the handle while Thomas remains unaffected and practical. Today has been just another moment in my life where he's come out on top. The Golden Boy wins again.

"Thomas *is* a bit of an ass."

Her comment surprises a laugh out of me.

She tilts her head to the other side, a smile playing on her gorgeous lips. "What? Is this one of those instances where you can insult your family, but no one else can?"

I reach for her, my hands sliding under hers on her hips, pleased when instead of her arms just dropping to her sides, they encircle my neck. "No, no. Insult away." My grip on her tightens, and thankfully, she lets me pull her closer. Lets me nuzzle the tip of her nose with my own.

She smiles then, a real smile, her body now flush with mine. "How about instead of wasting any more time on stuck-up T-money, we go get some breakfast tacos?"

"Breakfast tacos?" I smile wider, amazed that after such a long encounter with my brother I can smile at all. "You sure? I could probably get us into Wolfgang's for an exceptional late brunch."

"Nah. Who needs white linen and oysters when you can have tinfoil and chorizo?"

"You're a girl after my own heart, Ms. King."

Better yet, the one who is starting to own it.

* * *

A large gulp of Coke helps cool the heat from the chorizo. Bell was right: This is just what we needed.

Sitting on a bench in Central Park, the silence, for once, is comfortable as we alternate between people-watching and bites of spicy breakfast tacos.

"These are great." I raise the last of my taco. "I can't believe I've never tried them before."

"I can't believe the stand is there after all these years." She wipes a trickle of salsa off her chin, grinning. "I've missed New York."

Her smile is infectious, as is her joy at being back in the city. But something nags at me.

"I don't get it. If you love the city so much, why go back to Texas?"

She's silent, and I get the feeling the tables have turned. I may not want to elaborate on my family issues, but I notice she clams up when it comes to herself and her move back south.

"The job I had after college didn't work out," she finally says.

"But there are so many marketing firms in New York. With your education and experience, even just out of grad school, you could've gotten a job with another firm."

She shrugs before taking a large mouthful, finishing her taco and making it impossible for her to talk. Instead, she stands, walks to the nearest trash can, and throws away her wrapper and drink before walking over to a street artist, essentially ending the discussion.

I shove the rest of my taco in my mouth and follow suit, trying not to be annoyed. It's not like I would've opened up to her about the rest of my family had she not had the pleasure of meeting them herself. But seeing as she has, I should just be grateful she still wants to make the most of the two days she gave me instead of running for the nearest subway station.

I need to remember the game plan. Make the day and a half I have left so awesome that Bell can't help but want more. I can uncover her secrets later.

Plenty of time for that.

* * *

Bell

"What's next?" I ask after Chase tosses his taco wrapper in the trash.

He eyes me for a sec, like he wants me to know he knows that I've changed subjects, but he's giving me a chance to answer his previous question. I simply stare back at him until he sighs and glances at his watch.

"I planned on chartering a yacht to sail around on the Hudson." He slides his phone out of his pocket. "I'll call and see when they can take us."

As much as I'd like to try sailing on a yacht, something I've never done—because let's face it, that isn't something normal people do—I can tell Chase isn't over the family ambush. Or my lack of forthcoming information. His posture is stiff, and his smile doesn't quite reach his eyes.

For reasons I can't quite define, I need to cheer him up.

Maybe it's the guilt I'm carrying because I almost bailed on him at brunch. I'm not proud of that. But honestly, if Chase hadn't hauled me out of the booth when he did, I would've crawled over him to get to the door, leaving him to his familial fate. Or more likely, I would've lunged across the table and smacked that smug look off his brother's face.

"I have a better idea." I link my arm through his and rest my chin on his shoulder.

A bit of his smile creeps up to his eyes. "Is that so?"

I nod, my chin moving up and down on his arm. "Trust me, you'll like it."

He narrows his eyes over his smile. I flutter my lashes at him in response.

"Okay." He chuckles, smoothing his brow. "Lead on." He waves to the path ahead of us that will take us out of the park.

I reward him with a peck on the cheek before steering us in the right direction, glad the oppressing shadow of family drama and awkward silences are over. In the years since my parents passed, I've come to love my solitary life, free from uncomfortable family dynamics. Even when my parents were alive, there hadn't been any of that. At their age, they'd been too tired or too wise. Maybe both.

Suddenly, I'm jostled to the side.

"Whoa there, buddy." Chase stops and steadies the young boy who careened into him before squatting down to the kid's level. "You okay?"

Eyes wide, the kid just nods, his unruly, short brown hair sticking up every which way. He's about five or six, I'd guess.

"Ethan!" Another kid shouts, jogging over to us. "Sorry about that, mister." He places a hand on Ethan's shoulder. Must be his brother. Same eyes, same chin, same wild hair, but a few years older.

"No harm." Chase smiles, stands back up. The older kid takes Ethan's hand and leads him back into the park. Ethan waves his free hand at Chase.

"Cute kid," he says as he waves back, his eyes contemplative.

Looking at the boys, I wonder if Thomas ever looked out for Chase like that. Held his hand. The wistful look on Chase's face makes me think he might be having those same thoughts.

Growing up, I was jealous of my friends with their many siblings or large Thanksgiving dinner parties. Of course, I also bore witness to my friends being teased by their older brothers, or their parents' insistence that they share their toys with their brothers or sisters. Those were the only times I felt any sort of win by being an only child.

And today. Today, I definitely felt a win after meeting Thomas. I may not have a cool younger sister like Liz, but I also don't have an asshole older brother like Thomas.

In the distance, a woman swoops down on Ethan and his brother, giving Ethan a hug before shaking a finger at him. Followed by another hug. Then one for the older boy.

An image of Chase's mom pops into my head. She seemed nice enough at brunch, but I didn't exactly get a hugger vibe from her. I wonder briefly how Chase and Liz came by their ability to express affection so openly.

The young family gets swallowed up by the crowd at the park, and Chase wraps his arms around me. "So, where are we going?"

I settle into his embrace, giving him a side-hug. "My happy place."

* * *

"I have to say, your happy place and my happy place are two completely different places." Chase looks around, shaking his head.

"Oh yeah?" I head into another room of the Museum of Modern Art. "And what is your happy place, then?"

Chase trails after me. "Inside you."

An older woman gasps, and Chase cringes, having not seen her standing there. "Sorry about that, ma'am." He nods in my direction. "She kind of makes me crazy." The older woman looks unconvinced at his words. Chase winks.

And damn if that wink doesn't make one of the stuffiest-looking older women I've ever seen—wrist bag, pantyhose, and cardigan draped over her shoulders—blush.

"Here now, young lady. You shouldn't lead such a charming man on." She tsks at me.

I'm too dumbfounded to do anything other than gape as she walks out of the room, but not before patting Chase on the cheek like a good boy and wishing him luck.

Hands behind his back, Chase strolls farther into the room, whistling.

"What the hell was that?" Seriously. Have I transported back in time? Is feminism still a word? Can women still vote?

"Language, please, Campbell," he mock scolds me. "You don't want to be a further bad influence on me, now do you?"

"Oh, for heaven's sake," I huff, marching into the next room.

"Wait. You didn't even look at these paintings." Chase follows after me, but I keep walking through two more rooms until I find the one I want.

"Wow." Chase stands behind me, hands resting on my shoulders. "Your happy place is with a weird dude in a white wig."

I glare over my shoulder.

He raises his hands. "Hey, no judgment."

"His name is Andy Warhol."

Chase cocks an eyebrow. I huff.

"Okay, yes, he was a weird dude in a white wig."

There's that annoying but sexy smirk again.

"But he was *also* one of the most famous pop artists in America."

"Yeah, the soup can man, right?"

I laugh, unable to hold his opinion against him. Warhol *is* known as the soup can man. "Yeah, the soup can is a part of it."

Chase doesn't say anything else, just walks the perimeter of the room, looking over the art.

I've been looking forward to this pop art exhibit since my first flight to New York. Watching Chase, who's studying the Lichtensteins, Indianas, Harings, and yes, Warhols on display, I'm glad I'd waited to go.

I walk in the opposite direction, needing a smidge of distance now that I've taken him to someplace so meaningful to me. We pass each other once before meeting where we started.

Chase takes another glance around, lips pursed. "I'm surprised, but not surprised."

I laugh, though it sounds unnatural. "Okay," I draw out, not sure why I feel nervous. "Whatever that means."

When he looks at me, his usual smirk isn't there. "It means that sometimes you're so focused on brand exposure, distribution, and other tactical marketing concepts, I forget that marketing as a whole is a pretty creative business. Art is a big part of it."

I nod.

"Like that shoe display," he continues, and I nod again at the memory. "So I'm surprised at myself for *being* surprised when we first walked in here. Because really, it *isn't* very surprising that you'd like art. Especially pop art." He looks across the room where Warhol's iconic *Campbell's Soup Cans* is hung in a place of honor in the middle of the main exhibit wall. "It's like the most expensive and memorable product marketing ever."

I'm inordinately pleased by his words. "That's an interesting way of looking at it."

"What? You're saying *don't* like pop art because it's basically high-end marketing?"

"No. I mean, it is, that was the concept of pop art, after all. It conceptualizes things from popular culture: advertisements, comic books, the everyday, mainstream objects as opposed to anything elitist." I wave toward the soup can paintings before sitting down on the bench in front of the Warhols. "But that isn't why I like it. Or *just* why I like it." I pat the seat next to me, my hand shaking slightly. It's been a long time since I shared this part of myself with someone. It makes me excited and nervous all at once.

Chase sits, taking my hand in his. "Okay, I'll bite. Why do you like it then?"

Looking straight ahead at Warhol's hand-painted canvases, arranged on shelves just like they were in his first exhibit, I think back to the very first time I was introduced to pop art. "My father."

"Your dad?" He sounds surprised.

"Yep. My dad had the tomato soup can print hung in the den of our house. He brought it home from work after he retired."

"What'd he do?"

"He managed a large grocery store southwest of Houston. He told me that when he was promoted to head manager, Mom bought him the print for his office. He'd never been one for art and 'all that nonsense,' as he liked to say, but he really liked the Warhol print. I think he had a Brillo print and the Coca-Cola print too, but the soup can is the most memorable."

He nudges my shoulder. "See, I told ya."

"Yeah, you did." I laugh. "Warhol, the soup can man."

I'm quiet, lost in memories, before Chase urges me on. "You were saying about your dad?"

"Oh. Just that I remember one day, I was working on my history homework, trying to memorize dates that to this day I don't know why I needed to know, when I distracted myself by asking about the print. And from that one question, Dad and I had an hour-long conversation about art. About how he never paid attention to it growing up, because he couldn't afford it and didn't understand it.

And then my mom had gotten him this print for his office. Mom was a librarian, and Dad always liked to joke how she married down because she was so well-read and he was just a Texas boy with a high school diploma, working a low-end white-collar job."

"They sound like they were happy."

"They were. Even when kids didn't seem to be in the cards for them."

"I bet they were thrilled when you came along."

"Ah yes. Back to that." I nod at the soup can painting. "Even being the white-collar worker Dad was, for some reason, this small poster of a soup can interested him. Made him ask questions. Why is this art? Why does it appeal to me? Who painted it?"

I glance at Chase, amazed that this small story from my past has him so enraptured. Without thinking, I lean the right side of my body against his left, bringing our clasped hands to my lap.

"Five years after Dad's promotion, after my mother gifted him the Warhol print, he surprised her with a night in the city. He got tickets to the Museum of Modern Art's pop art exhibit. They got dressed up, had dinner in a nice restaurant beforehand, and rubbed shoulders with the socialites of Houston, which made them giggle. Wondering if all these rich people had any clue they were talking to a grocery store manager and a local librarian. Afterward, they stayed the night in a swanky downtown hotel. Dad said it was fancier than their wedding. Probably cost more too."

I close my eyes, remembering the day Dad and I talked about art for the first time. The way the sun slanted through the blinds, the rough texture of the tweed couch under my legs, my dad's soft smile as he told the story. "And nine months later, I was born. All because of a soup can." I nudge him. "Hence the name Campbell." I laugh. "Honestly, I'm surprised they didn't name me Andy."

Chase isn't laughing, though. When my chuckle tapers off, I risk a glance at him. His eyes are dark, brimming with emotion, but I don't think it's humor. His serious gaze makes me even more anxious than when I was working up the courage needed to tell him the story. It hits me that telling someone a simple tale of why I like pop art shouldn't be so nerve-wracking. That I probably have some issues I need to work on. And that the sudden anger I feel toward Chase's silence is unfair. But I can't seem to help it.

I jump up from the bench, abruptly enough that Chase lurches to the side I've been leaning against.

"Anyway, that's why I like this stuff." My speech is fast and my voice high. Is it hot in here? It feels hot. I pull my hair off my neck, fanning myself with my free hand.

"Campbell. Bell. *Bell.*"

Chase's voice finally breaks through my crazy-train of thought.

"Hmmm?" I blink at him, willing the beads of moisture on my scalp to stop forming.

"Thank you for telling me that story. And for bringing me here."

"Oh." I drop my hair and smooth down his shirt I'm wearing as a dress. "No problem. It, uh, probably wasn't as cool as yachting, but..." I shrug, out of sorts, and try to covertly wipe my brow.

Apparently unconcerned by my odd behavior, Chase wraps me in his arms again while we begin our exit from the museum. His touch does more to reassure me than any words could.

Out on the street, he hails a cab.

"Where are we going?"

"Well, you took me to your happy place." He opens the cab door and waits until I've slid in and over before ducking in after me and giving the cabby his address. "It's only fair I take you to mine."

18

BELL

"What is it with us and elevators?" I groan, head thrown back while Chase kisses, sucks, and bites down the column of my neck.

"Elevators are naughty," he manages between kisses. "Getting it up, going down." His hand squeezes my breast. "Otis was a dirty fuck."

I lift my leg to wrap around his waist. "Otis?"

The hand that's not on my breast glides up the side of my leg, disappearing under the dress shirt of his I'm wearing. "Yeah. Otis." His fingertips trace the edge of my panties along my ass cheek. "Ever notice the name Otis is stamped in every elevator?" He turns his head toward the doors and over to the row of floor buttons. Sure enough, OTIS is stamped above.

"Huh."

"He invented the elevator safety break." He slides his hand around and cups me over my panties. "To stop people in his elevators from going down too fast." His kisses continue down between my breasts.

I groan when he nips at my cleavage. We're back on track.

Everything's back on track.

No more childhood stories. No more family drama. No more feelings.

Just sex.

Okay, so I'm not so coldhearted that I don't feel *something* for Chase. Those feelings obviously led me to the museum today. But it's a dangerous slope. Feelings beget more feelings. I'm going to focus on the feelings he's stirring in my panties rather than in my chest.

I don't want to wonder at Chase's family dynamic or risk my job by defending him to his shareholder brother. Or unearth memories of my parents, long locked away.

The elevator doors ding, and like boxers heading into the ring, we both charge out, ready to take our latest elevator tryst to the bedroom. Hell, I'm so ready, the hardwood floor seems like a good option.

A beige missile leaps past me and detonates on Chase's crotch.

Chase sucks air in some sort of weird guttural inhale, sinking to his knees.

Mike lands gracefully and circles around Chase, who's still on his knees, bent at the waist, one hand cupping himself, the other bracing himself on the floor.

"Damn it, Mikey," he manages to choke out. "This is the second time you've tried to break my dick."

His words break me from my frozen shock. "Second time?" And then I'm laughing. Hard-to-breathe, tears-in-my-eyes laughter. "He's... tried to... break your dick... before?" At his nod I fall forward, unable to stay upright while laughing so hard. My palms brace on my knees, and tears of laughter fall to the floor before I manage a few deep breaths.

A glance up shows Chase looking a little green, so I try harder to rein it in.

"Are you okay?" I ease down on my knees beside him, awkward

in tall boots and a short dress. He leans toward me slightly, so I run my hand over his back in circles.

"No." His voice is still strangled.

Poor Chase. A minute ago, he'd been well on his way to his happy place, only to be sidelined by a dive-bombing, claws out, hairless pussy.

The image replays in my mind—the wild meow, the blur of skin, the wide-eyed shock in Chase's eyes, and the sudden, hard drop to the floor. Mikey and Chase. A giggle escapes, and I do my best to shut down the waves of laughter threatening to break free again.

"Is there... can I do anything?" I'm careful not to make eye contact. I may have stifled the laughter, but I haven't yet managed to wipe the grin off my face.

Chase grunts, and I'm not sure if it's an affirmative grunt or negatory.

Before I can translate Chase's junk-punched sounds, Mikey sashays between us, pushing me back from Chase.

The little menace looks so innocent, blinking up at me, rubbing his body against my hip. Unable to stop myself, I reach down to pet him. "Why'd you do that, Mikey, huh?" I ask, unclear if cats are known to crotch-bomb people or not. I haven't seen that video on YouTube before. I ask Chase, "Is that normal cat behavior?"

"No." His voice is stronger now, though his hand is still cupping his dick. "Nothing is normal about that cat." Chase heaves a sigh, settling back on his heels. "It may not excuse his *psychotic* behavior"—he eyes the cat I'm now giving a belly rub to— "but he's probably pissed because Saturdays are usually our day to go to the park, and I didn't take him."

Not quite so pale now, he pushes himself off the floor, hobbles over to the couch, and collapses, one hand still at his crotch, protecting his man bits from his ninja sphynx.

I follow, more gracefully than Chase, slip off my boots, and curl up on the cushion next to him. "So... up for a quickie?" I tease.

He groans. "Stop. Even thinking about getting hard hurts my dick." His eyes trail down my body, and he actually whimpers before his chin meets his chest in defeat. "I think I might cry. I've been imagining unwrapping that shirt off you all day."

"Maybe you can unwrap me later?"

Mike leaps up on the top of the couch and curls himself around my shoulders like a shawl, ass to Chase's face.

Chase eyes Mike's puckered asshole, aimed in his direction. "I hate you."

Mike's answer is to snuggle down around me, licking behind my ear once before purring contentedly.

I giggle, causing Chase's eyes to narrow in my direction.

I raise my palms up in surrender. "Sorry. Sorry."

Chase pouts.

"Aw, poor boy." I squeeze his leg. "How about I get you an ice pack?" Carefully, I get up from the sofa so Mikey doesn't fall forward. My effort is wasted when, unhappy with me leaving, the vengeful feline pounces onto Chase's already damaged crotch.

Air whooshes from Chase's lungs as his eyes roll back, watering. Mikey continues on his descent, landing on the floor before sauntering away without a care in the world.

Silence reigns.

Finally, Chase moves, inhaling deeply.

"Oh my god." Kneeling in front of him, I rest my hands on his thighs. "Are you... how can I help?"

His eyes flutter open only to shut fast on a groan when he sees me. "For a start, you could not kneel in front of me." He tries adjusting the crotch of his pants but stills on a whimper. "My dick is confused. He needs to rest, but with you looking like his next wet dream, he's trying to rise to the occasion."

I nod, pulling my lips between my teeth to keep from smiling and rise. "Sure thing, boss."

"Not helping, Ms. King."

* * *

Chase

Naked TV time is awesome.

Okay, so Bell made us both put on underwear because she didn't want me distracted from the movie with her nakedness.

Please. She can't fool me. We both know she really meant she'd be distracted by *my* nakedness. When I called her out on it, she just rolled her eyes, called me delusional, and commandeered the remote.

Whatever. Her boobs are still out, so I consider the boxer brief/panty compromise a win.

"Come out to the coast, we'll get together, have a few laughs." Bell whispers the words to one of her favorite movies before chuckling, her breath tickling my chest.

Her eyes lit up when *Die Hard* popped up on our streaming options. "A classic," she said. I'm pretty sure classics are more in line with *Citizen Kane*, *Gone with the Wind*, or even *The Godfather*, but I hadn't been stupid enough to argue with her.

Boobs out, remember?

Plus, feeling her lips move over my skin as she lip-syncs the *entire* movie from start to finish is far more entertaining than its over-the-top explosions and cheesy one-liners.

Before starting the movie, she ordered Chinese food. We ate as I iced my junk. By the time the last crab wonton had been fought over and devoured (she won), my dick was back to full strength (I won).

Don't worry, I was smart enough to lock Mike in the bathroom first. If I was going to finally unwrap Bell from my shirt, I didn't want to worry about a hairless bag of skin gunning for my dick. Fool me once and all that.

And now, Bell is curled into my side, bare breasts pressed against me, both of us basking in a post-orgasmic glow. Or maybe Bell is. I'm not sure guys are allowed to glow after sex. Hmmm. Whatever, I'm secure in my sexuality. If I want to glow, I'll glow, damn it.

I don't even care that Mike shredded all the toilet paper, making my bathroom look like a winter wonderland. Totally worth it.

He's been released from his containment area and is now stretched out on our laps (my junk protected with a throw pillow).

We've snuggled through the villain telling his minions to shoot the glass, through a bare-knuckle fight between the hero and the seven-foot German thug, and through two FBI agents named Johnson circling a building in a helicopter like it's Vietnam.

Best. Night. Ever.

No woman I've dated has ever watched TV with me. I'm not sure any of them even stepped into the living room. We went from doorway to bedroom. That includes my last ex, and we shared a cat. We may have had a conversation or two in the kitchen about which five-star restaurant she expected me to take her to that night, but that was the extent of it.

Bell agreed to two days. And yet, knowing the limited time frame we have, she's made no demands about where we go or what we do. She even chose a museum and Chinese take-out over a catered yachting excursion.

And I loved every second of it.

Sitting next to her on the museum bench, listening to her talk, telling me stories I never knew I wanted to hear, I realized two days wouldn't be enough. I think I've always known. Ever since my burnt man nipples.

"Oh! Listen, listen. The best part's coming up!" Bell squeezes my arm for emphasis. Like I haven't seen this movie a hundred times before.

I kiss the top of her head in answer, my dick cringing when Mike shifts his weight on the pillow. Thankfully, it's just to burrow closer to Bell.

Traitor.

This time, she doesn't whisper the words; she says them in a deep voice I'm guessing is supposed to sound like Bruce Willis, then makes gun noises at the subsequent shoot-out, complete with finger gun motions.

I think I just fell in love.

"Bruce Willis is so badass." Her last word is said in a yawn.

"Yeah." I smirk as my own little marketing badass snuggles deeper into me. "Total badass."

"Let's watch *Die Hard 2* next." She scratches behind Mikey's ears before resting her hand on his back. "The whole series, really. Have to watch the whole series. Can't just watch one." Another yawn. "That's like, sacrilegious or something."

I trace my fingers up and down her arm. "Sure thing, babe."

She hums, the noise vibrating through my chest and settling into my heart.

I've always thought that if I did find a woman for me, and it was a big if, she'd come from a large, loving family. Uncles, aunts, cousins, siblings, parents who hug and kiss every time they say hello or tell each other goodbye. People who call to check in, just because they want to make sure you're okay, not to tell you how wrong you're living your life. People who believe in you.

It hits me that I haven't been searching for a woman. I've been searching for a family.

It should sadden me that even as a grown-ass man in my thirties, I'm still hoping for the family I never had. Pathetic.

But with Bell draped over me, her wild, sunset-colored hair tickling my chin, and her smooth, soft, skin on display for me, I feel anything but pathetic. I feel fucking lucky.

Bell's lips press lightly against my chest. When I glance down, her eyes are still glued to the TV, but her lids are heavy. I press an answering kiss to the top of her head, stroking her exposed skin.

I laugh at the remaining fights, explosions, and one-liners, and by the time Ms. Gennaro punches that douchebag reporter in the face, Bell's passed out, her body soft and heavy over mine, with Mikey splayed out, belly up, on top of my dick pillow.

Yippee-ki-yay, indeed.

* * *

A guy in a multicolored sweater is gesticulating wildly around discounted blenders on the muted TV, Mike's tail is twitching, tickling my stomach, and my right arm is asleep.

If it weren't for the latter, I'd stay here all night.

Carefully, I move the pillow Mike's on to the side and slip out from under Bell.

The television's light plays across her face, casting her pale skin in a bluish haze and making her hair look slightly purple. Like an oddly colored Oompa Loompa.

She's beautiful.

Mikey takes advantage of the opening, claiming my spot on the couch and burrowing closer to Bell. He flicks his tail straight up, and I swear it's his version of giving me the finger.

Fucker. After all I've done for him, he throws me over for a woman.

I rummage through my pants on the floor, finding my phone. I don't know why this woman curled up with my cat makes me happy, or maybe I do and I don't want to jinx it, but I want to remember it. Especially if I only have two days.

I angle myself so I can't see her breasts, as it doesn't seem right taking naked pictures without permission, but rather the profile of her face and the long column of her neck and bare back. I focus the screen, Mike's head resting on her hip like the creepy fucker he is, and snap the picture.

Bell shifts in her sleep, sinking to one side, looking like a toddler passed out in a car seat. In a word: uncomfortable.

I take one more picture, this one for laughs, and lift Mike out of the way. He flicks his tail up again in annoyance, but otherwise gives me room to slip my arms under Bell and pick her up.

"Whaaat?" Her head lolls against my chest, her warmth instantly surrounding me, filling me up.

"Shhh. I got you," I murmur, my lips against her temple.

I want to tell her I mean that in more ways than just carrying her down the hall. I want to tell her I mean it in all the ways. And for much more than two days.

But I don't.

19

BELL

"Want to grab a cab or walk?" Chase wraps his arm around my shoulders as we near the end of the park.

It's a beautiful Sunday afternoon. Ice cream and hot dog vendors shout their wares, bicyclists fly by, children play tag, and meanwhile, the glow of the setting sun mirrors the warm feelings growing inside me. Even though they are dangerous feelings, I want to prolong this moment as long as possible.

My arm circles his waist. "Let's walk."

He smiles at my decision, as if my reasons are his reasons, and directs us toward the crosswalk.

In Texas, my typical Sunday afternoons are spent previewing the agenda for the following day. I make lists and draft emails so that I'm ready to tackle Monday head on. Though it isn't an opinion shared by many, I love Mondays. For eight years, my work life has been my *entire* life, so thoroughly preparing for the workday on a weekend never felt strange. It just made sense.

What doesn't make sense is the sinking dread I'm feeling just thinking about tomorrow. When Chase will go back to leading

Moore's into the twenty-first century and I'll go back to being the marketing specialist helping him get there.

Today, I haven't so much as logged on to a computer. Besides a quick scan of my inbox on my phone to make sure nothing urgent has come up (it hasn't), I haven't even opened an email.

Instead, I woke up, not from the annoying buzz of an alarm, but to the warm, soft, wet feel of Chase's tongue on my clit. After he rewarded me with an orgasm, he followed it up with a toasted New York bagel and a piping hot latte.

It was my most perfect morning ever.

I was positive I could sex Chase out of my system within our two days together. I've never been so wrong. Besides still wanting to use him for his body, I'm equally enjoying the other stuff, stuff I didn't even know I'd agreed to. Talking, holding hands, comfortable silences, learning new and interesting things about him.

Like the fact there seems to be nothing Chase can do to dampen his sexual appeal.

"How's your pussy doing?" I ask, a man jogging past nearly tripping when he overhears my question.

"Just fine, thank you." Chase smiles, patting the lump secured to his chest. The lump hisses and snuggles deeper into the sling.

That's right, ladies and gentlemen, Chase Moore, billionaire, playboy extraordinaire, is carrying around his hairless cat in an honest-to-goodness baby carrier on the streets of New York. And managing to look sexy as hell doing it.

We've had another great day in the city, doing all my favorite things, and things I've never thought of—riding a double-decker tourist bus, sex, browsing books at the Strand, sex, and then playing honest-to-goodness shuffleboard in an indoor club in Brooklyn. I've missed all the interesting and quirky things to do and find in New York.

And now we're "walking" the cat and people-watching.

But really, when you're strolling around hand in hand with a guy carrying a hairless pussy in a baby sling, people watch you.

"Thanks for doing this." Chase squeezes my shoulder. "Mike gets pretty pissed without a weekly outing." He adjusts himself, no doubt thinking of Mike's attack on his nether regions yesterday.

"No problem." I stifle another chuckle as a teenage boy gives Mike, who pokes his alien-looking head out of the sling, the side-eye. "This might be the most entertaining thing we've done all weekend." I finally give in to the laugh when the boy stumbles, nearly taking down the girl he has his arm around.

"Really?" Chase pulls me in closer, his breath tickling my ear when he whispers, "Even that thing I did with my hand under your dress on the tour bus while people—"

"Okay!" I yell, the heat rising in my cheeks.

Chase smirks knowingly.

I roll my eyes thinking of the orgasm he gave me as we drove through Times Square on the open top of the double-decker bus. Hopefully New Yorkers and tourists alike had been so enthralled with all the other interesting things going on around them that my flushed face, glazed eyes and low moan hadn't registered. "Maybe not the *most* entertaining."

We stop at another crosswalk, and Chase takes the moment to kiss my temple. The simple touch melts my heart. Who'd have thought my heart could still melt? That it had room, or even a need, for tenderness? That his public displays of affection wouldn't make me uncomfortable, but rather cherished and safe. All weekend Chase hasn't stopped touching me. And I'm not talking sex, although there has been *plenty* of that. I'm talking hand-holding, soft kisses, couch cuddling.

I slip my hand into his back pocket. Just one gentle squeeze of his ass sends a shiver running down my spine.

"You cold?" he asks, glancing down at me.

"Nope," I say, popping the p and trying to pretend like I'm not feeling him up in public. I'm pretty sure the heat spreading down my neck gives me away. I change the subject. "You think Mike's okay, though?"

"Yeah, he's loving it."

The spring weather really is lovely. There's a whole song about Paris in the spring, but I'd bet money New York is just as nice. The cotton dress I picked up from my hotel room yesterday (after Chase and I christened the room) flutters with the breeze, and my toes wiggle comfortably in my sandals. But Mike, being a sphynx, is just skin and bones. Worried he'd be cold, Chase sneak-tackled him earlier, forcing the uncooperative feline into a light blue sweater embroidered with wiener dogs. The struggle had been almost as hilarious as a hairless pussy wearing a bunch of wieners.

I'm pretty sure Chase chose the outfit in retaliation for last night's cat dick missile.

However, after the initial struggle, Mike didn't seem to care about his sweater. In fact, after it was tugged down his bare torso, he'd simply sniffed like a condescending bourgeois, then leapt into my arms to motorboat my boobs. Which prompted Chase to mutter about traitorous, cock-blocking pussies.

Chase isn't exactly wrong about the cock-blocking. Mike has claimed me as his own, even hissing at Chase if he tries to get too close to me.

Such a sweet kitty.

We pass by a Chinese place, reminding me of our takeout from last night. Chase didn't have much of an appetite after his junk got punched, and I don't remember much after falling asleep at the end of *Die Hard*. But in between, I'd felt content and happy, cuddled into Chase's side. It's a little unnerving that these feelings I have for Chase were present last night, even without the sex.

A loud gurgle disrupts my thoughts. I rub my tummy. "What's on the menu tonight?"

"You," he says, not missing a beat.

I pretend my panties didn't just start to tingle. "That's a given. I'm both the appetizer and dessert. But a girl's got to eat to maintain her stamina." I reach inside the carrier and scratch behind Mike's ear. "So what are you feeding me besides your dick?"

Chase barks out a laugh, causing Mike to hiss and swat at his face. Luckily, Chase's pretty visage is out of reach. "Sorry, Mikey. Your new girlfriend has a filthy mouth."

He kisses the top of my head while I try not to freak out about the word 'girlfriend.'

Continuing like he hasn't just given me a mini heart attack, Chase suggests pizza. "Have you had *real* pizza since you've been back to the best city on Earth?"

"That depends on what you consider real pizza."

"The only real pizza is New York style pizza, Campbell. You can't even try to argue with that. Do they even have pizza in Texas?"

"Yes." I glare. "They have pizza in Texas."

"Yeah, but *good* pizza?"

"Okay, smart-ass." I pinch his backside in retaliation, smiling when he jumps. "It may be true that New York has the best pizza, but are you smart enough to know which pizzeria has the best pizza in Manhattan?"

He narrows his eyes. "Is this a test?"

"Yep."

He chuckles again, but this time Mike stays content in his carrier. Probably 'cause I'm still petting him.

"Okay," I prompt. "Count of three we both shout out the place with the best pizza in town."

"Why are we both shouting it out? I already know I'm right; I just want to see if you are."

"One…"

I roll my eyes again, but honestly, he's so much fun.

"Two…"

He winks, and I bite my lip to keep from kissing him silly on the street. Mike would probably take his eye out if I tried.

"Three."

"Lombardi's!" we shout at each other.

Laughing, we stop right in the middle of the sidewalk and turn to each other, big, stupid grins on our faces. The moment stretches out, and I find myself wanting to freeze time, to stop the inevitable end, or even more dangerously, extend our time together in search of more moments just like this one.

Finally, I look away. "Who'd have thought?" I ask Mike, needing to lighten the mood. "The man has taste."

Chase's finger lifts my chin so that our eyes connect once more. "Of course. I'm with you, aren't I?" His smile remains, but his eyes are serious. Searching.

Is he with me? Like *with* me with me? The last two days have been amazing, but he has to realize that we've been in a bubble, untouched by outside forces. No work, no client–employer minefields. This isn't, can't be, real. We can't make promises and declarations with Monday just a few hours away.

I'm Cinderella waiting for the clock to strike midnight. But instead of being stranded with a pumpkin and a useless glass slipper, I'll be left with a broken heart and a potential professional disaster. Again.

"I…" I clear my throat, unwilling and unable to pop the two-day bubble early. "I want Lombardi's," I say with a playful, stern face. "Make it happen, Moore," I order.

There's a flash of disappointment in his gaze before he blinks, replacing it with his usual mischievous glint. "Yes, *ma'am*."

I gasp in mock indignation, relieved he's let the question of us pass unvoiced and unanswered. "You'll pay for that, mister."

He dips his head, brushing his lips against mine. "I hope so."

Mike growls between us, and we step back with a laugh.

I rub my hand over Mike's smooth head, which pacifies the temperamental cat, while Chase reaches in his pocket for his phone.

"One Lombardi's pie coming up."

But before he can call, an email notification lights up the screen.

An email from Denise Hampson.

Suddenly the breeze is too cold, the silence awkward, and my appetite vanishes.

My phone, also in my back pocket, remains quiet. Evidently, Denise hasn't copied me on whatever email she thought important enough to send on a Sunday afternoon. Even though Chase had been explicit that all information regarding marketing go through me.

Chase doesn't even blink, ignoring the notification and sliding his phone open. He captures my hand with his free one and resumes our walk back to his apartment. I barely hear him ordering our dinner, too busy wondering why Denise is contacting him and why, even though the question of us remains unasked, it rings in my head so loudly.

20

CHASE

Bell's moan is loud and deep. "God, that's good. Mmmm..."

It's official, I'm a sick bastard. Watching Bell eat pizza gives me a raging hard-on. I'm pretty sure that's not normal. When she wipes a dribble of grease from her chin with her thumb and then puts it in her mouth and sucks, I'm ashamed to say I come a little.

Shifting on the barstool, I concentrate on Mikey, who is once again licking himself. Dude must have the cleanest balls in all of Manhattan.

"Are you okay? You look like you're in pain." Bell's concern is amusing, considering she's the one who put the pained expression on my face.

"Uh-huh. Yep. Totally fine."

She gives me a well-deserved side-eye and continues eating her slice of pizza, folded in half like only good New York style pizzas can be eaten.

"So," I say, trying for distraction. "How well do you know Denise Hampson?"

Campbell chokes on her next swallow.

I get up and pound on her back. "Shit, you okay?"

"Fine," she coughs out. "Fine!" She leans back, warding off my hand with her arms. "Stop hitting me, you weirdo."

I stop, hand raised. "Oh. Sorry." In my panic I may have been a bit overzealous. Lowering my arm, I hop back on my chair.

Bell does that adorable eye roll she always likes to toss my way.

"So...?" She doesn't seem in any hurry to answer my question, making me all the more curious. I haven't forgotten the weird vibe from the meeting or the way her whole body had tensed up when she saw the email notification from Denise on my phone.

She lets out a huge sigh, as if resigned to her fate. "She was my co-worker once upon a time."

Dropping that on me, she picks up her pizza again and takes a large bite.

I remember what she said about her first job in New York not working out. "Co-worker, huh? I—"

"Why are you asking?" Her eyes narrow over her slice. "Did she say something in that email of hers?"

"No." I pull back, surprised at her tone. "Well, I don't think so. I haven't read it yet." She doesn't look like she believes me, so I go on. "I'm not doing *any* work this weekend. This weekend is ours."

Her body softens at my admission. "Oh. Okay." She opens her mouth to take another bite but stops. "Then why did you mention Denise?"

I don't exactly want to tell her I was hoping to distract my hard-on to limit any more of its premature ejaculating, so I go with, "No reason."

"Hmmm." But it isn't the good hmm from before when she was moaning over New York's dough and cheese combo. It's a contemplative hmm, like she doesn't like where my answer is leading her train of thought. When she places her slice back on the plate before glancing at her watch, my panic has me blurting out, "I was trying to ease my hard-on!"

Her head swivels to me, her eyes blinking. "*What* are you talking about?"

Resigned, I sigh. "The real reason I brought up she-who-shall-not-be-named."

"Denise?"

I nod, prompting a laugh from her that dissolves the frown between her brows.

"Voldemort and Denise?" She snorts. "Yeah, I can see the similarities."

"Exactly. She was the one thing guaranteed, even more than watching Mike clean his ball sack, to calm down the stiffy I'm rocking in my pants from watching you moan over your pizza."

That surprises another laugh out of her. "Is that right?"

"Yep." I reach for another slice. "Had to distract myself from how hot you are."

"I'm hot eating pizza?" Her voice is skeptical, but a spark lights up her eyes.

Note to self, next time don't try to dampen my arousal, just stoke hers up to my level.

Abandoning my pizza, I run my thumb over her slick bottom lip. "So hot. But then again, you're always hot." I smirk for good measure, my panic at the thought of her leaving early ebbing enough for my charm to pull through. Using both hands, I turn her more fully toward me before leaning one arm on the counter and dropping my chin to my palm.

Just inches away, she mirrors my pose and says, "If that's true, then we have something in common."

"And what's that?" I love the way her brown eyes shine. Those beautiful orbs that are like a smoldering fire, sparking with reds and ambers. Will they ignite in passion or anger, or stay banked with warmth? The suspense keeps me on my toes and my heartbeat racing. I love it. I could get addicted to this feeling.

If I'm not already.

Campbell leans in even closer, until her breath tickles my face. "We both find each other hot in what should be off-putting situations."

I chuckle softly, not wanting to break the spell. "We do?"

She nods, chin still in her hand.

"I admitted to the pizza turn-on. What's yours?"

She wrinkles her nose, like she can't believe she's going to tell me. She's so fucking cute.

Lifting her head up, she shows a small distance between her thumb and pointer finger. "I may have been *this close* to jumping you after you strapped your cat to your chest in a baby carrier."

I snort. "Women dig men wearing baby carriers. That's nothing new."

Her eyebrows rise. "A baby carrier holding a cat?"

I nod my head, conceding her point. "Okay. Yeah. That is weird. Probably weirder than me being turned on by you eating pizza." I slide off my stool, moving between her legs. "There's probably something wrong with you."

She slaps my shoulder playfully. "Hey—"

But I don't let her finish, instead taking the opportunity to drop my mouth over hers. She can eat pizza any old time. With anyone. I only have a few hours to remind her about all the pleasure she can have. With only me.

The greasiness of our lips should be off-putting, but it's not. Sex is messy. Love is messy. Love? No, it can't be. Can it? I've never been in love. I've never been around it enough to compare. Though I have a feeling, even if I had, nothing would compare to Bell.

My kiss started soft and playful, but is now deep and consuming. It's more than the usual combustible passion between us.

More than lust. My chest actually *aches* knowing tonight may be my last night with this woman.

I trail my lips across her jaw, nipping at her ear. "Stay the night," I whisper. I don't ask. Asking means letting her think she can say no. "Stay," I repeat before taking her mouth again, my arms wrapping tight around her.

The only answer I allow her is a moan. It's enough for me.

* * *

Bell

Stay.

The word echoes in my mind as he consumes me. That's the only word for it. His arms pull me in so close, not a whisper of breath between us. I want to move, to grind, to find some relief from this combustible current thrumming inside me. Yet I don't. Rather, I sink into his embrace, memorizing his scent, his touch, his taste.

There's an undercurrent of desperation driving both of us. We both know this is it. Our last night. It's all he asked of me. It's all I could promise. Two days.

Stay.

I don't answer. I couldn't even if I wanted to.

Small kisses, hard kisses, tongue and lips and shared breath. It's the kiss to end all kisses, and it would be sweet and momentous if it also wasn't heartbreaking.

It's only been two days. My heart has been safe all these years, so why does it suddenly feel so fragile? I thought I buried the fragile girl I once was, long ago.

Strong hands unfasten the tiny buttons down the front of my dress before gliding up to my shoulders and pushing the straps aside. The soft fabric grazes my nipples as it falls, catching once at my waist before Chase smooths it over my hips to the floor.

Still his kiss is gentle, reverent. His touch more so.

His fingertips float across my skin, barely grazing. Up my sides, over my breasts, around my nipples. My throat, my shoulders, my breasts again. Over and over, never the same path. As if he's memorizing me with his touch. My head drops back, and my eyes close, giving myself over to him. To this moment.

Suddenly his touch deepens, becomes purposeful. He lifts me, cradling me in his arms before taking us down the hall to his room.

It's almost déjà vu, being here, on his bed, Chase dressed and looking down at me. Except this time, there isn't a sense of urgency. Touches are slower, tastes longer, everything blissfully drawn out. By the time Chase finally makes his way between my legs, one tongue swirl over my clit and I come.

He flattens his tongue against me as I ride out the orgasm, moaning long and loud. I'm limp and warm when he crawls up my body, reaching for the nightstand. There's a crinkle of foil and finally the slow, full glide of his cock inside me.

"Bell. My Bell." Chase's words wash over me. "You feel so good, Bell."

* * *

"Ooof." All the air in my lungs whooshes out in one long, painful exhale.

An unpleasant way to wake up, to say the least.

Panicked, my eyes fly open, arms raised to ward off my attacker. Only to grab a lump of warm, saggy skin sitting on my stomach.

"Damn it, Mike," I wheeze, trying to suck in air.

He licks his balls once before leaping to the floor.

Freak-out over, my body relaxes back into the mattress. Light barely filters through the curtains, the bedroom still cast in shadow.

Stay, he'd said.

I could. It wouldn't be hard. This whole weekend has been easy. The two of us, we just... *mesh*. I can't think of another word to describe it. As cheesy as it sounds, being with Chase, being *here*, feels more right than my sad, undecorated, studio in Houston ever has.

I'd love to wake up next to him tomorrow. Make love. Tally orgasms. Watch action films. Protect his junk from his diabolical cat. Hold hands.

I *want* to stay.

Chase shifts in his sleep, facing me. He looks young and peaceful. Happy. Not that he isn't always smirking and winking. Lord knows he is. But this seems different. *He* seems different. Unguarded, genuine. I'd like to think I had something to do with that. I know he's made me happy. I feel like myself, as odd as that sounds. It's weird to realize that I haven't felt like myself these past few years. That I've just been running on autopilot, giving myself occupational goals, thinking each time I met and exceeded them that I'd achieved something meaningful.

It's sad to realize that I've just been filling a void. And not even that well, if two days with Chase has made me feel more myself than eight years of work.

I don't like to think of myself as easily duped. But it's clear that I've duped myself. I convinced myself that losing my parents hadn't affected me. That, because they were older, their deaths were expected sooner rather than later. So when it happened, when they were actually gone and I didn't have anyone else to lean on, I used work to cope.

I'm not sure if it was intentional or happenstance, but by

becoming such a workaholic, I conveniently didn't have time for new relationships.

And then Denise happened, and I was blacklisted from everything I'd worked so hard and so long for.

Chase lets out a soft snore, then grunts, sounding like a displeased gorilla.

Even in sleep, this man can make me smile when my thoughts are so unhappy.

If I stayed, I'm pretty sure he'd make me smile every day of my life. Pretty sure isn't sure enough, though. I'm finally back in the city I love, heading up a multi-billion-dollar company's marketing. Chase may think we can keep a relationship quiet, but he doesn't have at risk what I do.

His family already knows. And with Denise in the picture, it'll only take a whisper of impropriety for her to justify spreading rumors and undermining my success.

No. I may *want* to stay. But I *need* to go.

He asked for two days. I gave him two days.

Chase is my client. I will not fall for my client. I'd be doing the very thing Denise accused me of eight years ago. Except this time, it would be true.

His lashes flutter against his cheek, his mind far away in a dream. Reaching out, my fingertips graze the lock of hair over his brow.

Maybe after Moore's new media campaign is up and running, we could...

No. I pull my hand back. *Don't get ahead of yourself.*

Carefully, I slide out from the covers, grateful when Chase's breath remains deep and even.

On tiptoes, I cross the room, grabbing the bag I packed from my hotel, and slip through the door, quietly closing it behind me.

A Mike-shaped shadow slinks toward me. Little minx must be

nocturnal. He runs figure-eights between my legs while I scan the floor for my dress. Finding it by the island, I scoop it up and slip it on. My sandals are by the door. Now I just need to find my panties, and I can escape.

Not escape. It's not like I'm running. I'm just making a careful, silent exit after Chase's and my well-planned, time-limited fling concluded its natural course. Not waking Chase to say goodbye isn't cowardice; it's simple consideration.

For some reason, Mike's soft meow sounds very sarcastic.

Finally finding my panties draped over Chase's fancy espresso machine, I shimmy into them and collect my bag of stuff. I didn't bring much. Either I'm smart and efficient at bringing a weekend's worth of clothes, or I didn't want to tempt myself to stay longer.

Either way, in less than a minute, I'm ready to go.

The elevator's ding rings loudly in the quiet apartment, and I wince, hoping Chase won't hear it. Hurrying inside once the doors glide open, I hit the button for the lobby and pound the close-door button until they finally move toward each other.

The last thing I see before the elevator doors shut is Mike, sitting on his wrinkled, bare ass, looking at me with disappointment.

21

CHASE

She left.

A week later after our perfect weekend together, and I'm still distracted, staring out the window but seeing nothing. I still can't get over it. Over her.

She left.

It's not that I think I'm some sort of Casanova the ladies can't say no to (okay, yes, I do think that), but Bell and I, we had something. No. We *have* something.

And yet, for the past week she's dodged me. First by creeping out of my apartment without so much as a goodbye and now in my own goddamn store.

A week of no return phone calls or texts. Only business emails and polite indifference when we saw each other in the hall. And though I did have lunch with her team a few days ago, Bell was conspicuously absent. Even the former weak link for information, Alice, simply shrugged her shoulders when I asked where her boss was.

The woman is ghosting me.

My cell phone rings, and without thinking, I answer.

"Hello."

"Finally." My brother's superior voice makes my muscles clench.

I close my eyes in defeat. I've been avoiding him so well, and then I let Bell distract me.

"Did you hang up on me?"

I'd laugh at his incongruity if I wasn't so pissed at myself. "No, Thomas. I did not hang up."

"Wouldn't have surprised me, with how well you've dodged my calls lately."

"Lately? Seeing how you never tried to call me before I took over Moore's, you don't really know how well I dodge calls on the regular."

"So you *have* been dodging my calls."

Damn it. "What do you want, Thomas?"

"I want to talk."

"Yes, I gathered."

The phone buzzes with his long, drawn-out sigh. "Knock it off."

"Knock what off?"

"Acting like a pissed-off toddler."

"I see."

"What do you see?"

"I'm really not sure, but I was trying to appease you so you'd stop lecturing me and get on with the point of the phone call. Unless that was the point. Like father, like son, after all. At least Stan's superiority complex skipped Liz and me."

"Superiority complex? Are you serious right now?"

"No, Thomas. If you remember correctly, I'm the happy-go-lucky brother who's never been serious about anything. Have you forgotten that?"

"No wonder Father hates talking to you," he mutters but still loud enough for me to hear.

It shouldn't sting. I should be above his digs and the knowledge that our father prefers him over me. But after being rejected by Bell, having my lifelong paternal rejection thrown in my face cuts deeper than I thought it could.

"Yes, well, we all know how much I'm hated, Thomas. So nice of you to point out the obvious."

"I didn't... Fuck, I shouldn't have said that."

I start, barely registering his apology. "Did you just say fuck?"

A deep, rough chuckle, one I've never heard before, trickles through the line, making me smile. Who knew my brother could sound so human?

Shaking my head, I refocus on the conversation. "Okay, you've got my attention. Just what is it that you want to talk about?"

"Liz's shares."

And just like that, the smile is gone, and every word of my father's threat replays in my head.

"I should've fucking known." I stand, automatically shifting my weight like I'm about to throw a punch. Because I want to. I want to punch my brother's perfect face so badly, my blood is hot with it. "*You* walked away, Thomas. You don't get to play around with shares, and you sure as shit aren't taking them away from Liz."

He's trying to talk, but all I hear is Stan's voice, and all I see is Liz's face. Everything else is lost. "Did Stan put you up to this? Reissuing his threat against me? What, you report back to him that you saw me with Bell and now the old man wants to strip our sister of her inheritance?"

"No! What I'm trying to say—"

"Fuck you, Thomas. This is why I dodge your calls. This and a lifetime of your sick, superior attitude and subtle digs at those around you."

"Jesus, Chase." He sounds exasperated. "I'm not fucking superior."

But unlike my conversations with Stan, I don't get any satisfaction ruffling up Thomas's perfect feathers. Instead, I just feel tired. So fucking tired of this shit. "You're right. You're not, Thomas. Not by a long shot." Sitting down, I take a deep breath. "Now if you'll excuse me, I have our family's company to save. Don't call me again."

"Wait. Chase—"

Whatever Thomas had been about to say is lost when I hang up.

The death grip on my phone loosens when I catch a glimpse of my screen saver. It's the photo I took of Bell after she fell asleep on the couch. I'm not sure what possessed me to make it my screen saver, seeing as she already snuck out on me last Monday morning.

Looking at Bell, my shoulders relax, my blood pressure drops, and—even more improbable after the conversation I just had with my brother—a smile tugs at my lips. In the photo, Bell's head is tilted back, her hair draped over the cushions. Her wide, pouty mouth is slightly open. I remember the sound of her deep, even breathing. Not snoring, exactly, but a peaceful rumble. The sound of sleepy contentment.

It wasn't just her, either. I felt that. Especially in the moment after I took this picture, when I picked her up in my arms, her weight settled against me, her hair tickling my nose. The feeling of rightness as I carried her to my bedroom.

For two days, I had something I never thought I would. For two days, I didn't feel like an outcast, underserving or unwanted. For two days, I finally felt like I measured up.

And then she left.

Fuck this.

Reaching for the intercom, I bark into it. "Where is the marketing team right now?"

George, unfazed as always, replies, "Ms. King and her team are currently on the floor with the photographer."

"Photographer?"

"Yes, Mr. Moore. Campbell is getting a backlog of images for the new social media launch."

Campbell. My uptight, holier-than-thou, millennial administrative assistant calls our new marketing exec by her first name, but *I'm* still Mr. Moore.

"What floor?" I grind out.

"Their schedule shows that they should be in menswear on level two, sir. If running behind, they'll be in shoes. Same floor, other side of the escalator."

The intercom button cracks ominously under my finger. "Yes, George. I know where the men's department is. This is my family's store, after all."

"Of course, Mr. Moore."

Forcing my index finger off the intercom, I take another deep breath before standing and grabbing my jacket from the back of my chair. At this point, I'm going to hyperventilate before the end of the day.

I take my time smoothing the jacket arms, making sure my shirt cuffs peek out the appropriate amount at the wrists. Raymond always said if you look confident, you'll feel confident. And though I've overheard him tell that to numerous men throughout the years while guiding them into spending thousands of dollars on a new wardrobe, it doesn't make the saying any less true.

When I'm done adjusting my suit, I don't need a mirror to assure me I look my best. I know I do. Especially when every woman turns to check me out as I walk down the hall. One or two men, too.

Ghost me, will she? We'll just see about that.

22

BELL

Inhale. Exhale. Inhale. Exhale.

The scents of rich leather, warm wool, and Denise's pungent perfume fill my sinuses. But it's either that or pass out. Because if I don't remind myself to breathe, I may stop, just for relief from Denise's constant nagging. I'd be laid out on the hard tile floor, but it would totally be worth it not to hear her grating voice anymore.

"The angle you asked for is all wrong. You need to get the photographer off that ladder." She rolls her eyes. "This isn't *Project Runway*, for god's sake."

This is the first time Denise has deigned to convene with my team since the meeting between Warren and Baron and King Marketing. Oh, there've been plenty of group emails circulating, conference calls, etc. Denise's only responses thus far have been negative comments. *Loud* negative comments. Even in her emails, her vitriol screamed from the screen. I have to give it to her, that takes talent.

"Move to the right," Denise commands the poor man on the ladder. "God, this is such a juvenile approach. I thought you'd at least hire professionals."

The photographer doesn't even pause at Denise's voice. Not at this point. He tried to accommodate her suggestions (Demands. Suggestions. Same thing, right?) at the start of the session, but quickly got on board with the rest of us by ignoring her.

No matter how loud and annoying she got.

"I don't know, seems like a pretty cool idea to me," a smooth, sexy voice calls from somewhere behind me.

Not moving, I track Chase's saunter over to the group from the corner of my eye. He nods to Ben, Chris, and Alice before turning and giving the three employees from Warren and Baron the same greeting.

In. Out. In. Out.

I've done my best to stay out of his way, going so far as to sweet-talk his assistant, George, into giving me a copy of Chase's schedule. Well, sweet talk, and tickets to the Yankees–Astros game. Who knew the stodgy fellow loved baseball that much? But it was worth it to ensure I am anywhere but where Chase will be at any given moment of the day.

Like right now, Chase is supposed to be in his office catching up on emails and calls from the weekend. A weekend I spent holed up in a sub-par hotel just in case he decided to come find me.

I should've splurged for season tickets and had George put a GPS tracker in his pants like I first suggested.

"Chase, dear. I didn't know you'd be joining us today." In an instant, gone is Denise's sour attitude, replaced by a cheerful suck-up-ing-ness.

What? It's a word.

Her four-inch Tom Ford stilettos click sharply on the floor until she's an inch away from him. Red talon fingers encircle his bicep as she leans even farther toward him. "What a pleasant surprise." She tosses me a fake smile over her shoulder pad. "Isn't it, Bell?"

I nod like a robot, the saccharine lilt to her voice making my teeth hurt.

Oh, wait. That's my jaw clenching.

Denise pets his arm, purring at him. "I thought there may have been some falling out between you two. I've been told things were tense." She raises an eyebrow at me meaningfully while her spying minions shuffle awkwardly between suit displays.

Meanwhile, Chase doesn't pull away from her. Doesn't even flinch. "No. No falling out at all. Just busy. Isn't that right, Bell?" He doesn't wait for my response, his affable attitude and annoyingly handsome smirk in place. "Today there just happened to be a break in my schedule. Thought I'd see how the campaign preparation was going."

She curls farther into him, and with her other hand, she pats his chest. "Nothing for you to worry about, Chase, dear. I have it all under control."

At that, he does pull back. "Funny. I specifically remember putting Ms. King in charge."

"Oh, uh, well, you know." She waves her weaponized fingers in the air. "We're all just working so well together, there doesn't even seem to be a need to haggle over leadership." She turns a killer glare my way. "Isn't that right, *Ms. King*?"

Before I can calm down and temper my now erratic breathing, which is totally due to Denise's bullshit and not the fact that she's still touching Chase, Chase speaks up. "Great to hear, Denise." He pulls his arm from her grasp. "And I'm sure one hundred percent true." His arched brow says otherwise. "Now, if you'll excuse the boss here"—he tips his head in my direction— "she and I need to have a chat."

Fuck. As much as I love the pissed-off look on Denise's face, I'd rather not have a one-on-one talk with Chase. Nothing good for my resolve can come of it.

Chase slides his hand over my lower back, leading me away from the group. That simple touch, even blocked by a blouse and suit jacket, curls my toes. Not the most comfortable feeling when you're trying to walk in heels.

His hand remains in place until we reach our destination, a dark corner of the department with a large tie rack blocking us from view. His hand slides slowly around my waist when he turns to face me. His fingers graze briefly across my hipbone before falling to his side.

"In here."

Confused, I look to where his other hand is pointing. A hidden door, wallpapered the same as the walls.

He punches in a code on a small, inconspicuous keypad and pushes the door in.

I follow him, our movement setting off some sort of motion sensor. One after another, fluorescent lights flicker to life as we walk farther into the room.

"What is this place?"

"It used to be shoe inventory, but we outgrew it. Now it's just storage." He points to some boxes and mostly empty shelves along the wall. It's about the size of my apartment bedroom. Which isn't saying much. "My sister and I used to hide in here."

I smile, thinking of a young Chase, huddled with Liz, a ball of energy, outwitting their watchers. "Not your brother, too?"

"No." He looks to the side, brows pulled together in thought. "Thomas was always with Stan, I think."

"I see." And I do. I see that this smart, handsome, hard-working man cares. He cares for his sister, his employees, he even cares for the rest of his family. If he didn't, he wouldn't be so hurt by their actions. And he cares for *me*. Or he did, at least.

I search his face for answers, answers to questions I'm afraid to ask, but find none. Gone is his charm. His smirk. His features are so serious, he almost doesn't look like himself.

I want to tell him I'm sorry. That I didn't want to leave, but that it was for the best. For whom, I'm not sure at this point. But still, it seemed like the responsible, safe thing to do at the time.

I want to tell him that I cried when I left. In the elevator that we so nearly had sex in multiple times. I cried in the cab, and I continued to cry in my plush hotel room. I want to say I've missed his face, his wink, his all-too-knowing smiles. I've missed holding his hand and cuddling with him and his ugly cat. But mostly, I miss making him happy.

"You left." His voice is flat, detached, untainted with recrimination. But I hear it nonetheless.

I have no words. So I kiss him.

* * *

Chase

Everything wrong with this past week evaporates with the heat of her kiss.

I know this isn't the answer I need. Her lips on mine doesn't let me know where we stand, or what happens once we leave this hidden closet. But, please, I'm not stupid enough to stop the woman I'm jonesing for from taking advantage of my body.

Small hands run up and down my back, like she's trying to soothe me, take away the pain she caused. But it isn't my back that needs stroking.

With jerky movements, I yank open my belt and shrug my jacket to the floor. Bell does the same with her blazer, then reaches for the zipper on the side of her skirt. I bat her hands away, too impatient to wait.

I kneel, reach under her skirt, and rip her panties down her legs before standing once more and hiking her leg around my waist. She groans, pumping her hips, our urgent need for each other overriding common sense.

How? How is it still like this? How is it that my need for her just grows no matter how many times and ways I have her? No matter how long we stay away. How does it feel like *she* has *me*?

"Now," she demands. "I need..."

"What do you need, baby?" I bite her nipple through her shirt, and my hands squeeze fistfuls of her ass.

Her eyes lock with mine. "You. Please." She's begging, desperation coating her voice.

Good. The vindictive side of me hopes she feels half of what I felt when I woke up alone last Monday. The rest of me just wants her to want me as much as I want her.

I grind her down on my thigh again and again.

She bites her lip to keep from crying out. Even so, her whimpers echo in the room.

My dick practically jumps out of my pants when I unzip. In one motion, Bell tilts her ass up, and I slam inside her.

"Yes," she moans, circling her hips against me. "I need it."

I'll be damned if I don't give the lady exactly what she needs. I pull back only to slam inside, over and over again. She grabs fistfuls of my shirt every time I pound home.

"Oh my god, oh my god, oh my god," she chants quietly in my ear, and I feel her walls flutter around me. "I'm going to " Mouth open in a silent scream, her body stiffens, and her pussy pulls me deeper inside. I never stop, pounding through her orgasm, drawing it out. When her legs fall limp at my sides, I ground my pelvis against her clit, lighting up aftershocks inside her. She mewls in contentment, happy with what I gave her. But I want to give her more. Give her everything.

I pull out and turn her around, not giving her time to mourn the loss of my cock before I hitch her ass up and thrust back inside, my balls smacking her clit.

"Holy—" Her words are cut off when one of my hands wraps around her hair and pulls, turning her head and bowing her back. Keeping her where I want her. Where I can see her profile as another orgasm washes over her. Where she can see mine when I finally let go and let her have me.

All of me.

"Chase." A soft sob. It only makes me harder, rougher.

This is what she's needed, what we've needed, what she's denied us. Why can't she see that? Why aren't I enough?

Not able to hold back any longer, I grab her under her arms, pulling her back up against my chest. Hooking my hands around her shoulders, I ram up into her, as close as I can, burrowing inside her until my cock throbs out in release.

Once, twice, I grunt like an animal, trying to claim her from inside.

Finally, both of us having no more to give, we collapse. Side by side, we lie on the floor, in the very spot where I hid from my parents. Where I wondered why I wasn't good enough to be treated like Thomas by our father.

"Stay." I'm aware I'm begging. That I've said these same words before to no avail. But like an idiot, I say them again, hoping for a different outcome.

Bell's head, resting against my chest, looks up. Her face is flushed, her eyes molten chocolate. A lazy smile lights up her face, and for a moment, I think I might get what I want. *Her.*

"Campbell?" Chris's voice, distant through the doorway, calls out. "Campbell, you in there?"

In the blink of an eye, her expression turns frightened. She moves to cover herself, frantic. I still her with one hand and place my finger over my lips with the other. Neither of us wants to be found like this.

"I'm sure she and Chase are quite... busy." Denise's condescension and implication are clear, even with the door between us. That woman's a menace. There's a bit of murmuring back and forth before the sound of retreating footsteps.

Bell waits a beat more before pulling away. "I have to go to work." Her voice is flat and distant. Immediately, I know our time in my secret hiding place changed nothing. If anything, I feel even farther away from her than I have been this past week.

"Fuck work right now." I'm a sadist. I have to be. It's the only reason I can think of that I'm pushing this right now. Pushing her. "It doesn't matter." Even I know I'm lying. Both of us need Moore's to be successful. I just don't know what else to say to make her realize that *we* matter just as much. No. *More.*

"We can't... we just can't do this. Not anymore. It's not smart." Shuffling on her hands and knees, she grabs her panties off the floor. They're ripped and useless.

Kind of like my heart.

Her skirt is still rucked up, her ass exposed, and in this position, I can see my cum sliding down her thigh.

She pauses, looking down at the wetness coating her thighs.

I rub my palm down my face. "Fuck, no condom. I didn't think—"

She holds up her hand, silencing me. Grimacing, she uses her torn panties to wipe at the mess. "It should be fine." She takes a few deep breaths, as if counting each exhale. "I have an IUD." Once clean, she struggles to her feet, smoothing down her skirt.

"I'm sorry." Just one more thing I've messed up.

"Don't be." Over and over again, she runs her empty hand

down her skirt, not meeting my eyes. "This was my fault. My mistake."

Mistake. Yeah, I've been called that before. But it's never quite sliced through me like it does now, coming from the woman I love.

And that's the moment I give up all pretense of being charming and cool. Give up deflecting with humor and protecting myself by not saying exactly what I want. Because I love her. And she's worth it.

There, on my knees, dick out and still wet from her orgasm, I simply say it. The one thing I've been holding back.

"I love you."

23

BELL

My eyes jerk to his. "Wh—what?" There's no hiding my shock. Or the wonder that coats my voice. "You... love me?"

Chase tucks himself back into his pants and rises. Slowly. Like he's approaching a wounded, wild animal.

In a way, he is.

"Yes, Bell. I do."

I shake my head, just as slowly as his movements. "But it's only been—"

"It doesn't matter." His voice is harder, firmer, grounding me in the moment.

And yet I'm quiet. Processing what his words mean. To me. To us.

He must take my silence for uncertainty because he changes his approach; his tone lightens, his posture loosens. "Hey, what's that old adage? When you know, you know?" He pauses, his eyes meeting mine for one intense moment. "Well, I know." He shrugs like it's no big deal, when we both know it's a *very* big deal.

I fight the heat rising in my eyes. I'm being ridiculous. Crying when a man tells you he loves you? What's wrong with me?

But... how can I trust this? Him. When everyone I've ever loved has left. Just, poof, gone.

I start at the sudden realization.

The tears are running down my cheeks.

Chase gathers me in his arms. "Hey now."

Is that the real reason I don't open up? That I shut down when people want to get close to me? Because I'm afraid they'll leave?

That isn't fair or rational. My parents didn't *choose* to leave. Death is an inevitable part of life. Hell, even my dog dying had been inevitable.

But it also left me alone.

I give in to the tears for a moment, looking back at a time I try very hard not to relive. All those years ago when my parents died, I'd focused on my anger. Anger over double standards and back-stabbing co-workers. But did I just cling to that anger because it was easier than dealing with my grief?

I relax into his embrace as I come to terms with just how fucked-up I might be. Because even as standoffish as I am, even holding Chase off and sneaking out on him, he never left. I did.

I pull back, searching his eyes with mine. "You... love me?"

He nods, his expression tender. It isn't until the corner of his lip quirks up that I realize I'm humming "Can't Help Falling in Love." Elvis always knows what to say.

He kisses me quick on the mouth. "I love you, Bell. I love how smart you are, how creative. I love how hard you work and how you don't demand respect from the people who work for you; you earn it and give it right back." Another quick kiss. "And I love how sexy you are, how you light up when you come and how you hum Elvis tunes without even knowing it." His next kiss is longer, tender. It stops my tears and fills my heart. "Love me, Bell. Please. I'll be worth it. I promise."

Everything settles at his words. I notice he feels like he has to prove his worth to me to be loved, and I wonder how much of my own damaged responses to him he's taken as a personal rejection. Words, phrases, emotions war inside me as I try to piece together something powerful and romantic to let him know just how worthy he is.

And then he sings.

The chorus from "It's Now or Never" floats between us. He sings softly. Deeply. His eyes never leaving mine.

Just like that, emotions ebb, thoughts quiet, and the world becomes just this room, this man, and me.

The last words trail off, the lyrics answering any questions spawned by my fears and anxieties. So I do what the song says. I kiss him.

It's slow and seductive and so full of all the things I feel but am having trouble saying.

"You're worth everything, Chase."

Chase has many smiles. Seductive, playful, insincere, amused. I've clocked them all. But this one, the one spreading over his handsome face mere inches from mine, after serenading me with Elvis, is my new favorite.

It's pure happiness. It can't get any better than this.

I whisper the words we both need to hear. "I love you."

I was wrong. It *can* get better.

My hands are still shaking when I finally make my way to the conference room my team took over as their workspace.

Chase loves me.

We stood in that closet just staring at each other and smiling for a good minute or so before begrudgingly getting back to work. Don't get me wrong; there were plenty of one-last-kisses and whispered, filthy promises for later. But for now, there is reality to deal with. Like the reality of us having had sex in an inventory closet, just a few yards away from employees and, worse, Denise.

Speaking of Denise.

"Why we are even bothering with the men's department is beyond me. The numbers clearly show that Moore's strongest consumer is female." I stop outside the door, leaning against the wall, trying to shore up the emotional reserves needed to handle her. I heard what she said to Chris, what she implied, about Chase and me while we hid in the closet.

She wasn't wrong.

"We already shot the women's departments, Denise. On Friday." Chris's tone is bored. "When you couldn't make it, for some reason or another."

"Just like you couldn't make the previous meeting Campbell called last week," Ben mumbles.

Sensing that my team's patience is running out, I roll off the wall and around the door frame. Denise's back is to me, so she doesn't notice me in the doorway.

Alice, also turned away from me, clears her throat. "Um, maybe we should look over the photos from this morning. I've already uploaded them." She points to the projection screen. "I think the one of the mannequins dressed in Tom Ford and Yves Saint Laurent formal wear would be great for the men's department profile picture." Day by day, she becomes more confident, showing more of the talent I saw in her fantastical floating shoe display.

"*Alice*, is it?" Denise turns in her chair to address my new hire, giving me her profile. I can see her looking down her nose at Alice, taking in the younger woman's functional-looking shoes and professional, but by no means designer, outfit. Since hiring her, I've gotten the impression that things might be tight, financially, for Alice. She wore both the skirt and jacket earlier just this week, though not at the same time. Though her lack of designer duds doesn't faze me in the least, it's like blood in the water to a predator like Denise. "No one asked for the intern's thoughts." The words are drowning in condescension.

Alice's shoulders hunch, her head dropping forward.

Ben braces his palms on the table like he's about to pounce, but I beat him to the punch by speaking first. "Leave."

Startled, everyone jumps at my voice.

"You need to leave, Denise. It was a mistake thinking this could work." Looking back, I should have done this as soon as I was given carte blanche over personnel. But I wanted to avoid questions about why I refused to work with her. I didn't want to give her the chance to spout more lies about me and make me live through a repeat of the past. And if I'm honest, I also wanted to prove to Denise the mistake she made. Maybe by seeing how good I am at my job, how well my team works together, she'd regret her choices eight years ago.

Yet, looking around the room, I can see I've only made my team, and my friends, miserable.

Regaining her composure, Denise narrows her eyes at me. "Excuse me? I'm—"

"Out of line? Completely unhelpful? Vindictive? Yes, we know." I wave my hand at the room. "*Everyone* knows."

Ben snickers before turning it into a cough when Chris elbows him in the ribs.

"We've all had to listen to your diatribe long enough."

"See here, Miss Dougherty—"

"*King.* It's King. And you know it's King. You also know *why* it's Ms. King instead of Miss Dougherty."

An evil glint lights her eyes. "Exactly. And if you don't want all these people to know—"

"Know what? That you're a horrible person? No need. You did

that on your own." I take a step closer to her, pleased to see her lean back in her chair. "And now we're done here. You're done."

What I'm saying finally seems to penetrate. Her nostrils flare, her eyes slit. "You can't do that. I have a contract—"

"Correction." I walk around her, taking my seat at the head of the table. "Warren and Baron have a contract. *Nowhere* on that contract does it specify that *you* have to work on the account."

She shoots to her feet. "Stanley won't allow this."

"Stanley?" What does Chase's father have to do with this?

Denise's face flushes red, the death stare gone. She looks down, smoothing her skirt.

And suddenly it makes sense. I wondered why someone so incompetent at her job had retained such a large account. She has something going on with Stanley Moore. I can't help but snort at the irony of it all.

My expression must show I've connected the dots, because Denise recovers, pulling her shoulders back, hands going to her painfully slim hips. "Cut the high-and-mighty act, Campbell. You may be able to convince Chase to take me off the project, but we both know the only reason you have such authority is because your legs are as wide as your mouth."

I flinch, signaling the barb had landed.

She smiles. It's a wonder that someone with such beautiful features can look so ugly. She raises her voice, making sure it carries out the open door. "I wonder how much your colleagues and clients will respect you when they find out you like spreading your creativity around." She looks me up and down, her contempt fully unveiled. "On your back."

An uneasy quiet surrounds us. Even the hum of copy machines stops. No one moves. They don't even glance at each other to gather reactions. It's like someone hit a stop button in time.

I'm strangely calm. This is my worst fear come true... and I don't care.

The only thing flashing through my mind is Chase's face when I told him I love him. And I almost gave that up to protect myself from this? From this angry, hypocritical woman with a chip on her shoulder so large not even Michelangelo could chisel away at it?

I could easily out her in return, considering I'm pretty certain she's having, or has had, an affair with Stanley. However, looking at her, with her pretty features distorted into an ugly mask, I realize she isn't worth it. Rather, I wonder what the hell happened to her to make her this way. And if I would've eventually become just like her if Chase hadn't come along.

Now, instead of anger, I feel sadness. For her. For me. For all the wasted time. For what it might've cost me.

I rub a hand over my face, suddenly exhausted. "Just leave, Denise. Before I call security."

"Come," she snaps at the three Warren and Baron team members. "We'll just see what Mr. Warren has to say about this."

The three marketing employees shift uncomfortably in their seats, glancing at anything but Denise. Finally, the one woman of the bunch speaks. "I think we'll stay, Denise. You can sort things out with Mr. Warren on your own, I'm sure."

A confused look flashes across Denise's face, like she can't believe the whole room is against her. But in a flash, she regains her holier-than-though countenance. "Very well. I'm sure I don't want my name anywhere near this ridiculous marketing plan your inept team is wasting their time on, anyway. If you want to fail without my expertise, that's on you." She gathers her bag and notes from the table in swift, concise movements.

Alice jumps to her feet, picking up the cashmere coat draped on the back of Denise's chair. "Here, let me help you with your jacket."

This time Chris bows his head, cough-laughing into his fist.

I can't see Denise's face now that she's turned away from me, but from the smile melting off Alice's face, I'm sure she's giving my new hire one of her tried-and-true death glares. But rather than give Alice another snide comment, Denise plucks the coat from her outstretched hands, drapes it over her arm, and struts out of the room like a queen at court.

The intangible tension choking the room dissipates with her exit. Sighs of relief, even from the Warren and Baron team, resound, and Alice's smile picks back up.

"So," Ben says, cheeky grin in place. "You and Moore, huh?" Chris purses his lips in amusement, and Alice's smile grows larger. The thing missing from them all? Judgment.

I have a great team. Great *friends*.

I don't answer Ben, but I'm sure the smile I can't control says it all.

Even though I'm guilty of the very thing I'd been wrongly accused of and vilified for eight years ago, the shame I was so sure would drown me isn't there. But then, I'm not the same young girl, still grieving the loss of her parents, duped by her co-worker, shunned from her profession.

I'm the girl lucky enough to be loved by Chase Moore.

Chris snorts. "Like that wasn't obvious from the elevator incident after Winston's."

Oh my god. Kill me now.

* * *

Chase

Walking is good.

Walking the sidewalks of Manhattan is not like walking on a secluded beach. Your mind doesn't blank, and it isn't a good time to sort through your thoughts.

You do that in New York and you're roadkill.

Walking in New York calls for an active mind and sharp reflexes.

I waited in the closet for a good five minutes after Bell left, trying to simultaneously quell my goofy-ass smile and my ridiculously obvious hard-on. However, the mingled smell of Bell and sex had lingered in the air, and neither my smile nor my stiffy went down.

I escaped, hopefully without detection, and took refuge on the mad streets of Manhattan.

Bell loves me.

I've never been loved before. Or been in love.

It's true that I've had girlfriends in the past, but none like Bell. She puts what I previously considered a relationship to shame. I didn't know that I could feel this much, this fast. Or that it would actually be reciprocated. Because let's face it, Bell is smart, accomplished, sexy as hell, and can keep a smart-ass like me on his toes.

Now I have to figure out how not to screw it up. Tonight, I'll—

A shoulder slams into mine, sending me back a couple of steps.

Damn it. That hurt. The offending gentleman is already halfway down the block, not even slowing his stride.

New York, baby.

But it's cool. A bruised shoulder isn't going to dampen the fact that Bell loves me.

"Chase! Chase, dear!"

Fuck. How the hell did Denise find me? I turn my head, surprised to discover I'm just a few steps away from Moore's side entrance. I must have turned a corner at some point and circled back.

Way to be sharp, Moore.

Happiness lost me my edge. Though, on second thought, one look at Denise's sour face has fully cured my previous problems.

"Denise. How... unexpected." I'm pretty sure she's supposed to be upstairs with the marketing team, but Chris had mumbled something about her many recent no-shows.

"You're telling me."

On second glance, I realize Denise's normal stick-up-her-ass demeanor is gone. Beads of sweat form a line on her brow. Her lipstick is slightly smeared below her bottom lip. She looks almost frazzled. Annoyed.

I'm going to regret this. "Are you okay?"

"No. No, I am not okay, Chase."

Yep. Totally regret.

"Your marketing exec"—her tone implies incredulousness at that term— "just fired me."

Whoa. Though Chris mentioned about Denise not doing her job, not once has Bell said anything about it. In fact, Bell hasn't mentioned Denise *at all* since the email question over pizza at my place. Which now I find odd. Especially given their initial, frosty introduction.

I must show my surprise because Denise takes it as a green light to vent.

"I don't care how often she's putting out this time, Campbell's overstepped." Denise's red lips suck in a large gust of city air before continuing. "I'm the one with experience and knowledge. I'm not the one with a history of fucking her clients for work, like some backwater, Southern—"

"*What?*"

222 SARA L. HUDSON

The flutter of her lashes makes me wary. It's like a viper trying to feign innocence to a mouse.

"Oh, poor Chase. You didn't know?"

She's lying. She has to be. Bell isn't like that.

"You didn't think you were special, did you?" She pats my arm, then loops hers through my own. The snake beginning its choke-hold, going in for the kill. "I was there when Campbell *Dougherty* was fired the first time she got caught sleeping her way around the marketing pool." Even smudged, her red lips form a devious smile. "Guess that's why she changed her name and started her own firm. You know how word gets around in this city. No marketing firm would touch Miss *Dougherty* with a ten-foot pole." She snickers at her poor attempt at a juvenile double entendre.

"You're lying."

With one quirk of her eyebrow, Denise is back to looking like a shark. "Please. I don't need to lie when the truth is so much more damaging." In one fluid motion, she pulls away from me, maneuvering around me and down the street.

"Oh, and Chase?"

Still stunned, her venomous words coursing through me, I turn toward her.

"I'm sure your father will be *so* interested to hear how you do business."

* * *

"Chase?"

Auburn hair swings into the door frame, followed by brown eyes. Bell looks adorable poking her head into my office. Since the closet, since we stopped being wimps and owned up to how we felt, she seems... softer.

There's still a vulnerability there, one I hate to see, but at the moment, sadly, it reassures me. I'm annoyed with myself that I've given Denise's poisonous words any thought. *I* was the one who went after Bell. Not the other way around.

I have some serious shit-sorting to do if I'm damaged enough to believe Denise. Believe that the only reason Bell's interested in me is because of my job title.

And what was Denise's parting shot about? Why would my father care about Denise being fired?

"Is everything all right?" She steps fully into the doorway, straightening her skirt. The same skirt she pulled over her bare pussy because she'd used her panties to wipe my cum from her thighs.

Annnnd, I'm hard again.

"Yeah," I say, needing to clear my throat. "Everything's fine." Shaking off the doubt and nagging worry, I stand, buttoning my jacket. "It's quitting time. Why don't you and I head back to my place?"

"Oh." She grimaces. "All my stuff is back at the hotel."

"That's okay." I brush off the reminder of her sneaking out on me. "We can live it up hotel-style then." I cross the office to the walk-in closet (yes, this ridiculously large office has an actual walk-in closet), where I keep extra clothes. Grabbing a suit, I slide it into one of the garment bags, both of which Susan and George keep stocked, and drape it over my arm.

"Where does that go, Narnia?" I turn to see her pointing across the room at another door.

"No, smart-ass, that's the hallway. My dad had it installed so that his personal shoppers wouldn't have to step into his office."

Bell snorts. That pretty much sums my father's actions up.

She steps fully inside and spins in a circle. "Your office closet is bigger than my bedroom in Houston."

"I thought everything was bigger in Texas."

She gives me a long, leisurely look, ending with a pointed stare below my belt. "Not everything."

"Why, Miss Campbell, I do declare!" I mock with the worst Southern accent imaginable.

"Please. *Gone with the Wind* is Georgia, not Texas."

I tilt my imaginary hat. "My apologies, *ma'am*."

"Oh. Now those are fighting words." Her eyes light up, the brown sparking with mischief and seduction.

My favorite combination.

My favorite everything.

24

BELL

Something's up.

Chase is saying the right things, doing the right things, but something feels... off.

"Want to stop and get dinner on the way to the hotel?" he asks, opening the car door for me.

I bite my lip, handing him my laptop bag to put in the back. "Sure." Ugh, god, I hate being unsure. It's like I've unlocked a new part of myself that I haven't had practice with. Mentally slapping myself straight, I pause before getting in, going onto my tippy toes to whisper in his ear. "Or... we could grab a quick bite at the hotel restaurant? Makes the time between dinner and the hotel room that much shorter."

He doesn't answer right away. That's what I mean by something being off. Before I told him I loved him, Chase would've been all over getting me into a bed. "Or not." I drop back to my heels, feeling embarrassed.

"No. The hotel restaurant is fine." He waits until I've cleared the doorway before shutting me inside his sleek car. He takes a moment to hang the garment bag and place my bag on the backseat floor before sliding into the driver's seat. "You're right. It *is* that much closer to the bedroom." He throws me that signature smirk of his, but it's missing the wicked light in his eyes.

As soon as he pushes the ignition button, his phone goes off, the car dash displaying "Thomas" on the screen.

Chase cancels the call with a press of the button on his steering wheel, then pulls out into rush-hour traffic.

Thomas calls again.

With agitated movements, Chase stabs the button on the wheel, silencing the call again.

Well. Now it's just awkward.

"Are you okay?"

"Yep."

Uh-huh, sure. That's why his knuckles are turning white from his death grip on the steering wheel.

"That was your brother, wasn't it?"

He nods, but his eyes never stop staring in front of him. Even when traffic slows and we come to a stop.

I remember my mom being really upset once. So upset that even my dad couldn't lift her mood by putting on her favorite Elvis record. My dad turned to me and said, "It's time to bring out the big guns." He'd taken Mom's hand, sat her down in his study and told me to go play outside for a bit. After an hour of tossing the ball to Elvis, I'd come back inside to see my mom laughing, dancing with my dad to "Jailhouse Rock." That night I asked him how he made Momma happy again and he said, "Sometimes before a person can open up, you need to show them how."

I didn't really understand my dad then, but I think I might now.

I take a deep breath, mentally preparing to open a door I've had locked for a long time. "Chase?"

"Hmmm." His eyes are still on the stopped car ahead.

"My parents died in a car crash."

His head whips to mine, hands easing on the steering wheel. "What?"

"My parents," I say again, slower. "They died in a car crash."

"I thought because you said how they were older..."

"No." I brace my hands on my knees. "I mean yeah, they were older, but they didn't die of old age."

He takes one hand off the wheel to rest on mine. "That must have been hard."

Usually, at this point, I shrug and brush it off. Pretend that it was so long ago the grief is inconsequential to my life. But I remember Dad's words, and I try to show Chase how to open up by doing it myself.

"Yes. It was," I force out. "Where I grew up, it was a small town about an hour west of Houston. I told you my mom was the local librarian, but after I was born, she stayed at home with me. I was homeschooled." I smile, remembering how Dad turning the unused formal dining room into my classroom. "It was usually just the three of us. And Elvis, of course."

Chase smiles. "The singer. Or the dog?"

"Both, I guess." I was glad to be able to laugh. "So when I told you before, at the museum, that it was a big deal for *them* to let me go to New York, it was a big deal for *me*. They were my best friends as well as my parents. But at eighteen I could only think of a fast-paced life in the city with crowds and skyscrapers and classrooms full of students. Things I never had."

Traffic eases, and Chase puts the car in gear, moving forward slowly.

"And when I graduated, my parents thought I might come home. But I didn't." The twinge of guilt in my heart is still as strong as ever. "I got a job. A *good* job at a big, fancy office in the middle of it all. It didn't matter that I sat at a cubicle and had to do grunt work for a year before getting to work on an actual marketing campaign. I had a job and a life in New York, and that was all I'd ever wanted."

"I'm sure your parents were proud." His tone is placating, but it doesn't need to be.

"Oh, I know they were." I smile thinking of the calls, emails, and Skype sessions. "They told me every day." My smile falls, knowing what comes next. "Until they didn't. One day I got a call from the sheriff instead, telling me a deer had dashed out onto the road. Dad swerved, but he still hit the deer, and their car slammed into a tree. They died on impact."

"Oh, Bell."

We're silent for a while, me lost in my thoughts and Chase leaving me to them. His hand only leaves mine to shift gears.

Remembering why I started this, I clear my throat and pick up where I left off. "When I left to go to the funeral, I trusted the wrong person with my work. I came back to being fired and humiliated."

His fingers squeeze almost painfully around mine. "Denise."

My laugh sounds a bit hollow. "Yeah. I guess we didn't do a good job of hiding our animosity, huh?"

The look he throws me has me laughing.

"Yeah, well if you were grieving for your parents while she was busy logging on to your computer, stealing all your work, then sending inappropriate emails to all your clients under your name, you wouldn't like her either."

"Are you kidding me? She did all that?"

"Yeah."

"If you hadn't already fired her, I'd be tempted to do something much worse."

His protectiveness makes me feel cared for, makes the sadness fade away.

"That explains why you're fanatical about computer security."

"I wouldn't say fanatical." Am I?

He just raises his eyebrows.

"Hmph. Whatever."

"So what did you do? After Denise was a total bitch and all."

"Well." I take a deep breath, expelling the residual resentment, coming to terms with what happened. "I was blacklisted from all of the major marketing firms in New York, so I tucked tail and headed back to Texas. And for the longest time, I was so mad, so angry, that all I could think of was painting a spotless reputation. Because without my parents, my job was all I had." This time I place my hand over his. "That's why I told myself I couldn't be with you. That it would undo everything that I've worked for, and just make what Denise said all those years ago true."

Chase's skin pales. "God, Bell. I'm so sorry. I never should have pushed. I hope you don't—"

I cup his cheek with my other hand, somewhat awkwardly in the car. "I'm not sorry you pushed. I can't even begin to tell you how not sorry I am." Quickly, before we start moving again, I lean up and kiss his cheek before retreating back to my seat. "Because you made me realize that I was holding on to all that anger because it was easier than dealing with my grief."

He shakes his head, like he doesn't know what to say.

"This is the first time I've ever talked about my parents. Apart from the museum." I close my eyes, bringing their image to my mind. Images of happy times. "And though it hurts, it also feels... good. Like a relief to tell someone, finally."

"I'm glad."

Blinking my eyes open, I focus on his. "Me too."

"So who's Dougherty?"

"Huh?"

"Denise was always calling you Dougherty."

"Oh. Yeah. That." I lean back and grab my wallet from the front pocket of my laptop bag. Opening it up, I slide out an outdated license from my wallet and hold it out for him to see. "You're looking at Texas-born Campbell Hope Dougherty." My younger self smiles back at him. "I changed it to King in honor of my momma's love of Elvis." I pause before admitting with a smirk, "And for my dog." At Chase's look, I shrug. "What? He was a great dog."

Our laughter eases something inside of me. I may have started this sharing business with Chase in mind, but I came out feeling lighter than I have in forever, and closer to Chase.

His phone goes off once more, and this time he fishes it out of his pocket, shuts it off, and tosses it into the back seat.

Sliding my old license back into my wallet, I try to sound nonchalant. "So. Your brother, huh?"

* * *

Chase

My shoulders creep up to my ears. I'm thinking of playing it off, but after what Bell just told me, that would be a dick move. Especially as I already feel like a dick for my attitude earlier. At first, I thought her not wanting to go to dinner with me was a sign she still wanted to keep things quiet. Not be seen with me. Just wanted to keep it to sex. That maybe Denise was right, and all she wanted to do was sleep around.

God, I'm an asshole.

Preparing to open up to the wonderful woman I don't deserve, I let out a deep sigh and drop my head back. "Yeah. My brother."

"I mean, I've met him. He is..."

"Perfect? The golden boy? A man who can do no wrong?"

"Um... I was trying to think of a nice way to say ass-hat."

Stunned, I double over laughing. It takes the car behind me honking to get me to sober up and put the car in gear to inch ahead.

"Ass-hat, huh?" I snort. "I'll have to remember that one."

"Well, it's the truth. I don't know why you called him perfect." She looks so unimpressed with my older brother that I feel myself falling a little bit more in love with her.

Feeling good about this sharing thing, I dig deeper. "Because that is what my father drilled into me from the very start."

She throws me a questioning look.

"You have to understand, Thomas was perfect. Still is." She opens her mouth to interrupt, but I keep going. She needs to understand the whole picture. "He got the perfect grades, said the perfect things, dressed in the perfect way. He was the measuring stick I was always held up to and found lacking." I squint my eyes, thinking of an example. "In fact, I'm pretty sure my father said those exact words on my seventh birthday when I swung at the piñata and missed, only to have Thomas swing next and crack the thing in half in one go."

"Jesus." Bell sounds horrified.

"Yeah. That's what it was like growing up in Casa de Moore. It wouldn't have been so bad if Thomas had been a good brother or had even tried to be friendly. But the kid always had a stick up his ass, was always going off with Stan to do father–son things, never inviting me to come with. Though the old man probably wouldn't have allowed it anyway."

"What about Liz?"

"Ah." I smile, thinking of my sister. "The best day of my life was when Liz was born. I was ten years old, and I finally had a real sibling. Being that she's ten years younger than me, she was probably a bit of a surprise baby, but having a sister was awesome. Still is."

"I agree that Thomas isn't the easiest person to talk to, but why ignore his calls?" Bell gestures to the screen. "If he's trying that hard to get to you, it might be important."

I take a moment, trying to put my thoughts into words. "Hmmm." Actually, more like my *feelings* into words. "Well, I know it may sound childish, but Thomas was given *everything*. As Moore descendants, we all have equal shares in the business, but as first-born, Thomas was primed to take over the reins from Stan. Until he gave it up."

Bell sits up straighter. "He gave it up?"

I nod, changing lanes and turning the corner.

"But why?" She sounds as confused as I felt that day at lunch with my family.

"I don't know, and I don't care." At her look I try to explain myself. "See, I have always loved Moore's. Susan and Raymond are basically the parents I never had. I grew up with the store as my playground, and I loved every second of it, even though from the moment I could understand, my father drilled it into my head that it wasn't for me. That it was for Thomas."

The many, many memories of my father saying those exact words has me choking the steering wheel.

"Thomas never once called me before he quit the family business," I continue. "Not for birthdays, to catch up, or even if there was a family emergency. Only Liz did." I shrug, conceding, "Mom called on occasion."

Bell squeezes my hand.

"So if Thomas is calling now, I can only imagine it's because he regrets giving up the job. Or he wants to tell me how to do it." I sneer at my reflection in the windshield, seeing too many similarities between my brother and me for comfort. "Well fuck you, Thomas. You don't get to take this from me too."

I think I've shocked her into silence. I've shocked myself too, if I'm honest.

After a minute, Bell speaks, her voice soft and distant. "Hey."

I'm kind of embarrassed, so instead of answering, I concentrate doubly hard on turning into the hotel's valet drop-off point. If I can just get to the doors, maybe I can hold off whatever words of pity she's about to deliver. Bet she's wishing we went somewhere to dinner now. Nothing kills the mood like a pity party.

"Hey," she says more forcefully.

The valet still has one car to deal with. So close. Ready for whatever, I press the ignition off. "Sorry about that."

"Don't apologize. I mean, it isn't surprising that someone with an uncaring father and absent mother could have so much baggage to work through. I had loving parents, and I still have at least a carry-on."

That gets a light chuckle from me. Another valet runs over, but Bell holds him off with a wave of her hand.

Damn it.

She takes off her seat belt before fully turning toward me. "You, Chase Moore, are amazing."

That's unexpected.

She leans in, clasping my face in her palms, the smooth skin of her hands tickling my five o'clock shadow.

"Despite being told no, that you weren't good enough, you still grew into one of the most capable and confident people in business I've ever met."

Uncomfortable with her words, I make to pull back, but she holds me in place, touching her forehead with mine. The valet's peering through the windshield like he thinks we're crazy, but Bell ignores him, clearly not done.

"You not only deserve to run Moore's, you've earned it. Your father may never admit that, but you know who would? Raymond. And Susan. And everyone else at that store. They love you. *I* love you. And you are *very much* enough."

The only sound in the car is our mingled breath, mine choppy, hers smooth. I'm trying to keep my shit together, but her words ricochet from my head to my heart, and I'm afraid any minute now, one will pierce it, breaking the fragile thing I've spent most of my life trying to shield.

"My daddy was the one who had all the words of wisdom." Her accent is thicker than I've ever heard it, soothing the rough edges around my heart. "But my momma always said there was nothing that Elvis couldn't fix."

She begins to sing "The Wonder of You."

And oh my god, she sounds like a dozen squeaking rusty hinges. It's almost awe-inspiring how badly Bell sings.

After the first stanza and chorus, I nuzzle her neck. "Hey babe?"

"Hmm?"

"Do me a favor?"

"Anything."

"Stick to humming."

It takes a second for my words to sink in, but when my shoulders start shaking from laughing, she pulls back, gasping in outrage. "Why you—"

I silence her with a kiss before jumping out of the car, leaving her inside fuming, but also laughing.

I toss the key fob to the waiting valet, who is probably relieved that the weird intimate moment with my girlfriend is over.

Girlfriend. It seems like such an inconsequential word for what Bell means to me.

Rounding the car, I open Bell's door to find her looking like a petulant child, arms crossed, lips pouting, and a stink-eye directed right at me. But don't think I don't see that lip twitch she's trying to hide.

"Aw, don't be like that, babe." When she makes no move to exit the car, I lean in and pick her up, tossing her over my shoulder fireman style.

"Chase!" She tries wiggling off my shoulder, but the action only makes her skirt shimmy up her thighs. She freezes, probably very conscious of the fact that she's not wearing any underwear. "Let. Me. Down."

My answer is to slap her ass. It's a multipurpose ass slap. It shocks her quiet, stops her skirt from riding up any further, and, my favorite, gets my hands on her.

Striding toward the entrance, I slow only to toss a bellman a fifty and ask him to bring up our bags from the car.

The doorman opens both doors to make way for my caveman style entrance, which is gawked at by everyone in the five-star hotel lobby. The stares don't faze me as I make my way directly to the elevators and press the button.

"Wait." Bell finally finds her voice, though it's high pitched. "What are you doing? I thought you wanted to go to dinner. The restaurant is behind you."

An older couple braves the spectacle I'm putting on and waits for the elevator with us. "No need," I tell Bell, lightly spanking her ass again. "I plan to eat you instead."

The older man's eyes bulge, but the woman just smiles wistfully.

The elevator dings, the doors sliding open. Wisely, the couple stays back when I haul Bell inside.

"And besides," I say, as the doors slide shut, "if we really do get hungry for something other than each other, that's why God invented room service."

When the elevator starts moving, I slide Bell off my shoulder. She holds on to my shoulders, steadying her feet.

"You know something, Chase Moore?" Her voice is breathy and her eyes dark. I can't help crowding her into the corner, bracing my arms on either side of her body that I'd bet my shares is turned on.

"What's that, Bell?"

I let loose a low groan as she drags her hands up my sides, over my shoulders and around my neck, pulling me closer to her lush, pouting mouth.

"You're a hound dog."

One side of my upper lip twitches. "Thank you. Thank you very much."

25

CHASE

"I fed your cunt."

"Jesus, Liz." I shake my head at the hotel room's ceiling, hand holding my cell to my ear. "Way to take the finesse out of the joke."

Sunlight filters through the white sheers covering the hotel windows. Bell got up a few minutes ago and demanded I stay put and let her shower in peace. She ambled off, muttering something about not being able to walk.

My sister scoffs at me. "Please, that's what you meant when you named him Mike Hunt." Liz's usually chipper voice is deadened. "Might as well say what you mean."

"What crawled up your ass today? Mike attack you with his claws of fury?" Last night, via text, Liz said she'd stop over at my place on her way to class to feed the hairless wonder this morning. Now I'm thinking I should've called a service. Mike can be difficult. I have the bruised dick to prove it.

"Mike?" She laughs. "You're kidding me. That cuddle-cunt loves me."

I shudder. "Seriously, you've got to stop saying that. Hearing my sister say that is just... wrong."

I can feel her rolling her eyes at me. "Whatever. Like you don't say worse on a daily basis."

Liz "whatevered" me. Something must be wrong. "Okay, if Mike didn't attack you, then what put you in this rare foul mood?"

"Dad," she mutters. Her voice is flat and resigned.

Alert, I sit up. "What do you mean? What's the old man gone and done now?"

The phone fuzzes with a long, drawn-out sigh. "I don't know. It's weird. *He's* being weird."

My turn to eye roll. "Way to be specific, sis." Stan in general is weird. Although weird implies a sort of fun lightheartedness. Neither of those describe Stanley Moore. Personally, I'd go with an adjective more like demonic or malicious.

Liz sighs again. I hate when she's upset. When she was little and upset, I'd race her around the house, make up funny stories, or take her to the park. I kind of miss how easy it was back then to keep an eye on her.

"Okay. Explain what you mean by *weird*."

"Never mind. I'm fine."

I scoff. "Yeah, I'm not stupid enough to believe a woman when she says she's 'fine.'"

"That's extremely sexist, you know that, right?"

"Doesn't make it less true."

"Humph."

"Come on, spill. You know you want to."

She's silent for a minute before giving in. "Well, you and I both know that I've always hoped for more paternal involvement in my life. Some semblance that Dad cared. Any kind of effort on his part, you know?"

Boy, do I know.

"Well, he finally is, but..."

I fight my surprise at my father actually doing something other than be a jerk-off father and focus on Liz's concerned tone. "But what?"

"He's *hovering*, Chase. It isn't normal, and I can't take it. I am literally pulling my hair out while talking with you about it." Another pause. "Maybe I'm being contrary, but I want my distant, unfeeling father back."

Okay, this definitely deviates from Stan's normal daddy M.O. of ignore, shout/lecture, ignore, ignore. "How is he hovering?"

"He follows me around the house, asking if I've seen you. If I've seen Thomas. If I've talked to you. If I've talked to Thomas. Asking where I'm going all the time." She huffs. "He even asked if I wanted a ride to class today." She pauses as I take that in. "He doesn't even drive, Chase!"

I rub my chin, not knowing what to make of this. "Yeah. That *is* weird."

"I know! At first, I chalked it up to him trying to get in contact with Thomas, since I've heard him bitching at Mom about how Thomas won't return his calls. And maybe he wondered if I'd seen you 'cause he was trying to interrogate me on any inside information at Moore's. But now it's just... weird."

I know why *I* don't return Stan's calls, but why wouldn't Thomas? Before he walked away from Moore's, my brother and Stan got along just fine. Thomas is the only kid my dad actually likes.

"Did you know I actually skipped class to feed Mike? I was worried Dad would follow me to your place if I headed straight there. And we all know how you don't like Dad in your space."

Bless her. "I'm sorry you missed class. But I really appreciate you feeding Mikey this morning."

"Yeah, well, if I missed something vital to the mid-term, you're taking one for the team and sleeping with my professor to get me an A."

I bark out a laugh, relieved her sense of humor seems to be returning. "I'm not sleeping with your professor. You can't pimp me out to women for your benefit."

"Who said my professor was a woman?"

I snort. "Nice."

Her laugh relaxes me. I don't know what's up with Stan, but I don't like when my sister is involved in any of our dad's shit. He mentioned cutting Liz off earlier, but I don't know why he would now, as I've kept up my end of the deal. The quarterly reports are in, and Moore's is finally back in the black. Barely, but it's there. And now I'm sure that with Bell's help we're going to have a Renaissance year. So why is the old man pissed now?

"Sorry I'm out of sorts, bro. Things at the house have just been awkward. I meant to call you a few days ago, but I got distracted by this mid-term project coming up."

"That's okay. Class comes first, Lizzy."

"Ugh. Stop with the Lizzy."

"Sure thing." We both know that's a lie.

She mumbles something I can't understand before brushing me off. "Anyway, Thomas is going into Dad's office when Dad isn't home. I caught him coming out, and he asked me not to say anything. I just shrugged and walked to the kitchen, so I didn't *technically* agree not to say anything, so I'm not *really* lying. Right?"

Dad's office? What the hell is Thomas doing sneaking into Dad's office?

"Chase?"

"Uh, yeah, right. Fuck Thomas anyway."

Another sigh. This one I'm pretty sure is directed at me. "Even Mom is acting strange, being more reclusive than usual."

"Is she around when Thomas comes over?"

"She's in the house, but I haven't seen her go into the office with him. Why? You think something is going on? Want me to snoop?"

I'm distracted for a moment when I hear the shower shut off.

"Do you?"

"No." I rub a hand down my face, suddenly exhausted. "There seems to be enough snooping going on at the moment. I think you should move back into your apartment until whatever this is blows over."

"Really? Are you sure? I mean, I'm not going to lie, I'd move out in a heartbeat at this stage, but I'd feel bad if I left and I could've been useful. What if Dad tries to ambush you in your office again? I won't be at the house to warn you if I hear anything."

"Don't worry about that. Just get out of there. You need to focus on school. Besides, I told you that house is toxic."

"Yeah, yeah." She pauses. "Hey, on a side note, why couldn't *you* feed Mike today?"

The bathroom door opens, steam spilling out. Like a slow-motion movie reel, one bare leg, then another, emerges from the doorway. One of those too-small hotel towels barely covers the top of Bell's nipples, and when she turns to the closet, the bottom of the towel reveals the underside of her ass cheeks.

"Chase?" She waits for me to answer. "Bro?"

"Huh? What?" I clear my throat and wipe the drool from my chin. "Liz?"

"Where exactly are you right now?"

"Nowhere." Bell drops the towel, smiling over her shoulder. "I gotta go. Thanks for taking care of my cunt." Bell tilts her head in question, but I don't answer. Instead, I end the call, toss the phone, and make my way over to the seductress standing naked and wet before me.

"Who was that?" Her voice is breathy as I lick moisture from the valley of her breasts.

"Liz." I tweak her nipples. She moans.

"Why is... your sister... taking care of... your...?" She gestures rather than say the word.

"Doesn't matter." I drop to my knees, pushing her legs farther apart. "What matters is that now I'm going to take care of yours."

And I do.

Twice.

26

BELL

"Double shot latte, one pump white mocha please."

The barista smiles, not knowing that the one pump of white mocha in my order is very significant. That single pump of sweetness is the harbinger of good ideas. Whenever I studied in college for a big test, or now, when I'm stuck on a marketing design, that single white mocha infusion makes everything better.

"I'm all shook up..." Screw Chase. I can sing.

The barista falters with the steamer at my "yay, yay, yay." Okay, maybe I should stick with humming when invoking the power of Elvis.

I'm hoping that the combination of the King's energizing, jaunty lyrics and the almighty pump of sweet syrup can help me help Chase put Moore's back on top of New York City retail. And then... global dominance. Or, you know, build an international foundation with a strategic presence in foreign cosmopolitan areas.

I know that seems like a tall order, but the white mocha magic has yet to let me down.

The chirpy young girl in an apron holds out my finished latte. "Here you go, ma'am."

The warmth from the cup seeps into my skin, and I'm too focused on the delicious combination of caffeine and sugar that's sure to help me produce a global dominance plan to be mad about being ma'am-ed again.

"Ms. King?"

"Jesus!" My hand squeezes the paper cup, shooting a stream of latte into the air that arcs up over my head before landing on a pair of expensive men's shoes. Shoes with tassels.

It takes a confident man to pull off tassels.

Traveling up from the shoes, I find pleated-front suit pants, a skinny black belt, a white shirt smoothly tucked in behind said belt, and a maroon argyle silk tie. One perfectly groomed eyebrow rises above a set of serious brown eyes.

Thomas Moore.

What *the hell* is with the Moore brothers and hot coffee?

"I didn't mean to startle you." His voice is deep and steady, in direct opposition to my current frazzled nature.

Clearing my throat, I step back. "No, my fault. I guess I'm a bit jumpy today."

He pulls a few napkins from the dispenser. I fully expect him to work on saving his expensive shoes from coffee stains, but instead he wipes my fingers, sticky with milk, espresso and sadly, wasted white mocha.

"Oh." I startle at his touch, almost spilling the tiny remnants of coffee left in the cup, unprepared for his thoughtfulness. "Thanks." After his parting shot at brunch that Saturday, and everything that Chase told me yesterday, his gesture surprises me.

"No problem." Once my fingers are clean, he grabs some more napkins before bending down, making sure to clean the floor as well as brush haphazardly at his shoes. From my higher vantage point, I can appreciate his full head of blackish-brown wavy hair and the way his suit pulls across his broad back and shoulders.

What? I can look.

"Oh, Mr. Moore, you don't have to do that!" The happy-go-lucky, ma'am-ing barista from a moment ago is now panicked and flushed. "Please, let me." She bends down to take over, but he politely brushes her hands away.

"No problem. All done."

He pops back up and tosses the napkins into the trash, offering his hand to the girl still crouched down by his feet.

"Oh, ah, okay." Nodding, she maneuvers back behind the counter, leaving me with Thomas Moore.

"Well, okay, then." I lift my half-full coffee. "Thanks again for the napkins. I'll... uh, see you around." I turn toward the door, but he stops me before I can walk away.

"Wait. Please."

I stop, but at the questioning look I throw at him, he looks down, almost sheepishly. "I, uh, may have been waiting for you."

My expression remains the same. "I don't understand. Why would *you* wait for *me*?"

"I was hoping to speak with you."

I look behind me, then back again. "Me?"

His smile reminds me of Chase. It both guts me and endears me. "Yes. You." He gestures to an open café table. "Do you have a minute?"

"Well, I was going to..." How can I not think of anything I have to do, but a minute ago I was coming up with a plan for global dominance?

Thomas takes one step closer, his hand resting on my arm. "Please?"

The café employees are watching us, and it reminds me of how fast and furious work gossip can spread. I don't want to cause a scene that will get back to Chase. *Sigh.* "Okay. Just a minute."

"Thank you, Bell." My nickname sounds odd with his formal tone. Ever gracious, he relieves me of my heavy laptop bag, placing it on one of the four chairs around the open table.

I nod, sitting in the seat he pulls out for me. I rest what's left of my creative mojo juice on the table.

He's charming, but stiff. Thomas doesn't have the ease with which Chase moves or acts. Or his smile. I bet Thomas would look ridiculous if he tried to wink at someone.

Ugh. Stop thinking about Chase. You need to focus on making his beloved store a worldwide leader in luxury goods, not on how attractive your boyfriend is.

Oh my god. I have a boyfriend.

"Holy shit."

Thomas blinks. "I'm sorry?"

"Uh, nothing, nothing." I shake my head at myself. "You were saying?"

He gives me a strange look, one I deserve but ignore. Instead I focus on his tie. It's a Windsor knot. A perfectly symmetrical Windsor knot. Further study has me realizing that, with the exception of his part, which is on his left side, the rest of Thomas Moore is perfectly symmetrical. His hairline, eyebrows, eyes, even the bow on the top of his lips is evenly arched.

I read a study once that said symmetry is the leading factor in determining a person's beauty. That humans are subconsciously drawn to those with symmetrical features.

Yet nothing about Thomas's symmetry fires up my nether regions. I can appreciate his beauty. I acknowledge his handsomeness. But, all in all, I'd rather look at Chase's perma-smirk, the way one side of his mouth quirks higher than the other. The slight bump on the upper right side of his nose, and how the hair at the start of one eyebrow sticks up straight, while the other smooths perfectly over his eye. All of Chase's variations are slight, but as a whole they make for a more interesting picture. A sexier man. A man I love.

Who would prefer Thomas's cold perfection over Chase's warmth and realness?

"Campbell?"

Pulling myself from my thoughts, I offer Thomas a simple "Hmmm?"

"Are you humming 'Suspicious Minds'?"

"Uh... no?" I so totally was.

He gives me a skeptical look but continues. "As I was saying, I've been trying to reach Chase, but he's been dodging my calls."

"Okay." I draw out the word, unsure what to say. I mean, *I* know why Chase is dodging his calls, but I'm pretty sure that falls under boyfriend–girlfriend classified stuff.

He sighs, the look of defeat disturbing on his confident posture. "I know my brother and I don't have the best relationship."

I can't help but snort.

We're quiet for a moment before he tentatively places one of his hands on my forearm. "I'm sorry, by the way."

His words affect me more than his touch. He doesn't seem like a man to apologize all that often. But because of Chase, I can't help but be suspicious. I feel my eyes narrow. "For what, exactly?"

"That day at brunch. What I said." He pulls his hand back and runs it through his hair, reminding me once again of Chase. "I wasn't expecting to see my brother, though I'd been calling him for some time." He laughs, and I can tell it's directed mostly at himself. "However, instead of taking the opportunity to tell him what I needed to say and hopefully make a plan, I acted immature and got angry instead."

"I noticed."

"Again, I'm sorry." He lets out an exasperated sigh. "I'm not sure if you noticed, but Chase is damn near impossible to rile up. The kid can shrug off anything."

I recall the devil-may-care attitude he affected when talking with his father a few weeks ago in his office.

"Yes, he can seem that way," I say carefully, still unsure of this new Thomas.

"In my frustration at him not letting me talk, I took a cheap and uncalled-for shot at you, thinking if I couldn't get to him directly, I'd get to him through you." He looks stricken, and it reminds me of how he looked at brunch right after he'd insinuated about Chase and me sleeping together. "It worked, but instead of making me feel better, it will now go down as one of the more regrettable things I've ever done."

"I see." I'm not sure that I do, never having had siblings to fight with, but the man does seem sincere.

"I was an asshole," he declares, surprising me further. More for the foul language than the self-deprecation. "There's no excuse. Chase has a way of getting under my skin, but I'm a grown man, and I should've known better than to take it out on you."

Part of me wants to say something witty and snide, tit for tat and all that, but my more rational and mature part recently learned a lesson on what can happen if you hold on to a grudge. Reaching out, I offer Thomas my hand. "Apology accepted."

He takes my hand in his, a relieved smile on his weirdly symmetrical face. "Thank you. I want you to know that even if you don't want to help me, my apology is truly sincere."

Drawing my hand back, I tentatively get us back on track. "So what exactly *do* you need my help with?"

"I've been trying to reach Chase, but he's got me blocked from his phone, his office, and his condo."

I think of George and his guard-dog like position between the elevator and Chase's office. "Have you tried emailing him?"

He nods. "Yes, but only to tell him that I need to talk to him. I honestly don't know what type of tech security my father had in place before Chase took over. I didn't want to write anything that could be read." He leans back in the small café chair, blowing out a large breath. "I guess it isn't any wonder we don't have the best relationship, really. Our father did a number on us for sure."

"Oh." Not what I was expecting. "Well, I hate to tell you this, but normally when a person does all that, it means they really don't want to see you. And please remember, no matter what, I'll always be Team Chase. I'm not going to do anything to hurt him." Even if it would be nice to reconcile the brothers. No one knows as well as I do how hard it is being alone. Growing up, and especially since my parents died, I would've loved to have a sibling to lean on.

"I get that, but it's about our sister, Liz."

"Liz?" I think of the bubbly, bouncing blonde that Chase loves. "Is she okay?"

"Sort of."

My mouth drops open, and he hurries to continue.

"I mean, yes, she is *physically* fine, but her financial future is in jeopardy." His brown eyes are serious once more. "And I need Chase's help to fix it."

"Why?" I'm back to suspicious.

He spreads his hands wide. "Liz is the one thing Chase and I see eye to eye on. I'd do anything for her. Even if Chase doesn't believe me."

I take a sip of my now lukewarm white mocha, remembering Chase's affection for his sister. The easy camaraderie, the genuine love they have for each other. Far different from what I saw between Thomas and Chase that day at brunch. But looking at this man's stupidly perfect face, I can tell he cares just as much. Just... differently.

And I know he's right about Chase. He'd do anything for Liz.

Decision made, I put down my cup. "First, I'm going to need another one-pump white mocha latte." Thomas raises one eyebrow, and I suddenly get what Chase meant when he said Thomas always had a stick up his ass. "Hell," I mutter at his judgey expression, "this calls for two pumps."

Both eyebrows shoot up. "Um, okay. And second?"

"Second. Tell me how to help."

27

CHASE

He's touching her.

On her arm.

In our coffee shop.

Technically it's Moore's coffee shop, but ever since that day, I'll always think of it as Bell's and mine. Where we officially met. Where my nipples received third-degree burns at the hands of overpriced coffee. Where I saw her perfectly suckable nipples through her white shirt.

This café is *ours*, damn it. And he's touching her in it.

A saleswoman smiles at me. I try to return the gesture, but it sends her scurrying away. I have a feeling my smile was more feral than friendly.

Attention back on the café, I see Thomas briefly squeeze Bell's arm. Like he's trying to reassure her or something. It's a minute movement, but one I'm keenly aware of.

I love this store. But I'm not sure I love it enough to not burn the whole place down after witnessing my brother touching my girl in our café.

Especially after yesterday. I don't like talking about my family. It makes me feel weak, and other unmanly things. But Bell hadn't felt that way at all. In fact, I think she loved me even more for telling her about my fucked-up childhood. I'm not too proud to accept that. After all, it's the first time my daddy issues ever did anything beneficial for me.

But why isn't she walking away from him? Why is Bell even giving him the time of day after everything I told her? Is he trying to sweet-talk her? Bring her over to the dark side?

If the bastard thinks Bell is just one more thing he can take from me, he's got another think coming.

I'm about to do something stupid when Thomas finally pulls his fucking hand away from her arm. He doesn't even know how close he came to losing said fucking hand. Then being beaten in his perfect, smug face with it.

It would seem I'm feeling a tad violent today.

The small bit of relief from my brother's pause in mauling my girlfriend is short-lived. Because then Bell goes and smiles at the bastard. It's a small smile, but it's aimed at my brother. Is it wrong that I want *all* of Bell's smiles? They're mine, damn it. And even if I don't get all of them, Thomas damn well doesn't deserve a single one.

"Mr. Moore?"

I jump back from the pillar I'm hiding behind, nearly falling on my ass. Collecting myself, I run a hand down the front of my shirt, like me being a Creeper McCreeperson is nothing overly concerning. "Yes, Raymond?"

"May I somehow be of assistance?" He glances over my shoulder to the café. I can tell the moment he sees Bell, as his left eyebrow rises the barest millimeter. "Perhaps I can procure you a coffee?"

Hoity-toity bastard. Who says procure, anyway?

His lips twitch, and if I didn't know him to be such a well-mannered stick-in-the-mud, I'd swear he's laughing at me.

"No, no. Just, ah, making sure I don't have something in my teeth." I pretend to check my appearance in the small mirror perched on a counter to my right. That isn't anywhere near the pillar I was huddled against.

Whatever. I'm the boss. I can act sketchy if I want.

Raymond takes a long, bored look at me before deigning to reply. "Indeed." Then the way-too-perceptive man sniffs, actually sniffs like an old English butler of yore, before inclining his head.

"Then I guess I should inform you that your father, ah, stormed through the store about twenty minutes before you arrived."

"Fuck."

"Quite." He glances at the few early-morning customers browsing the floor. "I believe Mr. Moore Senior is awaiting you in your office." He gives me a knowing look. "George was most displeased not to have been at his desk at the time of his arrival."

"I bet." George does not take lightly to people invading what he considers his territory. Hell, half the time it's a miracle he lets *me* into the office. It wasn't until Bell that he—

"If I were you, I might want to make my way upstairs." Raymond glances behind me at the café. "Unless you were waiting for someone?"

Narrowing my eyes at him, I shake my head. "Nope. Not waiting for anyone."

"Indeed."

Nosy fucker.

Raymond inclines his head one more time before heading over to the group of women congregating around a makeup counter. I'm sure within minutes they'll be simpering over his hoity-toity ways.

Moore's is lucky to have him.

Hell, *I'm* lucky to have him.

When I glance back at the café, Thomas is at the counter ordering a coffee, and Bell's at the table rifling through her laptop bag. Hopefully that means their little chat is over. I'd go find out myself, but I trust Bell. I sure as shit don't trust my father.

I jog over to the elevators and swipe my security card, bracing myself for whatever new shit Stan is no doubt about to throw my way.

* * *

"Decided to make an appearance, huh?" My father is nearly vibrating with displeasure. A usual occurrence around me, though normally he does a better job of hiding it.

George jumps up from the couch in my office, where it seems he's stayed as a self-appointed overseer of my father. He pushes up his glasses and buttons his suit jacket before speaking. "Mr. Moore came in early this morning." His tone leaves no one wondering how he feels about this. "I called security and verified his arrival time. He was alone, in your office, a full ten minutes before I got here."

Stan's eyes narrow on George. "You insolent little... how dare you talk about me like I'm some sort of—"

"I found him at your desk," George goes on, ignoring my father. Handy trick. I'll need to remember it for future use.

"*His* desk?" Stan snorts. "We'll just see about that."

Making a mental note to give George a raise, I nod at him. "Thanks, George. I have it from here." My father blusters, like he's gathering wind for the new storm he's going to throw my way. Looking back to George, I add, "Why don't you go take a break? I think the marketing team brought in bagels again. Go get yourself one."

"The sniveling secretary just got here and you're already giving him a break? This is how you run things?" Stan glowers at George.

George just raises his eyebrow at the old man. His Uncle Raymond would be so proud.

"It's a mental health break, Stan. From having to deal with your shit." My voice comes off harsher than I'd intended, but honestly, I don't give a fuck.

My father blusters again. "You—"

I slice my hand through the air. "Enough."

Surprisingly, Stan quiets.

George's lips twitch, his proper exterior cracking slightly. "Are you sure, Chase? I don't mind staying. I could take notes." He throws a narrowed glance at my father. "Be a witness."

The fact that he called me Chase only signifies how much my father got to him, and how much he probably needs a time out away from my family drama. "Nah, you've done more than enough. Go ahead. Take a break."

"Very well." With a nod, he turns to leave, saying, "I'll be back in *ten minutes.*" Once he clears the threshold, he pointedly leaves the door open.

Being the mature man that he is, Stan walks over and closes it.

Might as well get this over with.

"So, old man, what's with the unscheduled drop-in?"

"Your little foray into heading the family business is over. Thomas is taking over."

"Thomas?" Suddenly, Thomas talking to Bell downstairs takes on new meaning. Maybe I should have gone over and confronted him.

"That's right. It just took him seeing you with that tramp to see the light." He sneers. "I can't believe you introduced that whore to your mother."

"Leave Bell out of this." I have to consciously unclench my fists.

"I would, if you hadn't given that *woman* firing privileges. It's obvious you're being led around by your dick." Stan snorts. "Thomas may have had doubts, but he's realized his duty. As first-born son, he has the right to run this company." He points a meaty finger at me. "You don't."

As archaic as it is, Stan is right. The by-laws state that another family member/shareholder can take over *only* if the firstborn turns over the reins willingly. Thomas had, verbally, but, since I don't like talking to him, I never asked him to put it in writing. Technically, Thomas can take over again.

Stan's face is grotesque with triumph. Me? I'm just tired of this merry-go-round our father has had us Moore kids on from day one. "Why?"

"Thomas is the first—"

"No. Not that." I roll my eyes. "I understand by-laws." I walk over to my desk and pick up the cracked family portrait. "I want to know why you hate me so much."

My father's smile slips. "Excuse me?"

I catch his eyes with mine. "You heard me."

His eyes narrow, like he's trying to figure out my angle. I really don't have one. I just want to know. It's something I've been afraid to ask my whole life.

He dismisses my question with a wave of his hand. "Don't be so sentimental."

"*Why?*" I slam down the picture, the glass cracking further.

Possibly shocked by my rare burst of anger toward him, he remains silent.

Annoyed, I state my case. No jokes, no self-deprecating humor. Just the facts. "I'm a self-made man. I didn't take *any* of your money. I earned what I needed and invested in start-ups and applications and became a billionaire in my own right. Something neither you nor Thomas ever did."

"You're right." A sneer. "Thomas or I would never get into porn."

His words sound pat, rehearsed. Like he's almost glad I created Pick a Dick, because that one application gave him the right to hate me. But there *has* to be more. "You always bring that up, but we both know that isn't why you look down on my success. That application is a small part of what I've done over the years." I sort through my thoughts, trying to find the missing piece. "It has to be something else. You've hated me ever since I can remember. Why?"

"Why does there have to be a why? You were a sniveling, rotten boy. Always misbehaving. And look at you, you're still sniveling."

"No." I shake my head, strangely calm. "That's not it. I mean, I may have misbehaved, but I was on the honor roll, a varsity athlete, earned academic scholarships. Just like Thomas."

His face turns red. "You're nothing like Thomas."

"I guess not." I shrug. "Though I did bring this company back from the brink of layoffs and bankruptcy. Something your poor management skills led us to, and Thomas didn't even want to try to fix." Stan's face is almost purple now. "*I* turned this company around. *I* saved the Moore legacy." My words come hard and fast. "So *why* do you hate me?"

Stan slams his hand down on an empty shelf as he yells, "Because you were born."

The blow of his words has me taking a step back like he hit me and not the bookcase. "What?"

Like I unlocked the floodgates, Stan paces in front of me, spewing angrily. "Your mother and I had a deal. A deal she agreed to. One kid. One! Just enough to ensure the legacy, but not any more, so I wouldn't have to divide up the shares." He looks up, his eyes narrowing. "But she *lied*. She tricked me and got pregnant with *you*."

"How is that—"

"She didn't even tell me she was pregnant until it was too late to get rid of you."

Bile climbs up my throat.

"I checked… you know. But you're mine. The DNA test was conclusive." He shakes his head in disgust. "I had to give you the shares as per the terms of the trust."

We're silent for a while. After all that, you'd think I'd regret asking the question. But I don't.

Now I know for sure that there's nothing I can do to prove myself to this man. It's fucked up, his reasons are *definitely* fucked up, but it's freeing to finally know.

"You and your precious golden boy can have Moore's then." I stand and walk to the door, not caring enough to look at the old man. Because that's all he is to me. An old man.

"I quit."

* * *

Bell

I'm shocked stupid.

My mouth, which has probably been hanging open the past ten minutes while Thomas regaled me with his family's secrets, finally closes. I open it again and try speaking. It doesn't go so well. Clearing my throat, I try again. "Are you kidding me?"

It's a dumb question. I don't think anyone would willingly make up a story like that about their own family. But a girl can hope.

Thomas, as expected, shakes his head. "I wish I was."

I whistle low. "Jesus."

"Nope. Just me."

Caught off guard, I blink at him. "Did you... did you just make a joke?"

He shrugs, the action looking awkward with his stiff shoulders. "Chase is the funny one."

"Yeah. I can see that." Standing, I grab my bag, hitching the heavy weight onto my shoulder, and pick up my latte. The latte I insisted Thomas get me before diving into his family's convoluted and downright ridiculous history and present-day shit show. "Come on, Chuckles. We need to find Chase."

Once standing, Thomas straightens his cuffs. "Chuckles? Really?"

"You don't like Golden Boy. I was trying something new out."

"Please don't."

"Fine." We begin our short trek to the elevator. "You actually like being called Thomas? Seriously?"

"Stan wouldn't allow anyone to call me anything else growing up." He shrugs again, this time a bit less awkwardly. "I got used to it."

I slide my free hand into my bag's front pocket to get my security card. "I've never watched a soap opera, but I have a feeling even they don't compare to the kind of drama your family creates." As I slide the card to open the elevator doors, I have to tilt my body to the right to keep my bag in place.

"Do you need help with any of that?"

"No, no. I've got it." I slip the card back in my bag and shift the strap higher on my shoulder. Once inside the elevator, I take a fortifying sip of my white mocha. "Hey, don't you think we should involve Liz in this? This affects her, and if what you said pans out, you're not going to be able to protect her for too much longer." I press the button for the main office level. "We should probably include your mom too, for that matter."

"I know. But not yet. Liz is in the middle of mid-terms, so I'd like to shield her from this as much as possible. At least until her exams are over."

"And your mom?"

"Mom's had it rough. I know it doesn't seem that way, but I'd like to keep her out of Stan's crosshairs."

I nod, trying to psych myself up for this unplanned turn of events. After Chase opened up to me yesterday, I can't say I didn't have a small ember of hope that one day I'd find a way to make things better between him and his brother. But I sure as hell didn't think that day would be today.

"Never wait for tomorrow." I whisper one of my mom's favorite Elvis quotes to myself. "What if tomorrow never comes?"

"What was that?"

"Nothing." I avoid his eyes and adjust my stuff again.

"Here, you really should let me carry something. That bag looks heavy." He reaches for the strap.

"No, really. I've got it. I'll just—"

Multiple things happen at once.

First, the shoulder strap from my laptop bag slides down my arm and hooks itself over Thomas's outstretched hand.

Two, the elevator doors open.

And three, unprepared for how heavy my bag is, the weight of it jerks Thomas down by his arm. His head nearly collides with mine as I step back, pressing against the elevator wall, trying to keep my latte from spilling by holding my arm out wide and out of the way. Which causes Thomas to fall further into me, his other hand, not caught in the strap, rising in an effort to brace himself.

On my boob.

"Bell?"

Simultaneously, Thomas and I turn our heads toward Chase, standing right outside the elevator doors with a confused look on his face, taking in the scene before him.

Which is basically Thomas plastered to my front, hand on my boob, our mouths inches away from each other.

I can't make this up.

"You...?" I can see the moment Chase's imagination turns this into something it's not.

"No. Chase, I—"

His laughter ricochets inside the small metal box, sounding hoarse and broken.

"This just figures, doesn't it?"

Thomas manages to shake off the strap anchoring his wrist down and stands up straight. I clear my throat, alerting him to the fact that he's still holding my boob.

"Oh. Apologies." He frees my breast and turns to his brother. "Chase, I'm here—"

Expression dark, Chase interrupts. "Save it. I know why you're here."

I push off the wall, sliding one hand out to stop the doors from closing on us, the other still wrapped around my now regrettable second latte. "You do?"

Chase ignores me. "Well, you can have it." His eyes focus on Thomas. "I quit."

"What? No," I start just as Thomas says, "Chase, please let me—"

"Thomas!"

Both Thomas and I jump at Stan Moore's voice.

"Father?" Thomas looks past Chase.

"Knew you'd come around, my boy. Come on, we have to..."

Stan's voice fades and his eyes narrow when he sees me. "What are you doing here?"

My eyes narrow right back. "I work here."

"No, you don't." A sly smile spreads across his face. "You're fired."

Chase stiffens. "You can't do that, old man. There's a legally binding contract between King Marketing and Moore's."

"Well now. Seeing how this one"—he jerks his thumb toward me— "probably earned that contract on her knees, I don't think I'll have a problem dissolving it."

Chase shifts toward his father, pulling his arm back. Quickly, I grab hold of his sleeve. "That's a bit hypocritical of you, isn't it?" I snap at Stan. "Seeing that you've been having an affair with Denise Hampson this whole time."

Everyone goes still.

Fuck. I hadn't meant to say that.

Chase's eyes bore into mine. "What?"

"I... uh..."

He whips his head back to Stan. "You've... you've been cheating on Mom?"

"I don't need to answer to you," Stan blusters.

Thomas tenses, as if waiting for his brother to strike.

Still holding his sleeve, I watch as Chase takes a few deep breaths, calming down enough to unclench his fists before shaking me off and turning his back on his father. "How long have you known, Bell?" His voice cracks on my name, echoing the one spreading across my heart. "And you kept it from me?"

Purposely, I don't look at Thomas. "I didn't... I mean... it wasn't like that." I sound lame even to my own ears.

But it doesn't matter. Chase's eyes sweep from me to Thomas and to the elevator behind us. "I see." And with that he walks off, heading toward the stairway door.

I go after him. "Chase, please, wait!"

Stopping at the doorway, he turns to me, hurt and anger in his eyes. "No. Like I said. I quit." His tone makes it obvious it isn't just Moore's he's quitting.

The heavy security door falls back in place with a bang, breaking open the fissure in my heart.

28

CHASE

"I don't understand how it's come to this."

Mike continues to lick his hairless testicles.

My apartment is dark. Not because it's evening. It isn't. I think it might be mid-afternoon or something. I don't know. I've lost track of the days, let alone the time.

My ass is numb from sitting in this same spot. Honestly, if I could piss from this position, I wouldn't even get up to use the bathroom. I guess my self-pity has some boundaries because I draw the line at that. But I have shut all the blinds like a vampire, in addition to not turning on any lights.

And with my speakers droning out a constant stream of Elvis's greatest hits, I've basically created the perfect mood for Mike to go after his balls like a porn star.

Looking at the debauched, hairless feline, I continue my bewilderment. "I mean, how did things go so wrong so fast?"

No answer. Not even an affectionate, sympathetic cuddle. Just another loud slurp to his nether regions.

For a pussy, he can be such a dick.

"Heartbreak Hotel" starts up, and it's so apt I find myself

saluting my speakers with my drink.

That's right. I'm drinking, too. For the past however many days, I've lived in sweatpants, eaten questionable leftovers from my fridge, and gone through two bottles of Scotch.

I'm wallowing. I'm a sad, pathetic wallower.

I can't shake off what happened.

Bell. Her boob. Thomas's hand.

My chest pangs, and I move on to the next present revelation.

It seems it is my very existence that curdled my father's heart. He would've rather had more company shares. And as much as his horrid insight answered the questions I've had my entire life about our relationship, I'd be a robot if it also didn't shred my soul.

I slosh some more whiskey into my glass.

"And Stan and Denise?" I ask Mike, even though I know even if he could, he wouldn't answer. I scoff into my drink before taking a long sip.

As sad as my childhood was, and as absent as my parents have been, I've always been able to say that my parents are still together. That their marriage isn't as broken as our family was.

Which brings me back to Bell.

Bell knew. Knowing about the affair, how could she listen to everything I said about my family and not tell me? Or even sit down and have a friendly chat with my brother in *our* café? And seriously, what the flying *fuck* was with her and Thomas in the elevator? Seeing my brother cop a feel on my girlfriend after my father eviscerated my soul is too much for any one man to take.

Okay. I replay my last thought and place the glass on the coffee table. I *might* be watching too many angsty teen shows on The CW. I'm getting a tad bit melodramatic.

More than a tad bit really. I mean, who 'quits' a relationship? A relationship with a wonderful, sensitive, sexy-as-fuck woman.

What the hell is wrong with me?

But I know what is wrong with me. I'm scared.

Because even though I know that Bell must've had a good reason to keep the information about Stan and Denise from me, and probably another good reason for spending time with my dipshit brother, and for whatever it was that blinded me with rage in that elevator, there is another part of me that is too scared to be sure. Scared that maybe everyone else is right. That maybe Bell would want Thomas, the golden boy who's once more in charge. That maybe Mom feels the same way about me that Stan does.

Fuck. I'm just as big a pussy as Mike Hunt.

The disco hit "We Are Family" blasts from under my ass. Sighing, I slide my phone out from the couch cushion I hid it under after I was tempted to answer Bell's calls and texts. And where I kept it after they stopped coming to stop myself from calling or texting her.

For answers? Forgiveness?

Who knows.

Palming the phone, I'm greeted with Liz's goofy face.

Here's hoping my baby sister can make me smile. "Hey, Lizzy."

"Chase, dear, it's Mom."

I pull the phone back and check the screen. Yep, still says Liz. "Mom?"

"Yes. Are you home?"

"Uh, yeah. But why are you—"

"See you in a bit then."

"Wait, what? Mom? Hello?"

The screen darkens. She hung up. Why is Mom using Liz's phone? And just how does she think she's getting into my apartment? Only Liz and Bell are on the pre-approved list.

Ding.

Oh, shit.

The telltale click of heels sounds from the hallway.

"Chase?" Tall and slender, Emily Moore enters my unkempt living room. Her eyes move around the room, taking in the drawn curtains, the empty food containers, and the half-empty bottle of Scotch on the table next to me. "Oh, Chase. My sweet boy."

I glance at my glass again, wondering how much I've had. If I've somehow drunk myself into such a stupor that I'm imagining my mother's caring tone.

Tentatively, Mom makes her way toward me, bypassing Mike, who seems to think licking one's nuts in front of someone's mom is a line even he won't cross.

Instead, he leaps up onto the armchair and lies down, watching the proceedings from his throne on high.

Mom comes to a bit of an impasse, not sure whether to take the seat next to me or keep standing. Finally, she perches on the edge of the coffee table. We're eye to eye.

We sit there like that, staring at each other, until I can't take the silence anymore. "Where's Liz?"

"Downstairs, keeping the floor manager busy so I could sneak up here."

"Traitor," I mutter.

That gets a small smile from her. I can't remember the last time I made my mother smile. Then again, do I even look for it anymore?

"Don't think that way. She was worried about you. *I'm* worried about you."

"Me?" I laugh, but even I hear the hurt laced through it.

"Oh, honey. This is all my fault."

"Why, 'cause you tricked Dad into having me?"

A long sigh. "I didn't trick anyone. I—" She regroups. "Let me start at the beginning." She nods once like she was asking herself what to do. Regaining her composure, she starts again. "My marriage to your father wasn't a love match."

I scoff. "What a surprise."

She continues as if I hadn't spoken. "We both went into it willingly, our families convincing us that a mutually beneficial marriage was a good option. Moore's needed the Hawthorns' influx of ready cash, and the Hawthorns wanted the prestige of the old and glamorous Moore name. The fact that my children would be guaranteed a part of that legacy was also compelling."

I snort, thinking where that legacy has brought us.

"But I misstepped," Mom continues. "At the very start, Stan said he only wanted one child. I agreed. At the time, I didn't know any better, didn't understand how much I'd love being a mother."

Her focus rests on the bottle of Scotch, but I don't think she actually sees it. She's lost in memories.

"For the first four years after Thomas was born, everything seemed to be going well. Your father had money to invest into the business, I had Thomas at home with me, and the three of us were content. But then it was time for Thomas to go to school, and things... changed.

"Your father insisted on certain schools. Only enrolled Thomas in specific extracurriculars. Didn't want me playing make-believe anymore or going to mommy groups or arranging playdates for him. Said I was making him too soft." Her delicate hands clasp tightly together. "In the span of a few months, I was shoved aside so that Thomas could be groomed to take over the Moore legacy." She looks at me, eyes pleading. "I fought it. I tried. But your father..." Her shoulders slumped, defeated. "Let's just say it was a battle I didn't win."

She takes a moment to compose herself. "When I got pregnant with you, please believe me, it wasn't a trick. Your father and I still shared a bed at that stage in our marriage."

I must make a face because my mom chuckles softly.

"As soon as I found out I was pregnant, I knew your father

wouldn't be happy. But I thought, since he genuinely seemed to care for Thomas, he wouldn't be able to help loving you too."

"You were wrong." I throw back the rest of my drink.

Another deep sigh. "Yes. I was."

In the silence that statement brings, I refill my glass.

"That was the beginning of the end of any sort of peaceful existence between your father and me." She leans forward, plucks the glass from my hand, and puts it aside before grasping both of my hands in hers. "*None* of that, or what came after, was your fault." Her eyes bore into mine, but I can't bring myself to answer. "Do you hear me? Not your fault, my darling boy."

I'm ashamed to say my eyes feel hot at her words.

"I mean it, Chase Hawthorn Moore. You are everything that is good. I just wish I had done things differently, or, I don't know, left your father once he became so hardened."

I blow out a hot breath, trying to will the tears away. "Why didn't you?"

She squeezes my hands once before sitting back, shrugging her thin shoulders. "I was afraid he'd take you from me. Both of you. Or even try to separate the two of you. So I stayed. For a while, it was like your father and I called a truce. Stan had Thomas, and I had you." She gets that faraway look in her eyes again. "We had great times together when you were little. Do you remember?"

I shake my head.

"Finger painting in the yard? Building Lego towers so tall we had to get a ladder? Making up our own lyrics to nursery rhymes?"

As soon as she says the words, the memories come back like long-lost childhood friends. Memories I forgot I had. Her calling me her darling boy. Her laughter, bright and loud. Her hugs and kisses.

"But as you got older, the more time I spent with you, the harder he was on you. Every time I praised you, he beat you down with words. Every special occasion, he made sure Thomas was center stage. It was like he was trying to punish me through you. Turn my children against me in a game they didn't know they were playing." Her voice catches, and she takes a deep breath, collecting herself.

"Until finally," she continues, "I thought, it's better if I stand back. Better if I don't engage anymore, if I stop showing you affection. Because then maybe he'll leave you alone." She picks up my glass and takes a sip of Scotch. "And then... and then Liz came." She downs the rest.

Clearing my throat and covertly wiping under my eyes, I take the glass from her and set it on the table. "If you and Dad were so... well, you know." I fight and fail to hide my cringe. "How did Liz come about?"

She stays silent, not meeting my eyes.

Carefully, I reach out to cover her hands with mine. I think this might be the first time since I was little that I've actively sought out my mother's touch. "Mom?"

"Liz isn't... well, she isn't..."

"She isn't what, Mom?"

"She isn't your father's." The words come fast and hot, like a shotgun blast.

They slam me back into the couch. "Holy fucking shit."

"Yes." She nods. "Holy fucking shit." Then, having purged herself of secrets, the proud and beautiful Emily Moore stands. And starts to straighten up my mess.

"Uh, Mom." I shift on the couch, prepared to get up. "You don't need to clean, Mom."

"I know." She shifts her glassy eyes around the apartment. "But I want to."

I'm not such a complete douchebag that I'd just sit back and watch my mom pick up my room. "Uh, okay, then. I'll help."

Fifteen minutes later, the curtains are open, the trash has been taken out, and Mom's forced two glasses of water down my throat. Well, not really. She simply suggested them, and I obliged. It's not too late to be a momma's boy, right?

Mom moves toward my bedroom. "Time for a shower."

I run a hand through my admittedly greasy hair with a smirk. "I know it's been a while, Mom. But I can shower all by myself these days."

"I always loved your jokes." She looks sort of sad when she says this, so I deflect the best way I know how.

"Of course you do." I flex for effect. "Because I'm awesome." The smell of my raised arm makes my eyes cross.

Her laugh sounds breathless and rusty, but to me, it sounds like magic.

"Yes, you are." She walks into my bedroom and heads for the closet. She pulls out a pair of jeans and a T-shirt that reads "Sorry I'm late. I didn't want to come," proving where my sense of humor comes from. "You're also going to finally have a chat with your brother."

Well, shit.

* * *

Bell

"Did you get everything I sent?"

My pen taps louder and harder the longer we talk.

"Yes." Thomas's calm voice is as infuriating as ever. "But I wish you'd reconsider."

The Houston skyline glows orange-red from the morning sun. I wanted to get to the office first thing to make sure all the information was sent to New York correctly and on time.

"You need to focus on more important things, T-money."

His sigh sounds exasperated. "You know what's scary?"

"What's that?"

"I'm getting used to your nicknames."

An unladylike bark of laughter escapes. In the past few days, Thomas and I have struck up an unlikely friendship. It probably helps that it was mostly over emails and phone calls so I didn't have to see his annoyingly superior facial expressions.

"Mom says Chase agreed to talk to me."

The sound of his name is enough to wipe the smile from my face. "That's good." I clear my throat to stop the emotion from coming up. "I've got to go, Chuckles."

Another sigh. This time sad. The man can run through the whole emotional dictionary on sighs alone. "Thanks for everything, Bell."

Ten minutes after we hang up, I'm still staring at the skyline. Déjà vu creeps in, but I shake it off. I may be back in the same spot I was before Chase Moore's call and New York, but I'm *not* the same person.

As if to make me prove it, Leslie saunters in. "This is bullshit, you know."

"Hello to you too, Leslie."

"Complete bullshit." She falls into one of the chairs in front of my desk. "If you had let me at the jackass I could've torn him a new one. We could have at least gotten a hefty price for them terminating the contract early."

"I know. You've said."

"Then why—"

"Why don't we go out on Friday?"

I take a minute to marvel at the wonder of a speechless Leslie.

She blinks a few times before regaining her composure. "I'm sorry, what?"

"Friday. You and me." I hate this idea. But I need it.

She flutters her lashes at me. "Are you asking me out, Campbell King?"

That has me laughing. "You're too high-maintenance for me. But if you already have plans…"

"No, no, no," she says, shaking her head. "And even if I did, I'd cancel. I am most definitely available for your… whatever this is."

"I just want to go out. People do that, you know."

"Not you. At least very rarely. And usually only to a wine bar for *a* drink." She stills. "Wait. Is that what you want? Another boring night at some wine bar?"

She looks too disappointed for me to tell her yes, that was exactly what I'd meant. So I go with, "No, of course not. I was thinking of Wild West."

She lights up again. "Wild West? Really?" Hooting, she kicks her legs up and down before popping out of the chair. "I'm going to find me a cowboy to ride!"

I can't help but laugh. "You have a cowboy fetish I didn't know about?"

"Um… who doesn't?"

She has a point.

One of her sharp, ladylike, French-tipped fingers points in my direction. "Don't you wuss out on me now."

"I won't," I promise, palms up.

Her eyes narrow, and I suddenly feel like the unfortunate opposition in court. "And don't think this is going to make me forget about the shit-storm in New York."

"Of course not." I nod solemnly. "You're much too sharp for that."

"Damn straight." She lowers her hand and walks to the door, a bit less stalk and a tad more swagger in her step. "Now if you'll excuse me, I've got to go see a man about a new pair of boots." She shimmies her ass in my direction. "We're going dancing."

I wish a new pair of boots would fix the so-called shit-storm.

King Marketing took a hit. Both its reputation and its bottom line. It's no secret that the first thing Stan did when he somehow wrestled control from Chase was fire me. There were enough people working near the elevator on the office floor that morning to ensure everyone in the business had some interesting opinions on what happened.

Even more so when Denise was reinstated seconds later, spreading her own rumors about what happened, and what she said happened with me years ago. The connection between Campbell Dougherty and Campbell King has been made.

I could tell it killed Thomas to just stand by and watch his father act like a pompous windbag. To not side with his brother or clue him in to what was really going on. But Thomas has to fake loyalty to Stan if he wants his plan to work.

A plan I hope Chase will be a part of if their conversation goes well.

I tried calling and texting, but Chase wouldn't pick up. The look of betrayal in his eyes when he realized I knew about the affair and hadn't told him... I see it every time I close my eyes. Needless to say, I haven't been sleeping well.

Though I know his family is just... wow, and me looking like I'd kept something from him must have hurt, at the same time I am so *mad* that he wouldn't listen. That he would just cut me off like that. *Leave me.*

Nope. I shake my head, blinking back the tears. I will not do this. Especially here in my domain.

I should just take a few days off and go to my parents' house in the country, but for some reason, I haven't.

Back at my desk, I sort through new projects, the ones that hadn't been canceled after the Moore's fiasco and pick the plumpest ones for Chris and Ben. It's the least I can do.

I tried to get Alice to come to Texas with me, but when she explained why she couldn't, I stopped arguing. Instead, I made Thomas promise she'd have a job, at her current pay, anywhere out of Denise's path until he could sort his family mess out. I'm mad I didn't have the time to help Alice more before I left. And even madder that she probably feels nervous at work while all this is being settled.

As if on cue, my phone alerts me to a text message.

Alice sent me a selfie, which makes me smile. After a second glance, I realize it isn't a selfie, but a picture of the mirror behind Alice, the one reflecting Denise and one of her minions rolling their eyes behind Denise's back.

It's hilarious.

We text back and forth a bit, her wanting to know if I'm coming back to New York any time soon, me making sure she's taken care of—professionally and personally. In answer to the former, she sends a picture of Thomas, looking aloof and bored in front of one of her displays, attached to an eye-roll emoji.

I resend it to Thomas with a reminder to lighten up.

Another picture pops up, and my heart stops. It's an older photo. One of Chase and me, the day of the storage room tryst. Alice must have taken it before Chase pulled me aside. We hadn't even said "I love you" yet, but the look in each other's eyes says it for us.

I save this one to my phone in a moment of weakness.

Alice is a bit of a romantic, I think. To cure her, and me too for that matter, of any hope of Chase and me reconciling, I text her that I'm going out with Leslie on Friday in search of cowboy comfort.

After a few minutes, when I think Alice is too disappointed in me to respond, she sends me a meme of Elvis from his cowboy movie *Charro!* with the words, "I'm just a hunk, a hunk of burning love" at the bottom.

She's photoshopped Chase's face on it.

Alice is surprisingly devious.

I save this picture too.

29

CHASE

I never would've taken my brother for the warm and fuzzy type.

His place has huge windows, showcasing a rare tree-lined street near Central Park. Surprisingly close to my own place.

And it's an actual *house*, not a condo or an apartment. It makes my place look sterile and bachelor-pad-esque. He even has family photos. And not just the obligatory professional family photo I kept in Stan's office when I took over. Thomas has *candid* shots. Shots I don't remember posing for, or even being aware of someone nearby with a camera.

There are off-kilter shots from when we were kids, like Liz and me running through the yard when she was around three. A younger version of Mom arranging flowers in the kitchen, the light behind her creating a halo around her. Me, lining up to take a penalty kick my senior year on the varsity soccer team. Dad hunched over his desk, papers fisted in his hands. And a stunning black and white of Liz as a teenager, curled up on the sofa, drawing in her sketch pad, a look of concentration on her face. As the subjects get older, the pictures become clearer, more vibrant, and the composition pretty fucking brilliant.

I stare at them while I wait for Thomas to return with whatever it is he wanted to show me.

It suddenly hits me what's missing. "You're not in any of these," I say when he enters the room, briefcase in hand. "You... took these?"

For once, my brother looks embarrassed. "Yes." That's all the answer I get. He walks over to the table and chairs by the windows, sitting in one and placing the briefcase on the table between them. Tearing myself away from the photo collage on the wall, I take the seat across from him.

This section of the large living room is set up like an area for cards or games. A long, white couch sits in the middle of the room, facing a TV, and on the other side of that, wall-to-wall bookcases surround a lone leather reading chair and floor lamp.

It's oddly homey. I would've pictured Thomas in a tall, dark skyscraper, in some minimalist condo decorated in black and chrome. You know, a villain's lair.

I need a hobby. My imagination is getting out of hand.

"Mom told you about Liz?" His suit jacket is gone, and his sleeves are rolled up. It's a more relaxed look on him. One I don't remember seeing before.

"Yeah." I can't help but glance back at the photos he took. "How long have *you* known?" And why am I the last to know everything?

"Not long before you. Just after I quit."

"After?"

He nods. "I don't actually think we ever would've known except that Mom came across some paperwork having to do with Liz's shares, and she panicked."

Stan's words about disinheriting her come to mind. "What about Liz's shares?"

"Stan's been stealing from Liz since she was eighteen and gained her shares."

I stand, bumping the table. The briefcase slides off, papers spilling onto the carpet. "Why didn't you tell me?" Another thought runs through my head. "Wait, did you know? All this time? Did you know he was stealing from Liz?"

"First," he says, still calm, "fuck you." He gets up from his chair and crouches down to gather the strewn papers. "Second, if you remember, I tried to tell you." He shoots me a look. "You wouldn't take my calls."

Damn it. He's right.

I help him gather the few remaining sheets. "Sorry."

"About what? Thinking I condoned stealing from our sister?" The sneer in his tone indicates exactly how he feels about that.

"Um, yeah." I run my free hand through my hair, feeling like a chastened kid. "And, you know, for not returning your calls."

He nods once before standing. "Apology accepted." He waits for me to stand before gesturing to the chairs. "Shall we try this again?"

I laugh, uneasy. "Sure." Once settled, I can't help but ask, "Do you think this is why Mom didn't want to be here? Because she figured we'd come to blows?"

"Actually, I think Mom wanted us to do this without her so we'd have a chance to *stop* fighting and work together."

"Oh."

We're silent for a minute before Thomas drops another bomb on me. "I quit because Dad was, and is, having an affair with Denise Hampson."

"When—"

Thomas cuts me off with a raised hand. "This will go a lot faster if you stop interrupting and stay seated."

I glance down to find I'm half out of my chair again. Clearing my throat, I drop back onto the cushion. "Ah, yes. Probably."

In his clear and concise way, Thomas tells me how he quit after finding out about the affair. He'd thought if he walked away, our father would wise up.

Stan didn't.

Then Mom, suspicious herself, snooped through our father's office and wound up finding documents that proved Stan was stealing money from Liz's shares. Shares that were supposed to be going into her trust until she turns twenty-five, when she gets full, legal access.

Stan's already bought a two-million-dollar love-nest penthouse and a Tesla for Denise, in addition to siphoning a bunch of money into an offshore account.

While I'm still processing this, Thomas outlines his plan to take care of Stan and reclaim Liz's money.

When Thomas is done, I can only open and close my mouth like a fish out of water, unable to form the words needed to truly do my father justice.

A rare smile peeks through my brother's sternness. "The great wise-ass Chase Moore is speechless?"

Laughing in spite of the situation, I return his smile. "Yeah, I guess I am."

He gives me a minute before moving forward. "So what do you think of the first part of my plan?"

"What? Pretend to hate both you and Stan until you can convince him to sign over control of Moore's to you, legally this time?" I pretend to contemplate the idea. "Sounds doable."

"Should be easy for you." He fixates on fiddling with the papers in front of him. "You just have to keep acting like you always have."

A pain pinches at my chest. We both say nothing for a while. Finally, I stop being a jerk about it. "But you know..."

"What?" I can hear a hopeful note in his tone, and it enables me to keep going.

"It would only be *acting*. Not, uh, how I really feel." I run a hand through my hair. "About you, I mean."

He just stares at me.

My exasperated sigh ruffles the paper on the table. "I'm saying I don't hate you, man. Don't make it weird."

Thomas puts on his best superior face. "Yeah. *I'm* making it weird."

Shaking my head and laughing again, I wonder at how I got here. To actually talking to my brother. To *liking* him.

It's then that the papers in front of me come into focus. "Wait. Why does this say Warren and Baron? King Marketing created this ad."

Sobering, Thomas turns the ad mock-ups so they face me. *Multiple* mock-ups with the Warren and Baron letterhead above each. And the step-by-step marketing strategy Bell and her team were working on. A sick feeling settles in my gut.

"What the fuck, dude?"

Sighing, Thomas brings me up to speed on Bell's sacrifice.

Shocked stupid, I can only blink at the papers in front of me. "She did all this for Moore's?"

"No, you idiot." Thomas collects the papers, breaking my stare, and stacks them neatly to the side. "She did it for you."

Guilt, self-pity, and hurt get swept aside by a rising tide of panic. "I... I fucked up."

"Yes."

"I need to go see her. Talk to her."

"Yes."

"Jesus, man. Be more helpful than just agreeing with me all the time!" I run my hands through my hair. "I need some advice here."

"You want advice?"

Feeling hopeful the Golden Boy will have some nugget of knowledge, I nod vigorously.

"All right, then. Here's some advice. Don't call me dude."

I stare at him, debating whether to break his nose or laugh. The corner of his mouth twitches, and I go with the latter. "Fuck you, man. Not helpful."

"Yeah, yeah." He stands. "Just go get her."

I stand too, once again knocking all the papers to the floor. "Uh..."

Thomas waves me off. "I'll get it, just get out of here. You're wasting time."

I take a moment to round the table and pull my brother in for a man-hug. After a strong pat on his back, I pull back and look as sincerely as possible into his eyes. "Thanks, dude."

Laughing, and with Thomas's glare burning a hole in my back, I jog out of the room.

It's time I made a trip. Deep in the heart of Texas.

* * *

Bell

"We should have gone to a wine bar."

"What? No way!" Leslie shouts to be heard over the blaring country music. "And miss you turn down not one, not two, but *three* hot guys? Never!" She hands me a shot. "And you have, like, no game. It's kind of hilarious."

"I think I like lawyer Leslie better than social, club-hopping Leslie." Leslie is in fine form tonight. Those boots she talked about? They weren't cowboy boots. She's in a bar called Wild West wearing over-the-knee leather stiletto boots with pointy-ass toes that look as lethal as cyanide. Most of the men in here want to flirt with death tonight, but Leslie's shot down more than I have.

I never knew my lawyer was as much of a shark outside the

courtroom as she is in it.

"Please, you love me." She knocks her drink back and then pointedly stares at me until I do the same. "Besides, how do you think I'm able to kick ass at law? Need to get a release *somewhere*." She eyes a twenty-something in a Johnny Cash T-shirt and baseball cap at the bar, showing genuine interest in a guy for the first time tonight. He eyes her right back.

"A bit young, isn't he?" I mean, Leslie looks hot—blond hair down, wearing a white, scooped-neck tank top, its front tucked into skin-tight jeans, and those man-eater boots of hers. Any guy would be lucky to have her. But that guy looks like he just celebrated his twenty-first birthday.

"Please. I'm a hard-working career woman with no time for the emotional baggage of men my age." Her face darkens for a moment, like she's remembering something. Or someone. "Young ones are more easily trainable, have less chance of emotional damage, and can fuck for hours." She brightens her face with a smile and waves to the Johnny Cash fan. "Everyone wins."

The disco-mirror-covered saddle floating above the dance floor casts twinkling lights over my plain black T-shirt and jeans. Leslie took one look at my loose-fitting tee and tied a knot in it, making it tighter and showing an inch of midriff. I humored her, because let's face it, Leslie scares the shit out of me.

Luke Combs is singing about how a cold longneck beer is the only thing that never broke his heart. And when the waitress comes back and I take a pull of my own longneck, I think he might be on to something.

I nudge her shoulder. "Want to talk about the heavily baggaged man your age that put you in this mood?"

She gives me a look. "Want to talk about the New York shit-storm?"

"Ah... no."

She salutes me with her beer. "Didn't think so."

After another minute or so of mutual eye-fucking with Leslie, the twenty-something walks over, the closer distance revealing a sexy, scruffy chin and snug jeans that any woman can appreciate. "Evening, ladies." He touches his fingers to the brim of his hat. "I'm Mike."

My heart lurches thinking of a hairy cat probably licking his balls in Chase's apartment right now.

"Leslie." My lawyer sticks her hand out, eyes wide when Mike turns it in his and kisses the back of it.

"Campbell." I just wave like a dork, because Leslie's right: I have no game.

He nods, his eyes crinkling with a smile, his eyes on Leslie. "Either of you ladies want to dance?"

I smile politely and shake my head, though he still isn't looking at me. "No thank you."

Leslie shrugs, chugs the rest of her beer, and lets him lead her out onto the dance floor.

I chuckle when he swivels his hat backwards and tugs Leslie close in one smooth move that has her hands digging into his shoulders for balance. Holding her tight, Mike maneuvers them onto the dance floor. Looks like the young ones also have confidence and swagger.

Leslie may have met her match.

They reach the floor just as the song changes. Luke Combs fading into... Elvis?

Sure enough, the haunting pick of guitar strings and soft hum of the background singers prefaces the King's sweet tenor from "Are You Lonesome Tonight?"

The crowd slows down, unused to this musical direction. A few old-timers here for a night of two-stepping take over the oak-planked dance floor. Mike just goes with it, moving Leslie back and forth to the sad song, even keeping time during the song's interlude where Elvis "talks" to his lady love.

When the King speaks about his love lying when she said she loved him but wanting to hear those lies rather than live without her, tears that I've managed to hold off ever since Chase left me by the elevator with a groped boob and half-empty white mocha surface.

I know Momma said there was an Elvis song for every occasion, but this just seems heartless.

Thankfully, the song ends before I can't hold back the tears any longer. Fanning my face like I'm hot and not about to cry, I signal the bartender for another shot. But before I can catch his eye, "Teddy Bear" starts up.

One Elvis song is unusual. Two back to back?

"Excuse me, ma'am?"

Startled, I swivel on my stool.

A good-looking man with blond hair and blue eyes, flashes me a dimple. I think he was sitting next to Mike earlier. He's just as young. "Would you like to dance?"

Trying to hide my disappointment, I shake my head. But the tears I'd been so successful at fighting back rear their ugly heads.

He looks mildly panicked. More so when the first one falls. "You okay, ma'am?"

"She just really hates being called ma'am."

Jerking my blurred gaze to the right, I can just make out the fine-ass form of Chase Moore. I blink a few times, shedding the fully formed tears from my eyes so I can focus.

He's wearing a tight gray Henley tucked into fitted jeans, with gorgeous calfskin Tecovas on his feet and a brown Stetson cowboy hat complete with braided band, just like Elvis wore in *Charro!*

Strapped to his chest in a baby carrier is Mike Hunt.

In a teddy bear costume.

30

CHASE

"He just wants to be your teddy bear."

Bell finally lifts her eyes from an extremely disgruntled Mike and looks at me. "Are you serious right now?"

I can't get a read on her expression. She doesn't look happy. But she doesn't look pissed either. "Uh, yes?" Personally, I thought Mike's costume was a stroke of brilliance.

"I'm just gonna go..." Neither of us looks at the guy who called her ma'am as he slinks away.

"Why are you here?" Her eyes narrow in a way that makes me nervous. Mike too, if the smell emanating from the baby carrier is any indication. Turns out Mike is a nervous farter. Something he proved on the flight here from New York.

People in first class have no sense of humor, by the way.

"I wanted to say I'm sorry?" I have no idea why I couched that as a question. Mike paws at me, and I think even he knows I've already fucked this grand gesture/apology up.

Bell's eyes narrow further.

Damn it. I should've done more research. Alice tried to give me a bunch of books for examples of swoon-worthy (her words, not mine) grand gesture examples written by someone named Audrey Cole, but I'd been too busy wanting to get here before some asshole cowboy tried to get in her pants.

Thomas may not have had any relationship advice to give, but he did tell me that Alice and Bell still talk. Then he'd muttered something about inappropriate use of work time and picture taking.

Whatever that meant.

And Alice had come through for me, telling me *exactly* where Bell would be. Then she mentioned that in all the romance books she's ever read, the guy always does something *big*. Something to sweep the woman off her feet in a moment of love-induced insanity (again—her words, not mine).

"Has Thomas gotten Stan to sign over control yet?"

Her change in direction has me confused. Is she not going to acknowledge the fact that Mike Hunt is in a freaking teddy bear costume? "Teddy Bear" fades into "Don't Be Cruel." Except for a slight eyebrow twitch, Bell's face remains impassive.

I really should have read those books.

"Um, no. But I told him to leverage my shares. Tell Stan I'd give up my shares as long as he wasn't in the picture."

"Wait, what? That's not smart. He may want it in writing when he signs over control."

I shrug. "Yeah. Probably."

"But... you love Moore's."

"No. I love what it represented. And what I thought it could give me. Family. But it turns out I already had that. I just needed to pick up a phone every once in a while."

Again, nothing.

"I love *you*, Bell. You're what I love. *Who* I love."

"You told me you loved me before." Her eyes shine. "And then you left."

Fuck.

I know I didn't technically leave, that in reality I'd been holed up in my apartment like a sad, pathetic lump of self-pity, but pointing that out here isn't going to help me. It doesn't take a genius to realize she means emotionally. That I promised her I was worth it, and at the first blip I bailed.

"I'm sorry, Bell." Unable to stop myself from touching her, I cup her cheek. "I'm so sorry." She doesn't pull away, so that's something. "I—"

Right then, the house lights flare, and "Viva Las Vegas" blares from the speakers. Surprised, Bell pulls back and watches as seven Elvis impersonators in full sequined-jumpsuit regalia take over the dance floor, hips swaying, arms swinging, upper lips curled.

In my head, this had played out differently.

I imagined a well-choreographed ensemble of on-point impersonators dressed in custom fitted and designed jumpsuits with Swarovski crystal embellishment impressing Bell with their nuanced routine—each sway of their hips hypnotizing her until she felt compelled to forgive and love me until the end of time. Thank you very much.

What I got was a group of sweaty middle-aged men, faces beet red and chests heavy with exertion, dancing off-beat like Vegas Richard Simmon's Rocking to the Oldies cardio class.

A few people duck, dodging the cheap metal and plastic beads flying off the Elvis' outfits. But as each Elvis is out of step to the music, there's no guessing when or where the next bedazzled projectile will fly.

I *knew* I should've asked for a video of a past performance before I booked.

"Did you... did you do this?" Bell, looking mesmerized not from love but horror, stands stock-still taking in the car-crash-like travesty.

Somewhere the King rolls over in his grave.

Here, people are taking bets on which Elvis needs CPR first.

Before I can answer, a wide-eyed blonde wearing the most badass fuck-me boots I've ever seen comes hurrying over. "Oh my god. Are you seeing this?"

A man with good taste in music, if his T-shirt is any indication, follows behind her. He nods in greeting.

"This has to be you," Blondie says to Bell. "Only you love Elvis this much."

"Actually..." Three pairs of eyes swing to me. "This was me."

Blondie goes from shock and awe to suspicious in a nanosecond. "Who the fuck are you?"

I stick out my hand, having to twist a bit to get Mike out of the way. "Chase Moore."

Her eyes flick to Bell and then back to my hand. She doesn't take it. "As in New York's Moore's?"

"Leslie..." Bell starts.

Blondie, or Leslie it would seem, tilts her head in my direction. "So *this* is Shit-storm?"

Who is Leslie? And what is shit-storm? And is *no one* going to acknowledge the hairless pussy teddy bear in the room?

How I, the person who arranged for seven Elvis impersonators to surprise flash mob a crowd of cowboys, ended up the one out of the loop, I have no idea. But there you have it.

"Yes," Bell acknowledges. "He decided to surprise me."

Mike starts shifting around in his carrier, probably pissed at the lack of attention.

"Do I need to file a restraining order? Because I may have had a bit to drink, but I'm not too sauced that I can't run legal circles around you right now."

A lawyer. Yeah. That makes sense.

The guy next to Leslie lifts his chin at me. "Mike."

I bro-code introduce myself right back. Chin lift. "Chase." I don't think I look half as cool as he does, though, not with the wiggling skin bag dressed up like it's Halloween I have strapped to me. He smirks, and my thought is confirmed.

I point at the skin bag. "Also Mike."

His smirk vanishes.

"I'm so glad the boys are now all introduced." The sarcasm is thick in Leslie's voice. "Now what about that restraining order?"

The final swell of music surges over the crowd with the disco saddle light lowering in the middle of the dance floor, setting off a rainbow of lights reflecting off the impersonators' jumpsuit sequins.

"No, Leslie," Bell starts. "I don't think—"

"Mike!" But my shout comes too late. The little fucker leaps from the baby carrier, his teddy-bear-covered ass tearing across the bar floor, pouncing on every moving dot of light.

It's a cat's laser light show fantasy come true.

His teddy bear hood falls off, and a woman with more sequins on her ass than all the Elvis impersonators combined screams. "Rat!"

Pandemonium.

The Elvises stop swinging their hips, too busy being body-checked by women hustling their high heels off the dance floor. Men in heavy boots are following, not wanting to lose sight of their dates. The music stops playing, but the disco lights are still in full effect.

All this means a shit ton of people in dangerous footwear are stomping around where Mike is playfully pouncing about like a nudist on acid.

Before I make it two steps toward the beast, a shrill whistle blasts through the air. Everyone slows and looks toward Bell, who takes her fingers out of her mouth and addresses the crowd.

"Stop moving! You're going to kick Mike Hunt!"

* * *

Bell

"It hurts!"

I swing my body away from Chase and the ice pack he procured out of nowhere as he tries to press it against my bruised hand.

"Yeah, well, so does my face." His eye *is* a little swollen.

"Yeah, well, you deserved it." Yes, I'm aware I'm a grown-ass woman pouting. But all I care about right now are the bones I'm pretty sure were pounded to dust when I connected with Chase's stupidly firm jaw.

"As Ms. King's legal counselor, I need to ask if you are going to sue for damages."

"What?" Chase and I say at the same time, turning to Leslie, who's standing over us in her superhero boots.

Still looking at Chase, she repeats, "Are you going to sue for damages?" She waves a hand at his face.

Looking affronted at the idea, Chase scoffs, "No, of course not."

Not relenting, Leslie continues her attack. "Are you willing to attest to that in writing?"

"Jesus, Bell." Chase looks at me for help. "Tell your lawyer friend I'd never sue you for accidentally punching me in the face while you were trying to save my cat. Or at all, for that matter."

Still hurt, both hand and heart, I don't say anything. Instead, I cuddle Mike closer to my chest, which he seems to love, going by his V-8 engine purr.

Mouth hanging open, Chase grabs a cocktail napkin from the bar. "Anyone have a pen?" Three cocktail waitresses with a front-row seat to my drama thrust pens at him.

And that's not all they're thrusting.

Chase grabs one, not even glancing at the copious amount of cleavage, and hunches over the bar, scribbling fast. "Here." He hands it to Leslie.

She scans it, nods, and pockets the napkin. "Everything's in order then."

"I'm not really sure a cocktail napkin would hold up in a court of law," Chase mutters.

Leslie gives Chase the eye. "Then you don't know me."

"Huh." Chase sits back in his seat, eyeing her like he's thinking. "You want a job destroying my father?"

I feel my eyes bulge.

Leslie taps her finger to her chin. "Stan Moore, the one who stole intellectual property from my client?" She gestures to me.

"Now wait, he didn't really steal—"

"That's the one." Chase nods.

She nods in return. "Yes. Call me."

"But you can't. I *gave*—"

She presses a manicured finger to my lips. "Now, if you'll excuse me, I have to see a man about some Elvis impersonators." She heads toward the side of the bar where the pissed-off bar owner sits. "This is going to be fun."

Chase smirks. "You can bill me for the hour."

"Oh, honey." Leslie laughs. "I'm going to bill you for a lot more than that." Then she sashays over and starts lawyering the shit out of the mayhem we caused.

"That's some woman." Human Mike, who's been surprisingly quiet and steady through this whole ordeal, takes a swig of his beer and watches Leslie talk down the owner.

With the crowd now dispersed, Leslie handling the damages Mike Hunt caused, and the pain in my hand receding, the adrenaline fades, and my eyelids get heavy.

"I need to go home," I tell cat Mike, who simply continues to motorboat me.

"I'll take you," Chase offers, hope lighting his features.

"I came with Leslie."

"I got Leslie," Human Mike says, his own smile telling me how he hopes the night will play out. And as Leslie hasn't told him to take a hike, I'm pretty sure she's okay with that.

I nod to him, then turn to Chase. "Fine, you can take me home." I squeeze the hairless ball of cuddles closer. "But I'm not giving up Mike Hunt."

Hands up, Chase nods. "Done."

* * *

"Take the next exit." I point at the upcoming sign. It's been forty minutes since we left Wild West, and the only time I've opened my mouth was to give directions. Anytime Chase tried to initiate conversation, I started baby-talking to Mike. Chase took note and stopped talking thirty-five minutes ago.

"Not that I'm not happy that you agreed to let me drive you home, but you aren't, by any chance, leading me out to the middle of nowhere to kill me and bury my body, are you?" He pulls the car off of I-45, heading west.

"As much as that might give me pleasure at this exact moment, no. I'm not." I cuddle Mike closer. "I'm taking you home."

"I thought you had an apartment downtown."

"I do. I'm taking you to my parents' place."

That quiets him for the next twenty minutes as we pass less retail shops and subdivisions and more split-rail fences and open spaces.

"This is it," I say when we pull up to the red brick ranch-style house.

Chase's headlights illuminate the metal wind chimes hanging from the porch.

"Home sweet home," I sing, a sense of peace coming over me just looking at my family's old house. I've kept it all these years. It's become a place of refuge for me. Where I grew up. Where I mourned. Where I started my company.

Oddly quiet, Chase gets out of the car, circling around to open my door and help me out. Gripping Mike extra tight, not wanting him to get loose and then lost in the woods, I lead Chase up the porch steps to my front door.

"Well. You came all this way. I might as well let you in for a bit."

A little of that trademark Moore smirk pulls through. "I'd like that."

Sighing like I'm put out, instead of oddly nervous at Chase seeing my childhood home, I kick the rock by the porch post and unearth the house key.

"Are you for real? People actually hide keys under rocks?" He looks up and down the street. "Aren't you afraid people will find it and rob you?"

"Come on, city boy." I unlock the front door, setting Mike down in the small foyer. "Let's sit you down a spell before you have a conniption right here on my momma's front porch."

He looks stunned. "I know I have a lot to apologize for, but right now, when you talk like that, I want to do more than have a conniption with you on your momma's front porch."

My treacherous nipples perk up at the thought.

"Let's just see how the apology goes, okay?"

"Yes, ma'am."

"You're not off to a very good start, Mr. Moore."

31

CHASE

Her house is like something out of an AMC western special. Like old-time America. I've traveled quite a bit in my life, but usually to places like Europe or the tropics. I haven't been south, except once to Miami, and that just isn't the same thing.

The chandelier over the breakfast nook in her kitchen is an honest-to-goodness wagon wheel.

I love it.

I'm not the only one. Mike leaps up onto the Formica counter and curls into an empty basket. Taking a fluffy tea towel from out of a drawer, Bell drapes it over him like a blanket.

Bringing the cat was a good move on my part, I think. Much better than the Elvis impersonators.

"Would you like some water?"

"Yes, thank you." I feel oddly formal with this woman who owns my heart. That's all my doing.

"We don't have bottled. Just tap." She opens a wood-grained upper kitchen cabinet, the kind with scrollwork on the front.

"We?"

Her hand stills on the glass. "Me. I, uh, I meant me." She plucks the glass off the blue-paper-lined shelf and shuts the door. "I've never really had anyone here since my parents died. I guess I tend to forget they're gone when I'm here." She runs the water in the kitchen sink for a moment before filling my glass. "Maybe that's why I never sold it. And why I like it here so much."

It's not fair that her parents died and yet my horrible excuse for a father is still alive.

She hands me the glass, and I gulp it down in one go.

She raises her eyebrows and takes the glass from me, placing it in the sink.

We stand awkwardly in the kitchen, lit up by the wagon-wheel chandelier. All around me are hints of Bell's past, proof of how loved she was. Pictures, school drawings, handmade ceramics probably made by a toddler Bell. They're everywhere.

"Well, I guess if that's it, then you should probably be go—"

"I'm sorry I'm such an asshole," I blurt out.

Wide eyes narrow as Bell crosses her arms. "Oh. You're *sorry*, are you? That's all you have to say?"

"No. I mean, yes." I run a hand through my hair.

"Well?" Her fancy cowboy boot taps the linoleum.

Channeling my mom, I take a deep breath. "How about I start over?"

She gestures to the curved-back dining chairs under the wagon wheel.

I hesitate. "Is it okay if we sit in your dad's study?"

"My dad's study?"

"The one with the soup can painting you told me about?"

Her breath catches. "Yeah," she says, having to clear her throat. "Yeah, we can sit there." She heads back the way we came, turning right when we get to the front of the house. There isn't a door, just an arch. The hardwood floor laid throughout the front of the house is covered with a worn braided rug. There's a tan and blue plaid tweed loveseat on one side of the wall, and on the other, a worn leather recliner.

Before she can move to the recliner, I take her hand and lead her to the loveseat. Warily, she lets me.

Once settled, I push my luck and wrap an arm around her. Her body doesn't relax into mine, but she doesn't junk punch me either, so I consider it a win.

Right across from the loveseat, in perfect view from either the recliner or the loveseat, is the small Warhol soup can print Bell had told me about at the museum. It's a very simple painting, the style devoid of too much detail, highlighting the ease of mass production that the artist found so intriguing. (I've been reading up on him since our day in the museum.) But for Bell, it doesn't mean any of that. The picture evokes happy memories of her childhood, of her parents' love.

"My father never wanted me. He told me, to my face, that he would've gotten rid of me if my mom hadn't waited so long to tell him."

Bell's body freezes next to mine.

"He said he only wanted Thomas. That Thomas represented the continuing legacy. I just represented split shares in the company."

"Oh my god." She struggles to sit up. Reluctantly, I let her. "Thomas told me about Stan stealing money and the affair, and even about Liz, but he didn't say anything about your father feeling that way."

"I'm not sure if Thomas knows, to be honest." I frown, considering. We never got around to talking about that. "I mean, we talked about all the other stuff, and we have a plan to fix all the shit my father's fucked up, but I didn't tell him about that particular conversation."

"When did he tell you this?"

"One minute before I ran into you and Thomas at the elevator."

Understanding dawns in her eyes. "Oh."

"Yeah, oh." I cover her hand resting on her thigh with mine. "It wasn't my best moment. In fact, I'm pretty sure it was my worst. What my father said to me... it really blindsided me."

She nods.

"It doesn't excuse, in any way, how I acted, but I was just so..."

"Hurt? Angry?"

"Yes."

She turns her hand in mine, interlacing our fingers.

"A few days later, Mom came by and helped me realize a few things. And one of them is that it isn't my fault my father's a horrible person. It isn't Thomas's either, for that matter."

Bell releases my hand so she can cup the sides of my face. "Of *course* it isn't your fault. Anyone who thinks otherwise is obviously a douche-canoe."

"Douche-canoe?" I laugh, causing her to smile. She moves to lower her hands, but I hold them in place with my own, careful of her sore knuckles. "That's just one of the many reasons I love you. Your ability to insult with flair." I slide her hands together in front of me, planting a gentle kiss on them.

"You didn't love me enough not to leave."

Guilt slices at me. "I know words are just words. As Elvis says, more action, less talk."

She rolls her eyes, but she's smiling, so I keep going.

"I know I left. I really wish I hadn't. Please know that once I finally stopped being a douche-canoe"—her smile gets a little bigger— "I realized leaving was the complete opposite of what I should've done." I kiss her hands again. "I'm not very good at talking about... feelings stuff."

She snorts.

"But I promise you I will get better. I won't shut you out. Because I love you so goddamn much, Campbell Dougherty."

She leans forward until her forehead rests against mine. "Chase Moore. What *am* I going to do with you?" Her Southern twang sends shivers down my spine, putting my hopeful dick on alert.

"Love me tender?"

"Chase," she warns, pulling back.

"No?" I wink at her. "How about loving me sweet?"

"You can't keep using the King against me." She tries to look cross, but her smile wins. "It's not fair."

"Never let me go," I whisper.

Sighing, she lies back on the loveseat, opening her arms for me. "Okay," she whispers back.

Shifting forward, I brace my arms on either side of her, stopping just short of kissing. The moonlight filtering in through the front window ignites amber sparks in her brown eyes. "I love you."

Her eyes crinkle slightly at the corners. "I love you too, Chase."

And then *she* kisses *me*. Soft and searching. I kiss her back, putting everything I feel for her in every touch, every breath. My hands tangle in her hair, hers drifting up and down my back.

"I missed you, Bell. So much."

She tilts her head, giving me access to the column of her slender throat. "Show me. Show me how much you missed me."

I do. I kiss her for what seems like hours. Until she's yanking my shirt out of my jeans.

"Ow." She pulls back her hand, cradling it to her chest.

"Careful, baby." I kiss her bruised knuckles. "Let me."

"But you're taking too long." The whine in her voice is adorable.

"Patience."

She scowls. I kiss it away.

After a moment, I give in to her, peeling off her clothes piece by piece, until she's naked, laid out before me. Moonlight catches the fire in her hair, the desire in her eyes. I reach back, yanking my shirt over my head, hating that I need to move back away from her, and stand to shuck off my boots and jeans.

The little minx tries to reach for me, but I shake my head. If she wants me to show her how much I missed her, I'm going to show her.

Dropping to my knees, I lift her foot to my lips, kissing the arch. She flexes her foot and giggles, but I hold on, moving my lips to her ankle, and then her calf. Taking my time, I kiss upward, making sure to savor each kiss, each noise she makes while I explore. While I memorize her body.

Reaching her inner thigh, I smile as Bell tilts her hips expectantly, only to curse me when I drift back down, holding her other foot up to my lips. I repeat the process, cherishing her. Once again between her legs, I give in and inhale, savoring her arousal. Only to lift my head and kiss her belly.

"I swear to god, Chase Moore..."

I hide my grin against her ribs, nibbling the underside of her breast, then soothing the sting with my tongue. "Do you feel crazed right now?"

"Yes," she pants.

"About to come out of your skin with need?"

"Yes." Her answer is more moan than word.

"Do you feel like you're missing something? That the one thing you need is just out of reach?"

She nods, biting her lip, turned on past speaking.

"Then I've shown you how I've missed you." I draw a lazy circle around one nipple, pinching the other. "I've felt like that every day since I pushed you away."

She grips my hair, holding me to her while I tease and suck before yanking me up to her mouth.

This time I let her pull me up and press our bodies together.

"Now I'm going to show you how much I love you," I whisper.

She comes as soon as I thrust, the buildup having been too much. I hold her as she tenses, muscles locked in pleasure, before she softens in my arms. Only then do I begin to move, slowly, deliberately, building her back up.

Impatient as ever, she lifts her hips in time with mine, fucking herself on me as I make love to her.

God, I love this woman.

"Chase, Chase, Chase..." she chants, like the mere reminder of who is making love to her is bringing her that much closer to the brink.

My balls draw up, and I know I'm reaching the end of my limit. My hips piston harder, my thrusts deeper.

"Look at me, baby. Look at me."

Blinking wildly, nearly unable to focus, Bell's eyes finally lock on mine.

"Never let me go." Reaching down, I lift her ass, thrusting once more as hard and as deep as I can, our orgasms clashing together in one wave of pleasure.

"Never." Her body shivers with aftershocks. "I love you."

"Me too." I sag against her, my body spent. "And I always will."

EPILOGUE

CHASE

I slip my hand under Bell's skirt and palm her ass.

"Chase, pay attention," she whispers, as harshly as a whisper allows.

"I am." The tip of my middle finger slides under the lace.

"To what's happening in your office, not my ass."

She's so cute when she pretends to be annoyed.

"But it's such a fine ass," I murmur against the column of her neck.

The sound of a door opening quiets us both.

"This way." Thomas's deep, steady voice sounds through the small opening of the closet door that Bell and I are hiding behind.

"Everything is in order?" Stan's voice booms.

"Yes." Denise's shrill voice sends chills down my spine. "I was hoping to have this over with so your father and I could celebrate at Jean-Georges."

They make their way to the desk, where Bell and I can see them from our hiding spot.

"I can't believe that boy would give up his shares. He never could hack being a *real* Moore. Doesn't have the stones."

Thomas makes a noncommittal sound while rifling through the papers on the desk.

"And Denise is working out great, isn't she? The new campaign she's rolled out has really set Moore's up for a great year."

Denise coos and smooths down Stan's lapels with her talons.

Bell stiffens. I move my hand from under her skirt and wrap both arms around her, drawing her back up against my front for a hug. I know she says it doesn't matter that she 'left' her work behind when she went to Texas, knowing Denise would take it. That it was her choice, and she'd do it again. But it still hurt, and I'm planning on making it up to her.

"I'm going to junk-punch your father and then stab Denise with my new Jimmy Choos," Bell mutters softly.

I shh her, but honestly, I'd pay money to see that.

Thomas ignores the question and lifts a stack of papers from the desk. "This is the paperwork from Chase turning in his shares. It's already signed. But its legality is contingent on you signing away daily control of Moore's." Thomas places that paperwork aside and presses the intercom. "George, could you come in here?"

A second later, as if waiting for the invitation (because he was), George steps into the office.

"Why the devil haven't you fired this—"

"George is a notary, Father. And very good at his job." Thomas picks up the other stack of papers, turning it toward Stan. "I've marked the places where you need to sign and initial. Starting here." He points to a spot on the page.

Stan glares at George for a moment more. George remains impassive as ever.

"Hmph." Stan pulls a gold pen from his suit pocket before ignoring George and focusing on Thomas. "Great work, Thomas. I knew you would do amazing things for the company, but I didn't know you could get your wayward brother out of the picture so efficiently." He pats Thomas on the back. "I should've though. You're just like me."

Too busy leaning over the contract, Stan doesn't see Thomas's face. And as Stan's words don't have their usual effect on me, I'm not too busy licking my wounds not to see the sick expression Thomas has trouble suppressing. Being compared to Stanley Moore would do that to anyone.

Hopefully, what I have planned for after we finally oust Stan will make up for all the shit-eating he's had to do this past month.

With a final flourish of his gaudy pen, Stan straightens from the desk. "There. Now we can take care of Chase's shares."

Thomas holds up a hand. "One moment."

George steps forward and notarizes the paperwork. "I'll just go file these, sir," he says to Thomas before walking out.

Once the door closes behind George, Stan reaches for the second contract. My father, the man whose blood runs through my veins, eagerly leans down to sign away my birthright from me with a large smile on his face.

This is going to be so satisfying.

He turns the first page, only to still. "It's blank." He rifles through the rest of the pages. "They're all blank."

"Hmmm," is all Thomas says.

"Really, Thomas, you need to be more on top of things now that you're in control. Your father doesn't want the income from his shares slipping due to bad management." It's obvious to everyone who's not Stan that Denise means *she* doesn't want less money to spend.

"Fix this, Thomas." The old man's voice is steely. "Now."

Thomas's placid expression breaks for a moment with a look of smug satisfaction. "I *am* fixing this, Father. I've been fixing it for quite some time." He nods in our direction—our signal.

Bell pulls the closet door open, revealing us inside.

"What the—"

A loud pounding on the door cuts him off.

"Come in," Thomas calls.

A group of men enter the room, some in New York police uniforms, others in suits. As do my mother and Leslie, Bell's lawyer friend from Texas.

Leslie speaks up first. "Stanley Moore"—she hands him a manila envelope— "you have been served."

"What's this?"

"Divorce papers." Mom, looking every Chanel-clad inch like the New York princess she was born, sneers at her husband.

Then she flips Denise the bird.

Everyone, including me, gapes at the gesture.

A suit speaks up next. "Stanley Moore, you are under arrest for embezzlement."

Before Stan can open his mouth, a uniformed officer takes his turn. "Denise Hampson, you are under arrest for the theft of intellectual property from King Marketing."

"What? How dare you!" Denise screeches, causing everyone to cringe before the officers begin reading both her and Stan their Miranda rights.

Stan looks from me to Thomas, obviously confused, as the FBI agent cuffs his hands behind his back. "Thomas, you can't let them do this."

Casually, at odds with the whole vibe in the room, my brother walks over to me and our mother. We all stand side by side, staring Stanley down. "This wasn't Chase's idea." Thomas's eyes drill into the old man. "It was mine."

The color drains from Stan's face. "What?"

"The staging was my idea, though," I pipe up, unable to resist. "I thought being arrested with your side-piece in the very office you coveted for your firstborn was a bit of poetic justice." I wink at him. "You always did tell me I was too sentimental."

"This is ridiculous!" Denise shouts, trying to pull her arms away from the officer. "I've done nothing wrong." Her eyes swing wildly around the room, landing and narrowing on Bell.

Bell just smiles.

Stan and Denise are pulled from the room, their crazed, panicked voices getting softer as they go farther and farther down the hall. Until finally, they're gone.

"Well. That felt wonderful." Mom turns to Bell. "Now don't forget, lunch tomorrow."

Bell nods, and they hug tight. "Thanks, Leslie," she says over my mom's shoulder.

"Eh, don't worry. You'll get the bill soon enough." Leslie places a hand on Mom's shoulder. "Come on, Em. Let's go get our ducks in a row so we can really bleed Stan dry in the divorce. It'll be fun."

And with the shares Stan just signed over, plus most of the family assets coming from Mom's family, not Stan's, I have a feeling that with Leslie at the helm, Mom's divorce *will* be fun.

For her at least.

With a light laugh, my mother follows her out, making Thomas and me promise a family dinner soon.

"I wish we could call Liz," Bell says after my mother leaves.

When Thomas and I planned this out, we knew we had to tell Liz what Stan had done and the truth about her parentage. It was a conversation Mom had with her, so Thomas and I don't know what was said, but the end result was Liz dropping out of school and leaving town. She left a note for us saying she needed time, and that she'd call when she could.

At first, Thomas and I were determined to find her and bring her back. Even had a private detective all picked out. But then Bell and Mom talked us down. Said to trust Liz and give her the time she asked for.

Time for what, I'm not sure. But I said I'd give her a month, and if I didn't hear from Liz by then, all bets were off.

Thomas walks back to the desk, opening the top drawer. He grabs yet another stack of papers and holds them out to me. "Here you go. I've signed control of the company back over to you. It's all legal this time."

Taking it, I smirk at my stodgy older brother. "Thanks, dude." I smile wider when his eyes narrow. Then I toss the paperwork in the garbage. "But no thanks."

"What the hell?"

"Tommy-kins, did you just curse?" Bell's shocked voice rings with humor.

Thomas pinches the bridge of his nose. "Between Chase calling me dude and you making up the most ridiculous nicknames, you're both going to spike my blood pressure." He points to the garbage. "Why the *hell* did you do that?"

"Because I don't want that. I want something else." I turn to the open office door. "George!"

My PA walks in holding a large file folder and hands it to Thomas. "Will that be all, Mr. Moore?"

"Chase, George. You'll need to call me Chase now for sure. Especially since there'll be *two* Mr. Moores in residence now."

The uptight fellow just quirks an eyebrow and leaves.

Thomas's eyes narrow farther on George's retreating back, then shift to me. "What are you talking about, *two* of us?"

"Open it." I nod at the file in his hands.

Bell leans into me, and I wrap an arm around her as we watch my brother open the file and read over the paperwork inside.

"You want"—he clears his throat, sounding emotional for the

first time ever— "you want *both* of us to run Moore's?" He looks up, confused and maybe a little hopeful. "Together?"

"Yep." I'm sure I'm grinning like an idiot, but I'm too happy to care.

Until Thomas remains quiet a little too long.

Shit, maybe I read this wrong.

I unwrap my arm from Bell and move closer to Thomas, placing a hand on his shoulder. "Hey. Uh, you don't have to. I mean, I thought you'd want to, but if you don't…" I run my free hand through my hair. "I just thought, with us talking again, that maybe—"

Thomas finally looks up from the file, his smirk throwing me off. "Why do you always have to make things weird?"

"You fucker." I punch his arm in retaliation for making me squirm. You know, as manly men do.

"Great!" Bell claps her hands, smiling broadly. "Now we can get started."

Thomas and I share a look. "Get started with what, babe?"

She wags a finger at me, tsking. "I told you, no calling me babe in the office." She walks over to the door, her pert ass swaying beneath a short, flowy skirt. "Alice," she calls out. "You can bring it in now."

I'm pretty sure my brother just choked on air at the mention of the new marketing exec.

I throw him a curious look. "Dude?"

He glares at me, the Golden Boy façade firmly in place.

Interesting.

Alice rolls a large whiteboard into the room. Thomas stalks forward, pulling it out of her grasp. "Did you push this here your-self?" His voice is harsher than usual. "You should've called someone."

Alice flushes, and I'm about to call my brother out for being a douche, when the normally timid marketing exec places her hands on her hips and glares at my brother. "I am perfectly capable, thank you very much."

"Uhhhh..." I look to Bell for help, but she just continues to smile.

Alice flips the board, revealing blueprints, sketches, and swatches of carpet and fabric.

"Ta-da!" Bell does a weird jazz-hands gesture at the whiteboard.

"Um, what's this, ba—" I pause at her death stare. "I mean, Ms. King?"

"It's the plan for your new offices. Alice and I contacted an architecture firm and got all the blueprints made up. We're taking this boring monstrosity and dividing it into two offices." She looks between Thomas and me. "One for Chuckles and the other for you. Construction starts on Monday." More jazz hands. "Surprise!"

God, I love this woman.

I step up to her and cup her cheek with my hand. "As awesome as that sounds, we'll have to leave the office as is for a while."

Bell's smile falls. "But why?"

"Because now that Stan has been dealt with and the Moore brothers are back in action, my brother is going to give me the month off to fully apologize to you for being such an ass hat." I shoot my brother a look. "Isn't that right?"

"Typical." Thomas's expression remains aloof, but I don't miss the way his eyes keep glancing at Alice every few seconds. "But, yes, you may go."

Bell's lips twitch slightly as she settles her palms against my chest. "And just how are you planning to redeem your past ass-hat tendencies?"

I rub my nose against hers. "First I'm taking you to Pittsburgh so we can visit the Andy Warhol Museum."

A full-blown smile lights up Bell's face. "Really?"

"Really." I shift the hand at her jaw into her auburn hair, my other hand wrapping around her waist. "Then we're off to Memphis, where I've scheduled a private tour of Graceland."

Her mouth drops open. "Graceland?" She whispers the words like it's some sacred, religious site. Which, I guess to her, it is.

"And *finally*, I'm going to spend two weeks in Texas impressing you with my inner cowboy at your parents' house." I kiss the tip of her nose.

"Inner cowboy, huh?" She chuckles, tears forming in her eyes.

Alice clasps her hands to her chest and sighs.

I knew I'd get this romance shit (aka Grand Gesture) right at some point. "That's right, baby."

Bell doesn't even object to the pet name this time, just continues smiling, her eyes glassy with emotion.

I lean in to kiss her, but she stops me with pressure on my chest.

"But there's one thing missing."

"And what's that?" I lean to the side, kissing the column of her neck. She shivers, and I pull back, eager to watch the arousal burn out the tears in her eyes. They may be happy tears, but after recent events, I've promised myself never to make her cry again.

"This is hardly appropriate," Thomas intones, only to be shushed by Alice.

Bell's eyes, the ones I fell in love with as hot coffee burned my areolae, darken with desire, but they also spark with mischief.

Tipping forward on her toes, she brushes her lips against mine. "We're going to need to bring Mike Hunt."

And that, ladies and gentlemen, is one of the many reasons why I love this woman.

MORE FROM SARA L. HUDSON

We hope you enjoyed reading *Anyone But The Billionaire*. If you did, please leave a review.

If you'd like to gift a copy, this book is also available as an ebook, digital audio download and audiobook CD.

Sign up to Sara L. Hudson's mailing list for news, competitions and updates on future books.

https://bit.ly/SaraLHudsonNews

ABOUT THE AUTHOR

Sara L. Hudson is a bestselling romantic comedy author living in Houston, whose books include the hilarious Space series, featuring the men and women of NASA and their panty-melting happily-ever-afters.

Visit Sara's website: https://www.saralhudson.com/

Follow Sara L. Hudson on social media here:

 facebook.com/SaraLHudsonWriter
twitter.com/_SaraLHudson
instagram.com/sara_l_hudson

Boldw∞d

Boldwood Books is an award-winning fiction publishing company seeking out the best stories from around the world.

Find out more at www.boldwoodbooks.com

Join our reader community for brilliant books, competitions and offers!

Follow us
@BoldwoodBooks
@BookandTonic

Sign up to our weekly deals newsletter

https://bit.ly/BoldwoodBNewsletter

Printed in Great Britain
by Amazon